DOUBLE JEOPARDY

By the same author

THE STOCKHOLM SYNDICATE
AVALANCHE EXPRESS
THE STONE LEOPARD
YEAR OF THE GOLDEN APE
TARGET FIVE
THE PALERMO AMBUSH
THE HEIGHTS OF ZERVOS
TRAMP IN ARMOUR

Colin Forbes

DOUBLE JEOPARDY

COLLINS
St James's Place, London
1982

William Collins Sons & Co Ltd
London · Glasgow · Sydney · Auckland
Toronto · Johannesburg

First published in 1982
© Colin Forbes 1982

ISBN 0 00 222657 X

Composition in Ehrhardt by Filmtype Services Limited,
Scarborough, North Yorkshire.
Made and printed in Great Britain by
William Collins Sons & Co Ltd, Glasgow

FOR JANE

CHAPTER 1

Sunday May 24

After the murder it was assumed that Charles Warner – always so vigilant – had let down his guard because of the atmosphere. When he left the harbour at Lindau, Bavaria, and took his powerboat out on to Lake Konstanz it was a sunny, peaceful afternoon.

'And it was a diabolically clever and audacious killing,' Tweed commented to Martel two days later in London.

The powerboat, with Warner as its sole occupant, moved slowly as it passed through the harbour exit, flanked on one side by the stone statue of the Lion of Bavaria; on the other by the towering lighthouse. Conforming to regulations, he sounded his hooter.

A lean, agile man of forty, Warner was wearing a German suit. On the seat beside him lay a Tyrolean hat. For his secret crossing to his landfall on the Swiss shore he had substituted a peaked, nautical cap which merged into the holiday scene.

There was nothing ahead of him on the huge lake to arouse suspicion. In the glare of the afternoon sun a fleet of yachts with coloured sails drifted like toys. Beyond rose the jagged, snow-bound peaks of Liechtenstein and Switzerland. To his right one of the many white steamers which ply the lake disappeared towards the German town of Konstanz.

To his left a group of wind-surfers was using the light breeze to skim over the glassy surface of the water. He counted six of them as they moved across his bows.

'Kindly get out of the Goddamn way,' he muttered as he throttled back his engine.

They were all young, fine physical specimens, clad only in

7

bathing trunks as they propelled their strange craft in an enclosing arc. Two of them were blond. Warner was about half a mile
from the shore when he realised they were playing games,
circling round to stop him opening up the throttle.

'Go and play elsewhere,' Warner growled.

He had a damned good mind to open up and scare them – but
they were so close he might run them down. The tallest blond
waved and brought his craft alongside the powerboat. He held
the sail steady with his left hand while his right gripped the
sheath knife strapped to his thigh. Too late a flicker of alarm
alerted the Englishman. The wind-surfer abandoned his sail and
jumped into the powerboat. He wielded the blade with speed and
lethal efficiency, plunging it into his victim at varying angles.

The other five wind-surfers formed a screen of sails, masking
the powerboat from anyone who might be watching them
through glasses onshore. And the *Wasserschutzpolizei* – Water
Police – had a unit and a launch at Lindau.

They maintained the screen while the tall blond completed his
butchery. Then he left the powerboat, slipped into the water and
upended his own sail. They resumed formation, heading for the
deserted shore between Lindau and the Austrian border at the
end of the lake.

'Multiple stab wounds – like the work of some maniac . . .'

Sergeant Dorner of the Water Police stood up from his
examination of the body in the drifting powerboat. He looked at
the launch with *Polizei* painted in blue letters on the hull drawn
up alongside. The youngest policeman aboard who had been
watching the examination began to retch over the side. Baptism
of fire, Dorner thought.

He frowned as he noticed something gleaming by his foot.
When he picked it up and saw what he had found he slipped it
quickly into his pocket. A triangular-shaped badge very like the
Greek letter *delta*. He glanced down at the body again; it was a
pretty grisly mess. He opened the passport extracted from the
corpse's jacket together with a wallet.

'He's English. Funny, the wallet is stuffed with money . . .'

'Maybe those wind-surfers panicked . . .' From his high point on the bridge of the launch, Busch, Dorner's deputy and the third man in the team, shielded his eyes and stared east. 'No sign of the bastards. They moved off fast . . .'

'It takes only seconds to snatch a man's wallet,' Dorner persisted. 'This is the strangest killing I've come across . . . Christ!'

Sifting through the contents of the wallet he had found a small card made of plastic rather like a credit card. But this was no credit card Dorner thought grimly as he studied the green and red stripes, the embossed number – which identified the owner – and a five-letter code reference which meant London.

'What's the matter?' Busch called down.

Something in his chief's expression warned him they had found trouble. Dorner slipped the card back inside the wallet and beckoned Busch to leave the bridge and come close to the powerboat. He kept his voice low when Busch faced him over the narrow gap between the two vessels.

'This has to be kept quiet. First we inform the BND at Pullach immediately . . .'

'You mean he's . . .'

'I don't mean anything. But I think there are people in London who will want to know about this before nightfall . . .'

Sergeant Dorner was very silent as he stood on the bridge of the police launch, leaving the handling of the vessel to his subordinate as they approached the harbour of Lindau. Attached by a strong rope, the powerboat with its ghastly cargo was being dragged at the stern, the body carefully concealed by a sheet of canvas.

It was the macabre condition of the corpse's back which worried Dorner, a fact he had not mentioned even to Busch. And the horror of what he had discovered seemed such an appalling contrast to the holiday atmosphere of Lindau where visitors strolled in the sun along the short harbour front.

Keep close watch for group six wind-surfers possibly approaching

*your shore now. If seen apprehend and hold in close custody. Proceed
on basis group armed and dangerous.*

This was the top priority signal Dorner had told the young
radio operator to send before they began the return trip to Lindau. By then the latest addition to his crew had fortunately
recovered from his bout of vomiting. And the signal had been
sent to police headquarters at Bregenz on the Austrian shore as
well as to Dorner's home base.

'I thought I saw some weird markings carved on his back,'
Busch remarked as he sounded the siren prior to entering the
harbour. 'Almost like some kind of symbol – but there was so
much blood . . .'

'Keep your mind on your job,' Dorner told him tersely.

With the sun blazing down on their necks they entered the
small harbour and turned east to the landing-stage where the
launch always berthed. Dorner was most concerned about how
to smuggle the body the short distance from harbour to headquarters without anyone seeing it. He need not have worried.
The early discovery of Charles Warner's body was already being
observed.

The ancient town of Lindau with its medieval buildings, narrow,
cobbled streets and even narrower alleys stands on an island at
the eastern end of Lake Konstanz. There are two quite separate
routes to reach this geographical oddity.

Coming by car you drive over the Seebrücke – the road
bridge. Travelling to Lindau by international express from
Zürich, you cross a rail embankment further west. The train
stops at the Hauptbahnhof perched by the waterfront; it then
moves back over the embankment and proceeds on to München.

The pavement artist was located outside the Bayerischer Hof,
the most luxurious hotel on Lindau which faces the station exit.
From here he could easily observe arrivals by train or boat.

A lean, bony-faced man in his early twenties, he wore a faded
windcheater and jeans. The clothes were spotlessly clean. There
are few beggars in Germany but those who exist preserve a

respectable appearance. Only in this way can they hope to obtain money from passers-by.

His work was a picture of the Forum in Rome drawn in crayon on the stones of the sidewalk, a small cardboard box by its side for coins. At frequent intervals he paused while he walked up and down slowly, hands clasped behind his back.

He was now watching the police launch entering the harbour. As it swung round, broadside on, heading for its berth, he saw the powerboat being towed in its wake. Turning away, he made sure no one was watching him and checked his watch strapped well above the wrist. Then he strolled across the road, pushed open a door and walked into the Hauptbahnhof.

Before he entered the phone booth he checked to make sure no one was coming out of the office marked *Polizei*. Once inside the booth he called the number and waited. From an apartment block in Stuttgart a girl's voice answered.

'Edgar Braun,' he replied.

'This is Klara. I'm just going out so I only have a minute . . .'

'A minute is all it will take . . .' He paused. The agreed opening had confirmed to each the other's identity. 'I thought that you would like to know the expected consignment has arrived . . .'

'So quickly?'

She sounded startled. The man who called himself Braun frowned. It was most unlike the girl to lose her detachment. Whoever's body was inside the powerboat had clearly been found much earlier than expected.

'Are you sure?' she demanded.

'Of course I'm sure.' He bridled. 'You want the details?' he suggested nastily.

'That won't be necessary.' Her voice had resumed its normal cold tone. ' Thank you for calling . . .'

'And my fee?' Braun persisted.

'Waiting to be collected at the Post Office in the usual way two days from now. And continue in your present job. Remember, jobs are not so easy to get at the moment . . .'

He was left staring at the phone. The bitch had broken the

connection. He shrugged, left the booth and returned to his pitch on the pavement. Braun knew what he had to watch for but beyond phoning a girl called Klara he had never met – and the fact that she had a Stuttgart number – he knew nothing about the organisation he was spying for.

In the luxurious penthouse apartment in Stuttgart Klara stared at herself in the dressing-table mirror. An ex-model with a superb figure she was twenty-seven years old. Her sleek black hair was attended to weekly by the city's top hairdresser and there was a small fortune in her wardrobe of clothes.

She had dark, sleepy-looking eyes, a fine bone structure and was a chain-smoker. She was hesitating before she picked up the white telephone and called the man who owned the apartment. She lit a fresh cigarette and dialled the number in southern Bavaria.

Inside the moated *schloss* many miles north-east of Lindau a firm, leathery hand picked up the receiver. On his third finger the man wore a large diamond ring. Beneath his strong jaw he wore a solid gold tie-slide. Attached to his left wrist was a Patek Philippe watch.

'Yes!'

No identification, just the single curt word.

'Klara calling. It is convenient to talk?'

'Yes! You received the fur I sent? Good. Anything else?'

The voice had a gravelly timbre, a hint of impatience that they must go through this identification rigmarole before they could get to the point. Like Klara earlier, he sounded startled when she relayed Braun's message.

'You say the consignment has arrived *already*?'

'Yes. I knew you would be relieved . . .'

The sixty-year old man she was talking to was not relieved. He concealed his reaction but he was alarmed at the speed with which the police had discovered the body of the Englishman.

The reference to the 'consignment' confirmed that Warner had been liquidated on schedule as planned. The further reference to 'has arrived' told him the corpse was already in police hands. He repeated almost the same words Klara had used to Braun.

'Are you quite certain? It is very quick ...'

'I wasn't there to witness the collection,' she said, her voice tinged with sarcasm. 'I'm reporting what our observer told me less than five minutes ago ...'

'Remember who you're talking to,' he told her. He replaced the receiver, took a Havana cigar from a box on his desk, clipped off the end and lit it with a gold lighter.

In her Stuttgart apartment Klara was careful to replace her own receiver before she used the four-letter word. He might share her bed, pay the rent, buy her clothes but he didn't bloody well own her.

She lit a fresh cigarette, studied herself in the mirror and began manipulating an eye pencil. The trouble was Reinhard Dietrich was a millionaire industrialist, a considerable land-owner and a well-known politician. And she never let herself forget that she was consorting with one of the most dangerous men in West Germany.

CHAPTER 2

Tuesday May 26

Tweed sat behind his desk in the first floor office of a house which overlooks Regents Park in the distance. Through thick-lensed spectacles he gazed at the pile of relics taken by the Lindau Water Police off the dead body of Charles Warner.

The hub of Britain's Secret Service is not – as has been reported – in a concrete building close to Waterloo Station. It is situated inside one of many Georgian buildings in a crescent, most of which are occupied by professional institutions.

The location has a number of advantages. On leaving the building there are different directions one can take. To check whether anyone is following you the simplest route is to walk straight into Regents Park. In the open parkland it is impossible for a shadow to conceal his presence.

Only a few paces away is the entrance to Regents Park Underground. Unlike most other stations you descend in a lift to reach the platforms. Again, anyone following has to show himself by stepping into the same lift.

'Pathetic what a man carries about with him,' Tweed remarked.

Keith Martel, the only other occupant in the room, lit a cigarette and wondered whether Tweed was criticising the relics because they offended his sense of order or commenting on the poverty of what a man left behind. He decided it was the latter.

There was about twenty years' difference in the ages of the two men. Martel, tall, well-built, dark-haired and with an air of supreme self-confidence, was twenty-nine. His most prominent feature was his Roman nose. His most outstanding characteristic was insubordination.

He chain-smoked, using a black holder. He spoke German, French and Spanish fluently. He was a first-rate pilot of light aircraft and helicopters. He swam like a fish and hated team sports.

No one knew Tweed's age. Five feet eight inches tall, wiry and with a ramrod back, he had the appearance of an ex-Army major – which he was – and his grey moustache matching his thatch of hair was neatly trimmed. Behind the spectacles his eyes bulged and held a haunted look as though expecting the worst.

'It usually happens – the worst. Count on it,' was his favourite maxim.

Events had an uncanny habit of proving him correct. It was this fact – his reputation for solving problems – and his caustic manner which had persuaded the new head of the department to sidetrack him into the post of Chief of Central Registry. Also the new supremo, Frederick Anthony Howard, had taken an instant dislike to Tweed when they first met in some mysterious past.

'What do you make of it all, Keith?'

Tweed gestured to the possessions of Warner spread in a gap on his desk he had cleared amid tidy piles of dossiers. Martel picked up several slips of paper and tickets extracted from the dead man's wallet.

Warner had been a squirrel, stuffing his wallet with odd items other agents would have thrown away. But Martel knew it was not carelessness: Warner had worked on the basis that if ever anything happened to him while on an assignment he should leave his successor clues.

'What was he doing in Germany?' Martel asked as he examined the collection.

'On loan from me to Erich Stoller of the *Bundesnachrichtendienst*. I owe Erich and he needed an outsider who could pass for a German to infiltrate this Delta outfit in Bavaria – neo-Nazis, as you well know. They cleverly keep just inside the law so they can't be banned.'

The *Bundesnachrichtendienst* – the BND – was the German

Federal Secret Service with discreet headquarters near Münich. There was a dull *clink* as Tweed took something from his pocket and dropped it on the desk. A triangular-shaped silver badge like the Greek letter *delta*.

'That's their latest version of the swastika,' Tweed remarked. 'The badge was found under Warner's body. The killer must have dropped it without realising he'd lost it ...'

'How *was* he killed?'

'Brutally.' Tweed took off his glasses and leaned back in his swivel chair, settling himself on his favourite cushion. 'The BND pathologist reports that Warner was struck with some kind of knife twenty-five times. Twenty-five! And they completed the job by carving their trademark on his naked back – the Delta symbol.'

'We're relying on that to identify it as a Delta killing?'

'We're relying on an impartial eye-witness – whose name Stoller won't reveal even to me. Some German tourist was sitting on an elevated terrace above the harbour at Lindau ...'

'Sounds like the Romerschanze,' Martel interjected.

'Of course, I'd forgotten. You know Lindau. Rum-looking sort of place – I checked it up on the map. From the air it must look like a raft linked by a couple of planks to the mainland. As you know, it's an island linked to Bavaria by two bridges ...'

'One road bridge and a separate rail embankment with a cycle and pedestrian track running alongside the railway.'

'Nice to have an eye for detail,' Tweed commented with a hint of sarcasm. Martel appeared not to notice: the reaction showed Tweed was concealing considerable anxiety.

'As I was saying,' Tweed continued, 'this German tourist using his binoculars watched Warner take his powerboat out on to the lake. He saw a crowd of wind-surfers – six to be precise – get in Warner's way so he had to stop his boat. When they pushed off he saw Warner's boat was drifting – with Warner slumped over the wheel. He thought he must have been taken ill so he immediately contacted the Water Police who berth their launch just below that Romer-what-not terrace . . .' He consulted Stoller's report. 'Chap called Dorner went out to have a look-see . . .'

'And the rest is history – past history, unfortunately.'

'Except that I want you to go out and replace Warner for me,' Tweed said quietly.

Frederick Anthony Howard came into the office without knocking. It would be more accurate to say he *breezed* in. It was the essence of Howard's personality that you dominated a room the moment you entered it.

He was accompanied by Mason, a new recruit. Mason had restless eyes and a lean and hungry look. He said nothing and stood behind his chief like a commissionaire.

'Tweed, I suppose you know we need all *active* personnel mustered for the protection of the PM during her trip to the summit conference in Vienna?'

He invested the word 'active' with a significance which included Martel and specifically excluded Tweed. Florid-faced and with a choleric temper, Howard was a well-built man of fifty who had an unruly shock of grey hair and a brisk manner. He had a reputation for being a devil with the women, a reputation he relished.

The fact that his wife, Cynthia, lived at their 'small manor' in the country and he rented 'a pied-à-terre' in Knightsbridge could not have been more convenient. Tweed's privately expressed comment had been rather devastating.

'Pied-à-terre? I've been there once. When he has a girl with him it must be standing room only . . .'

'What's all this bumf?' Howard demanded, picking up the wallet from the desk. Martel had palmed the slips of paper he was perusing and slipped them into his pocket as Howard entered the room.

'That *bumf*,' Tweed said grimly, 'happens to be the personal effects of the late Charles Warner. The BND kindly flew them straight to London from Münich so we can begin our investigation at the earliest moment.'

Having delivered his statement in a calm, cold voice Tweed put on his spectacles. Without them he felt naked, especially in the presence of people like Howard. And he was well aware that wearing the glasses made it impossible to judge his expression.

'Getting touchy in our old age, are we?' Howard enquired lightly, trying to bluff his way through what he now realised had been the height of bad taste.

'The man is dead,' Tweed replied, giving no quarter.

'I don't like it any more than you do.' Howard strolled over to the heavily net-curtained window and gazed through the armoured glass. He clasped both hands in a theatrical pose before making his pronouncement.

'I simply must insist that all active personnel are available to travel aboard the Summit Express from Paris to Vienna one week from today. Tuesday June 2 . . .'

'I do have a calendar,' Tweed commented.

Howard looked pointedly away from Tweed and at Martel who said nothing, his cigarette holder in his mouth – which to Howard was insubordination. He had made it very clear he preferred no one to practise the filthy habit in his presence.

'Well?' he pressed.

Martel stared back at Howard, puffing away, his expression hard and hostile. 'I'm otherwise engaged,' he said eventually, still clenching the holder. Howard turned to Tweed and erupted.

'This is too damned much. I'm taking Martel and attaching him to my protection group. He speaks good German . . .'

'Which is why he's going to Bavaria,' Tweed told him. 'We were suspicious something strange is going on in that part of the world. It looks as though we were right. Otherwise why was Warner killed?'

Howard glanced at Mason who still stood by the door like a commissionaire. Time to assert his authority. '*We?*' he repeated in a supercilious tone. 'May I enquire the identity of "we"?'

'Erich Stoller of the BND and myself,' Tweed said tersely.

Time to get rid of Howard. 'I have a minute from the Minister – authorising me to investigate the Bavarian enigma and full powers to use my staff in any way I see fit. May I also point out that the route of the Summit Express carrying the four top western leaders to Vienna to meet the Soviet First Secretary passes through Bavaria?'

They were alone again. Howard had stormed out of the office on hearing of the existence of the special ministerial minute. Mason had followed, closing the door carefully behind him.

'He was memorising my appearance,' Martel said.

'Do let's get on. Oh, all right, who was?'

'The new boy, Mason. Who brought him in off the street?'

'Ex-Special Branch, I gather,' Tweed replied. 'And it was Howard who recruited him – interviewed him personally, I heard. I think he'd been angling to join us for a while ...'

'We don't take people who apply,' Martel snapped.

'We do now, apparently. How are you going to pick up Warner's trail? And since you've had your breakfast your stomach should be strong enough to study these pictures taken by Stoller's man – two show clearly the triangular symbol of the Delta Party carved out of Warner's back ...'

'Delta being the neo-Nazis,' Martel ruminated as he studied the glossy blow-ups. 'Delta is run by that millionaire electronics industrialist, Reinhard Dietrich. He's also running for office in the Bavarian state elections which take place ...'

'On Thursday June 4 – the day after the Summit Express crosses Bavaria,' Tweed interjected. 'Which is something else Howard may have overlooked. You know, Keith, I have the oddest feeling the whole thing interlocks – the Bavarian crossing by the express, the state elections, and the murder of Warner before he could reach us.'

Martel dropped the glossy prints back on the desk and extracted from his pocket the pieces of paper he had secreted while Howard was in the room. He showed Tweed one particular piece of paper.

'I'll start in Zürich to try and find out what got Warner killed.'

'Why Zürich? I did notice a first-class ticket from Münich by train to Zürich – and another from Lindau to Münich, but ...'

'This little scrap of paper. Go on, have a really good look at it.'

Tweed examined it under a magnifying glass. It was some kind of ticket which carried the printed legend *VBZ Zuri ... Linie*. The words *RENNWEG/AUGUST* had been punched in purple on the ticket together with the price 0.80.

'From the last time I was in Zürich I'm sure you're holding a tram ticket,' Martel explained. 'A tram whose route takes it along Bahnhofstrasse – Rennweg is a side street running off Bahnhofstrasse. Warner travelled about inside the city. Why? Where to? He never wasted time.'

Tweed nodded agreement, unlocked a drawer and brought out a file. From inside he produced a tiny black notebook and thumbed through the pages. Then he waved the key he had used.

'I suppose you know Howard waits until everyone has gone home in the evening and then prowls – hoping to find something he hasn't been told about? He spends more time spying on his own staff than on the opposition. Still, it will help to keep his hand in ...'

'You're just about to play your strongest card,' Martel observed. 'You're enjoying the anticipation. Could I now see what you hold in the way of aces?'

'It came with Warner's possessions Stoller flew to me with such commendable speed.' Tweed riffled the pages of the tiny notebook. 'Only I know Warner carried two notebooks – a large one inside his breast pocket, which is missing. Presumably filched by the swine who mutilated him. That was full of meaningless rubbish. This little fellow he kept in a secret pocket Stoller himself found when he flew to Lindau – or the nearest airstrip – when he heard from Dorner of the Water Police.'

'Am I to be allowed to see it?'

'You have a viper's tongue, Mr Martel.' Tweed handed over the notebook. 'The trouble is the jottings in it don't make sense.'

Martel went through the pages. The references seemed disjointed. *Hauptbahnhof, Münich ... Hauptbahnhof, Zürich ... Delta ... Centralhof ... Bregenz ... Washington, DC, Clint Loomis ... Pullach, BND ... Operation Crocodile.*

'Charles ...'

They had always called him Charles. Warner was the kind of man they would never dream of calling Charlie; he would have resented it.

'Charles,' Martel repeated, 'seems to have been fixated on the main stations – the Hauptbahnhofs in Münich and Zürich. Why? And if the note sequence means anything Delta is somehow linked with Zürich, which is odd, wouldn't you say?'

'Delta is the official neo-Nazi party with candidates standing in the coming Bavarian state elections,' Tweed remarked. 'But it also works underground. Rumour has it Delta cells are operating in north-east Switzerland between St. Gallen and the Austrian border. Ferdy Arnold of Swiss counter-espionage is worried ...'

'Enough to give us support?' Martel enquired.

'At arm's length. You know the Swiss – policy of neutrality so they feel they have to be careful ...'

'With that bunch of thugs? Look what they did to Warner. And who is Clint Loomis – Washington, DC?'

'I can't fathom that reference.' Tweed leaned back and swivelled his chair through small arcs. 'Clint is an old friend of mine. *Ex*-CIA. Kicked out by Tim O'Meara, now chief of the Secret Service detachment which will protect the US President aboard the Summit Express to Vienna. Makes no sense ...'

'Who provides most of the funds for this link-up with the BND if Howard is against it?'

'Erich Stoller of the BND – and he has plenty of money at his disposal. Delta is scaring Bonn ...'

'So Charles, being the secretive type he was, could have flown on a quick trip to Washington from Münich without your knowing?'

'Yes, I suppose so.' Tweed sounded dubious. 'I don't see

why.'

'But we don't see anything yet, do we? Least of all what Warner found out that provoked his cold-blooded murder.' He checked the notebook again. '*Centralhof*. That rings a bell.'

Tweed stirred in his chair and the expression behind his spectacles went blank. Which meant, Martel knew from experience, he was going to be told something he wouldn't like. He lit another cigarette and clamped his teeth on the holder.

'You at least have some help on this thing, Keith,' Tweed said cheerfully. 'Ferdy Arnold put his best operative at the disposal of Warner and that operative may have more to tell you. Outside of his killers, she may have been the last person to see Warner alive ...'

'*She?*'

'The pronoun denotes a woman. Claire Hofer. Her mother was English, her father Swiss – and one of Ferdy's best men, which is how she came to join the Swiss Service. She lives at Centralhof 45 in Zürich. Hence the reference, I presume ...'

'Except that Warner seems to have used his secret notebook for suspect factors ...'

'You may need all the help you can get ...'

'All the help I can *trust* ...'

'She could be a major asset,' Tweed persisted.

'You do realise,' Martel began vehemently, 'that Warner was betrayed by someone who *knew* he was making the crossing to Switzerland – by someone he *trusted*. And tell me again why Stoller asked for outside help.'

'Because he thinks the BND may have been infiltrated. You will find an atmosphere of suspicion everywhere you go. And with the Summit Express leaving Paris at 2335 hours on Tuesday June 2 you have exactly seven days to crack this mystery.'

22

CHAPTER 3

Wednesday May 27

Will Mr Keith Martel bound for Geneva please report immediately to the Swissair reception desk . . .

Martel was inside Heathrow on his way to the final departure lounge when the message came over the tannoy. He went back down the stairs slowly and paused where he could see Swissair. Only when two more passengers had called at the reception desk did he wander over.

The Swissair girl told him he was wanted urgently on the phone and left him as he picked up the receiver, fuming. It was Tweed. His voice held that quality of detached control which meant he was alarmed. They went through the identification routine and then Martel quietly exploded.

'What the hell do you mean broadcasting my name so everyone in the bloody terminal can hear . . .'

'I did change the destination to Geneva. Didn't they . . .'

'They did. Thank you for that small consideration. I now have ten minutes to board my flight . . .'

'My office was bugged – while we were talking yesterday. About Delta, the lot . . .'

'Where are you calling from.'

'A phone booth at Baker Street station, of course. You don't imagine I'm such a damned fool as to call from the building, do you? I found the bloody thing purely by chance. The cleaning woman had left a note that my main light bulb had gone. I checked it – the bug was inside the shade . . .'

'So anyone could have overheard our conversation, could have taped it, could know where I'm going and why?'

'I thought you ought to know – before you boarded the plane.'

Tweed sounded genuinely concerned. Unusual for Tweed to display any emotion.

'Thanks,' Martel said shortly. 'I'll keep my eyes open ...'

'Probably it's the Zürich end you should watch. A reception committee could be waiting for you ...'

'Thanks a million. I must go now ...'

The Swissair flight departed on time at 1110 hours. In London it had been 50°F. As they lost height over Switzerland Martel, who had a window seat, watched the saddleback ridge of the Jura mountains which he felt he could reach down and touch. The plane had come in over Basle and headed east for Zürich.

As the machine tilted the most spectacular of views was framed in a window on the other side of the plane, a sunlit panorama of the snowbound Alps. Martel picked out the savage triangle of the Matterhorn, a shape not unlike Delta's badge. Then they landed.

At Kloten Airport, ten kilometres outside Zürich, a wave of heat enveloped him as he disembarked. 50°F in London; 75°F in Zürich. After Heathrow it seemed unnaturally quiet and orderly. When he had passed through Customs and Passport Control he started looking for trouble.

He was tempted to take the train from the airport's underground station to the Hauptbahnhof, the second location recorded in Warner's notebook. Instead he took a cab to the Baur au Lac.

He was staying at one of the top three hotels in Switzerland and the room tariff would have caused Howard to have apoplexy. But Howard was not paying the expenses. Before Martel left London a large amount of deutschemarks had been telexed to Tweed for the trip from Erich Stoller.

'The Germans are paying, so enjoy yourself,' Tweed had commented. 'They're conscious of the fact that the first man I sent to help is no longer with us ...'

'And that I may be next?' Martel had replied. 'Still, it's good cover – to stay at the best place in town rather than some grotty little *pension* ...'

Good cover? He recalled the remark cynically as the cab sped along the two-lane highway into the *centrum* of Zürich. It had been made in Tweed's office which they now knew had been bugged. He could change his hotel – but if the opposition sought him out at the Baur au Lac it might present him with a golden opportunity.

Just so long as I see them first he thought as he lit a fresh cigarette.

It was good to be back in Zürich, to see the blue trams rumbling along their tracks. The route the driver followed took him down through the underpass, sharp right across the bridge over the river Limmat and into the Bahnhofplatz. Martel stared at the massive bulk of the Hauptbahnhof, wondering again why the place had figured in Warner's notebook.

To his left he caught a glimpse of the tree-lined Bahnhofstrasse, his favourite street in his favourite European city. Here were the great banks with their incredible security systems, their underground vaults stacked with gold bullion. Then they were driving down Talstrasse, the street where the Baur au Lac was situated at the far end facing the lake.

A heavy grey overcast pressed down on the city and, as was so often the case when the temperature was high, the atmosphere was clammy. The cab turned in under an archway and pulled up at the main entrance. The head porter opened his door and Martel counted five Mercedes and one Rolls Royce parked in the concourse. Beyond the entrance the green lawns of the mini-park stretched away towards the lake.

From the airport to hotel he had not been followed. He was quite certain. The fact somehow did not reassure him as he followed the porter inside. The hotel was almost full. On the phone he had accepted a twin-bedded room overlooking the park. When the porter left he checked bedroom and bathroom for hidden microphones and found nothing. He was still not happy.

He went down the staircase after checking his room – avoiding

25

the lift because lifts could be traps. The atmosphere was luxurious, peaceful and disturbingly normal. He strolled over the concourse to where tea and drinks were being served under a canopy near the French Restaurant. He ordered coffee, lit a cigarette and waited, watching the world's élite arrive and depart. He was looking for a shadow.

His appointment with Claire Hofer at her apartment was eight in the evening, an odd hour which he had wondered about. Normally he would have scanned the area in advance but the bugging of Tweed's office changed his tactics. He was good at waiting and he counted on the impatience of the opposition.

By 7.30 he was swimming in coffee and people were starting their evening meal in the nearby restaurant. He suddenly scribbled his signature and room number on the bill, stood up and walked out under the archway. Crossing Talstrasse, he turned left up Bahnhofstrasse away from the lake. He had spotted no one but could not rid himself of a feeling of unease.

Stopping by a machine in the deserted street, he inserted four twenty-centime coins obtained from the Baur au Lac cashier, took his ticket and waited for one of Zürich's 'sacred cows'. These gleaming trams had total right-of-way over all other traffic – hence the Zürichers' irreverent description.

The ticket gave him a slight twinge. Inside his breast pocket was an envelope which contained the contents of Warner's wallet – including the tram ticket with the destination RENNWEG/AUGUST inscribed. This stop was not far away and the ticket could have been used by Warner when he called on Claire Hofer. A tram glided up the street, streamlined and freshly-painted. Martel climbed aboard and sat down near the exit doors.

From the hotel it would have taken him five minutes to walk to Centralhof 45, Claire Hofer's address. Taking a tram and travelling only one stop he hoped to flush out anyone following him. He played it deviously at the next stop. Standing up, he pressed the black button which would automatically open the double doors when the tram stopped.

The doors opened, he checked his ticket and stared about in

26

a perplexed manner as though uncertain of his destination. People left the tram, came on board. Still he waited. The doors began closing. Martel *moved* . . .

He knew how the tram worked. He stepped down on to the outside footboard just when it began to elevate in conjunction with the closing of the automatic doors. As a safety device, when there is weight on the footboard, the doors remain open – or open again if they are closing. Reaching the sidewalk he paused to light a cigarette, to see if anyone rushed out after him. The doors shut, the tram moved off.

Centralhof is a square enclosed by buildings. One side overlooks Bahnhofstrasse. There are four entrances under archways at the centre of each side of the square – one leading off Bahnhofstrasse – to the interior garden beyond.

Martel crossed the street, walked down Poststrasse, turned right and continued along the third side of the block. Walking under the archway he saw the trees and the fountain he remembered. Nothing had changed. He sat down on a seat.

He had never visited this apartment in Centralhof before – but on an earlier visit he had used exactly the same tactic to entice a shadow to show himself. On that occasion it had worked.

The only sounds in the semi-dark were the chirruping of invisible sparrows in the foliage of the trees, the gentle splash of fountain water. It was impossible to imagine a more peaceful scene. He looked up at the windows masked by net curtains and the silence was almost a sound.

No one had followed him into this oasis of peace. He began to think he had evaded detection. He got up and headed for the archway Tweed had shown him on a street plan which contained the entrance to the apartment.

There was only one name-plate, a bell-push by its side. *C. Hofer*. He pressed the bell and a woman's voice responded through the metal grille of the speakphone almost immediately. In German – not Swiss-German, which he would not have understood.

'Who is that?'

'Martel.'

He kept his voice low, his mouth close to the grille. The other voice sounded disembodied, filtered through the louvres.

'I have released the catch. I am on the first floor . . .'

He went into a bare hall and the spring-loaded hinge closed the door behind him. An old-fashioned lift with open grille-work enclosing a cage faced him. He ignored it and ran lightly up the staircase to arrive a few seconds before she would expect him.

Height: five feet six inches. Weight: nine stone two pounds. Age: twenty-five. Colour of hair: black. Colour of eyes: deep blue.

This was the description of Hofer Tweed had supplied to Martel in London. It was typical of Ferdy Arnold's consideration and efficiency that he should supply the girl's vital statistics in this terminology: he knew Tweed's detestation of the Common Market and the metric system.

Martel was not armed with any weapon when he reached the first floor. He expected Hofer to supply a hand-gun. A closed door faced him on the deserted landing and he noticed that – blended in with the grain of the highly-varnished woodwork – was a spy-hole. At least she took *some* precautions when strangers arrived.

'Welcome to Zürich, Mr Martel. Please come in quickly . . .'

The door had been opened swiftly and the girl examined him as she ushered him inside, closed the door and double-locked it. Martel had stubbed out his cigarette as he waited inside the archway below. He held the black holder between his fingers and studied her without any show of enthusiasm.

She was wearing dark-tinted glasses with the outsize exotic-shaped lenses so many girls affected these days. Her hair *was* very black, her height *was* about five foot six and he calculated she *would* turn the scales at around nine stone. She was also very attractive and wore a flowered blouse and a pastel-coloured skirt which revealed shapely legs.

'Satisfied?' she demanded in a waspish tone.

'You can't be too careful,' he told her and walked out of the tiny hall into a living-room whose windows overlooked the garden inside Centralhof. His manner was off-hand and he inserted a cigarette and lit it without asking her permission.

'Yes, you may smoke,' she told him.

'Good. It helps my concentration ...'

He looked round the room which was filled with heavy leather arm-chairs and sofas and the usual weighty sideboard. The German Swiss went in for solid furniture which was probably a reflection of their sturdy character. He thought he knew what Hofer was thinking. *Hell, do I have to work with this bastard?*

'I'm just making some coffee,' she said in a more friendly voice.

'That would be nice ...'

He went towards the window and changed direction as she vanished through a swing-door into a kitchen. From a quick glimpse it looked expensively equipped. Quietly he turned the handle of a closed door and eased it open, peering inside.

The bedroom. Large double bed. Large dressing-table with a few cosmetic articles neatly arranged. A pair of large double doors which presumably led to a large built-in wardrobe or dressing room. Everything spotless. He left the door half-open.

She had the percolator bubbling away when he walked uninvited into the kitchen. On a wing counter there were plates of half-eaten food, an unwashed glass, unwashed cutlery and a pair of scissors with a piece of sticking-plaster attached to one of the blades. She swung round, her mouth tight.

'Make yourself at home, Martel ...'

'I always do ...' He smiled briefly, the cigarette-holder still clenched between his teeth. 'Did Warner sleep here often?'

It threw her. She almost caught the percolator with her hand and knocked the whole thing over. He waited, watching her, smoking his cigarette. She unplugged the percolator, which had stopped bubbling, went to a wall-cupboard and opened it.

'Spring-cleaning – that's when I change things around to stop life getting boring ...'

She took coffee-cups from another cupboard next to the one

29

she had first opened and Martel was relieved to see they also were large. He drank coffee by the gallon. He said no cream and she poured two cups of black coffee, put them on saucers and looked at him.

'You're in my way . . .'

'Allow me . . .'

He picked up both cups and carried them into the living-room where he placed them on mats on a low table. She followed him, talking as she came through the swing-door.

'You're agile – I can't get through that swing-door with two cups. I have to take them one at a . . .'

He looked up as she stopped in mid-sentence. She was staring through her dark glasses at the half-opened bedroom door. It was impossible to see the expression in her eyes but her mouth compressed into a bleak gash.

'You've been in the bedroom . . .'

'I like to be sure I really am alone with someone . . .'

'You've got a bloody nerve . . .'

She started towards the bedroom but he reached forward, caught her arm and sat her down on the sofa beside him. Still gripping her arm with one hand he reached up towards the outsized tinted glasses. She clawed her other hand and struck at his face with talon-like nails. He had to move fast to grab her wrist to protect himself: she had moved like a whip-lash.

'Martel, I've had you in a big way,' she hissed through perfectly formed teeth. '*If* we are going to work together we have a few things to get straightened out . . .'

'You never answered my question about you and Warner . . .'

He had released her and picked up his cup of coffee, sipping at it while he watched her. She got herself under control very quickly, picking up her own cup before she replied.

'That's one of the things. First, it's none of your damned business. Second, the answer is no – he didn't even make a pass at me in all the time I knew him. It was strictly a business relationship – like ours is going to be . . .

'Oh, that you can count on, Claire. When did you last see

Warner before he was murdered? And I may call you Claire?'

'I suppose so. I last saw Charlie three days before he went off on a trip to Lindau. He was frustrated – said he felt he wasn't getting anywhere ...'

'With Delta?'

She paused. Martel sat thinking and guessed if she could have read his thoughts they would have surprised her. He was recalling Tweed's comment that the dossiers never lied.

'If the facts conflict with your expectations, always believe the facts,' was a maxim Tweed had hammered into Martel. Hofer had worked out her reply.

'You're referring to their neo-Nazi background?'

'I'm referring to Delta's underground organisation he was tracking.'

Martel's attitude now was one of complete relaxation but inside his nerves were tingling as he forced himself to lean back and cross his legs. Hofer drank more coffee and then stood up. When she had followed him in from the kitchen she had brought with her a shoulder bag which she left on a chair behind the sofa close to the window. She went round the back of the sofa, talking while she moved.

'He did leave a notebook with me. There's a lot in it but I'd have remembered any reference to Delta ...'

Martel was like a coiled spring. There was a faint thumping sound which came from beyond the half-open bedroom door. Hofer continued talking as she undid the clasp of her bag.

'The workmen next door are a nuisance – they're making alterations to the apartment before redecorating. The people cleared out to Tangier until it's all finished ...'

Martel had chosen the sofa to sit on because it faced a large mirror over the fireplace. There were vases of flowers on the ledge but between them he could watch Hofer behind him. He had made a bloody awful mistake when he was so careful to check that he was not followed to Centralhof. He had got it the wrong way round. The danger had been in front of him, not behind. *The enemy was waiting for his arrival at the apartment ...*

31

'I'm sorry if I was uptight when you arrived,' Hofer continued, 'but the news of Charlie's death shook me ...'

He heard the click, watched her coming up behind him through a gap in the flowers in front of the mirror. He swung round suddenly, grasped Hofer's right hand by the wrist. The hand held an object like a large felt-tip pen.

The click had occurred when she pressed something and a blade shot out from inside the handle, a blade unlike any he had ever seen, a blade like a skewer with a needle-thin tip. She had been pushing the needle-point towards the centre of the back of his neck.

He twisted the wrist brutally and she yelped as she dropped the weapon and he hauled her bodily over the back of the sofa and sprawled her along its length. Her skirt was dragged up to her thighs exposing a superb pair of legs. She arched her supple body in a sexual movement, using her free hand to try and pull him down on top of her.

'Bloody cow ...'

He hit her a hard blow on the side of the jaw and she went limp. Standing up, he undid his leather belt and tightened the adjustable fasteners on either hip. When he bent down to turn her over on her face she suddenly came awake and jabbed two stiffened fingers towards his eyes. He became rougher, gave her a tremendous slap.

'Start struggling and I'll break your Goddamn neck ...'

For the first time he saw her mouth go slack with fear and she remained passive as he turned her over, pulled the upper part of her body towards him, then used the belt to strap her ankles to her wrists.

It was the most uncomfortable position anyone can be forced into: if she struggled she would suffer excruciating pain. He tightened the belt to the limit of his strength. Soon the circulation would start to go. He left her on the sofa after using his handkerchief as a gag.

'It's not too clean,' he assured her.

Then he walked into the bedroom where the faint thumping

was repeating itself. He opened both doors of the built-in wardrobe cupboard and looked down. The dark-haired girl on the floor had been trussed up like a chicken and her mouth was sealed with a band of sticking plaster.

'Hello, Claire Hofer,' he said. 'Thanks for the warning. Now let's make you comfortable. You have got guts . . .'

CHAPTER 4

Wednesday May 27

Hofer was emerging from the state of shock brought on by her ordeal inside the cupboard. She had cleared up the mess in the kitchen and was making coffee for herself and Martel.

'How did you know that girl was impersonating me?' she asked.

Their prisoner was lying on the living-room floor. Martel had released her from his belt and replaced it with the ropes used to bind up Hofer. Her mouth was sealed with a fresh strip of sticking-plaster Hofer had provided from the kitchen.

'She made a lot of mistakes,' Martel explained. 'Although her physical description fitted the one I had been given she wore dark-tinted glasses – in a room where the light was dim anyway. Now we know why – her eyes are brown . . .'

'There must have been more . . .'

'When I peered into the bedroom your cosmetics were neat and tidy on the dressing-table – one hell of a contrast with the food remains and dirt in here. The bit of sticking-plaster stuck to the scissors intrigued me. She had no visible injury. The normal one is when a woman cuts her hands in the kitchen. There were other things, too . . .'

'Such as?'

'More damning was the fact she didn't know which cupboard held the coffee cups. She denied Warner had ever made a pass at her – he always made one try for an attractive woman. And she called him Charlie. He always insisted on Charles.'

'You really are observant. Coffee in here?'

'No, in the living-room. I have questions to ask our imposter. She also over-reacted to my leaving the bedroom door half-open.

Plus her elaborate explanation to cover your thumping the inside of the cupboard. You took a chance there . . .'

'I heard a man's voice and guessed you had arrived. I felt such a fool that I'd let her overpower me I had to warn you. Was she going to kill you?'

They had moved back into the living-room where their prisoner was rolled on her side in front of the fireplace. Martel lowered his voice so she couldn't hear him.

'Was she going to kill me?' He picked up the needle weapon he had earlier rescued from the floor and placed on a table. 'I think so. This ingenious little toy is very like a hypodermic. When I grabbed her she was about to ram it into the back of my neck. Press this button a second time and I'd say it injects the fluid. Let's test her reaction to her own medicine . . .'

Holding the weapon out of sight he knelt on the floor and rolled the girl on her back. With the other hand he took a grip on the plaster and ripped it off her mouth. She screamed. He placed a hand over her lips.

'No more noise. I'm going to ask questions. You're going to answer. Your real name?'

'Go stuff yourself . . .'

'What would happen if I jab this into you and press the button?'

He showed her the needle weapon. He moved the point close to the side of her neck. Her brown eyes glared up at him with a mixture of hatred and apprehension.

'For God's sake, no! *Please* . . .'

'She says *please*,' Martel observed sarcastically. 'And yet she was about to give me the same treatment. Oh, well, here we go . . .'

'Gisela Zobel . . .'

'Where is your home base?'

'Bavaria . . . München. For pity's sake . . .'

'Pity?' Martel glanced up at Hofer who was staring intently, wondering how far he was prepared to go. 'She wouldn't know the meaning of the word, would she?'

'Not from the way she treated me . . .' Hofer responded with deliberate callousness. 'You decide . . .'

She lit a cigarette and the girl on the floor watched her with bulging eyes. Sweat beads were forming on her forehead. Martel moved the needle closer as he asked the question.

'Who do you work for?'

'He will kill me . . .'

'How could he? If you don't give the reply – the right reply – and we have certain information Warner sent by a secret route, you will be dead anyway. That is, unless I'm mistaken about what this instrument you were going to use on me contains. So, once again, here goes . . .'

'*Reinhard Dietrich* . . .'

Then she fainted from terror – whether from uttering the name or because of Martel's threat to use the weapon he was not sure. He looked into Hofer's deep blue eyes, shrugged and withdrew the needle tip from the proximity of Zobel's neck.

'Get me a cork to protect this damned thing,' he suggested and while she fetched one from the kitchen he gazed at the weapon. He was convinced that the contents injected into the victim would be lethal, that Gisela Zobel *had* planned to kill him. He would hand it to the counter-espionage people: Forensic could then check it.

At ten o'clock night had descended and Martel decided they could safely leave the apartment. Hofer packed a bag and Martel arranged with the police to send a plain-clothes man to the Baur au Lac to pay his bill and collect his suitcase. The bag was now standing in the small hall outside the apartment.

'We take a train to St. Gallen,' Martel told the Swiss girl in the living-room. 'We have to pick up Warner's trail there . . .'

'We have very little to go on,' the girl reminded him. 'Only that he stopped off there on his way here from Bavaria . . .'

'So we make use of what little we have got . . .'

The evening had been packed with activity. Hofer had looked up the number in her pocket diary and Martel had phoned Berne. While he was talking to her boss, Ferdy Arnold, he had studied her in the mirror.

Her description fitted the one provided by Tweed perfectly but he was puzzled by her passive personality. She was a nice girl with long dark hair, a soft voice and graceful movements. Already he liked her. But he had expected someone more dynamic.

The Swiss counter-espionage chief had flown by private plane to Zürich. The atmosphere changed the moment he entered the place. A small, serious-faced man with rimless glasses, Ferdy Arnold resembled a banker. He took immediate decisions.

'We smuggle her out in an ambulance,' he announced, indicating Gisela Zobel who was now propped up in one of the deep arm-chairs. 'She will be taken to a special hospital. She will be kept under heavy guard. She will be intensively interrogated.'

He looked at Martel, ignoring Hofer. 'Phone me at this number at ten in the morning ...' He scribbled a number on a small pad, tore off the sheet and handed it to the Englishman. 'I've left off the Zürich code in case you lose the paper ...'

Arnold, smartly dressed in a dark blue suit, looked at Martel with a wry smile. 'It isn't that I don't trust you ...'

'But one English agent, Warner, was spotted – even posing as a German – so you're playing it to cover all angles. And why do I phone at ten in the morning? Surely you'll only just have started Zobel's daily interrogation ...'

'On the contrary, we shall just have *finished* since she will be interrogated throughout the night without a break ...'

Martel was not happy. There was an atmosphere which did not ring true. Something in the relationship between Ferdy Arnold and his 'top operative', Hofer. He was damned if he could detect why he sensed he was being tricked – but his instincts had never let him down yet.

'Come into the bedroom,' Arnold suggested, glancing at Gisela Zobel, who sat motionless watching and listening. 'Keep an eye on her,' he told Hofer. When he had closed the bedroom door he accepted a cigarette from Martel.

37

'All that I said in there was strictly for Zobel's ears. It can help the breaking-down process if they worry about what is in store for them.'

'She admitted she was working for Reinhard Dietrich,' Martel told him.

'I see.'

Arnold showed no interest in the statement. Martel recalled a remark Tweed had made in London. *At arm's length ... you know the Swiss. Policy of neutrality ...* It was understandable – that the Swiss counter-espionage should not want an open war with a German neo-Nazi movement. Understandable but unhelpful. Arnold was, he suspected, maintaining a watching brief.

'Berne,' Arnold commented, 'is disturbed about rumours that an underground organisation has spread its tentacles into northern Switzerland ...'

'St. Gallen?'

'What made you mention that place?' Arnold enquired.

'Because it is one of the chief towns in north-eastern Switzerland,' Martel replied casually. 'I find the choice of the word *delta* interesting – the Rhine delta is located just beyond your border with Austria. The Vorarlberg province ...'

He watched Arnold's reaction closely. One of the references in Warner's tiny notebook had been to *Bregenz*. This was the only port Austria had on its narrow frontage of lake shore at the eastern end of Lake Konstanz.

'We've been in touch with Austrian counter-espionage,' Arnold commented vaguely. 'Nothing has come of it so far. Berne is sensitive about the recent unprecedented student riots here in Zürich. It is suspected they are organised by a secret Delta cell.' He checked his watch and seemed disinclined to linger. 'I must go now.'

He left without saying a word to the girl except for a brief exchange before walking out. Martel frowned as he looked round the living-room. Gisela Zobel had disappeared. Hofer explained before he could ask.

'A team dressed like ambulance men came. They took her

38

away on a stretcher.'

'Arnold doesn't waste much time, does he? By the way, as he was leaving he said something to you. Did you mention that we are on our way to St. Gallen?'

'No.' She looked surprised. 'Is something wrong? I'm beginning to know your intonations ...'

Martel passed it off lightly as he picked up both bags in the hall. 'When you get to know me better you'll realise I often ask random questions. We board one of the trams for the Haupt-bahnhof?'

'It will be quicker – the tram goes straight to the station. A number eight. And it's an unobtrusive way of travelling ...'

'Warner thought that, too ...'

The brutal assault – the insane shock – commenced as soon as they closed the street door to the apartment and emerged from the archway leading into Bahnhofstrasse. Ten o'clock at night. Illuminated by the street lights, the trees lining one of the most famous thoroughfares in the world cast patches of shadow on the wide pavement. It was very quiet and few people were about.

One essential addition to Martel's equipment since he arrived at the Centralhof apartment was the Colt .45 he now carried in a spring-loaded shoulder holster. Hofer had provided this, taking it from a secret compartment in the floor of the wardrobe cupboard where she had been imprisoned. She had also given him ammunition.

Martel was committing a strictly illegal act carrying the gun but they would cross no frontiers on their way to St. Gallen. He had asked her not to mention to Ferdy Arnold the fact that he was now armed. He was not sure why he made this request.

'The ticket machine is over here,' Hofer said and he followed her with the two cases. 'I'll take my own case once we're on the tram.'

He watched her inserting coins. Light from a lamp shone down directly on her. She really was a very beautiful girl and he wondered why she had ever joined the service. He'd try to find

39

out when he knew her better ...

A tram was coming in the distance from the lake direction so, if it was the right number, it would take them to the top of the street which faced the Hauptbahnhof. That was the reason he stood with a case in each hand, ready to board the tram – which put him at an initial disadvantage.

He was listening to the rumble of the approaching tram, the faint hiss of the traction wires, when the huge six-seater Mercedes appeared and charged like a tank. It came out of nowhere and swung up on to the sidewalk alongside the ticket machine, alongside the girl ...

The shock hit Martel like a physical blow. Men were pouring out of the Mercedes, men dressed in respectable business suits and wearing dark glasses. He saw two of them grab Hofer, one of them pressing a cloth over the upper part of her face. Beneath the glare of the street light they had another common denominator – a triangular silver badge like the Greek letter *delta* in their coat lapels.

He heard the oncoming tram ringing its warning bell – the car was positioned diagonally, its front on the sidewalk, its rear in the street, blocking the tramline. A second car appeared, a Rolls Royce, and swung across the tramline blocking it completely. The tram's bell continued clanging as the driver jammed on his brakes and stopped a few feet from the Rolls Royce.

Martel had dropped his bags and was moving. The Colt .45 was in his hand as the Rolls turned slightly and swivelled the glare of its undipped headlights full on him. Shielding his eyes with one hand he snapped off two shots. There was a tinkling of glass and both lights died. One of the men from the Mercedes produced an automatic and aimed point-blank at Martel. The Englishman shot him and the gunman sagged back against the Mercedes, blood cascading from his forehead.

Martel ran towards the two men still grappling with Hofer. She had torn the cloth away from her face and in the clammy night air a waft of chloroform reached Martel's nostrils. The first man was turning towards Martel when the Englishman lashed

40

out. The savage kick reached its target – the assailant's kneecap. He screamed and dropped in a heap. More men appeared from the far side of the Mercedes and now Hofer was screaming at the top of her voice.

Martel found it a nightmare. This was anarchy, violence, kidnapping on the main street in Zürich. Another attacker levelled an automatic at Martel who fired in a reflex movement, still trying to reach the girl. The man clutched at his chest and his hand came away covered in blood as he toppled forward.

More men were appearing – from inside the Rolls. Martel ducked and weaved, never still for a moment, lashing out with the barrel of his Colt, catching one man a terrible blow on the side of his face, raking him from his ear to the tip of his jaw.

The arrival of reinforcements distracted Martel. He was fighting for his life. He went on using the Colt as a club, preserving his remaining bullets. He took refuge with his back to the ticket machine so they could only come at him from the front – and something very hard struck his skull, blurring his vision. As his sight cleared he saw an appalling sight. Hofer was being dragged head first inside the rear of the Mercedes, her legs kicking until another man grabbed her ankles and twisted them viciously over each other. She looked as though she were being sucked inside the maw of a shark.

And now there was smoke. One of them had thrown a smoke bomb – probably several – in the direction of the tram. The street began to fill with fog. A car engine started up. A man grappling with Martel let go and tried to flee. They had Hofer inside the Mercedes. *He had to reach the Mercedes*! As the man ran Martel shot him and he sprawled with a crash on the flagstones.

The Mercedes backed off the sidewalk. The injured and the dead had been collected and taken inside the two cars – except for the man on the flagstones. The Rolls Royce also was moving. With the Mercedes leading both cars sped off up Bahnhofstrasse, then turned left at the Paradeplatz.

It was suddenly very quiet and the stationary tram was still hidden in drifting smoke. Martel slithered in a pool of blood. He stumbled back to the man they had abandoned, the one who had grappled with him.

The body was lying on its face and Martel quickly felt the neck pulse, cursing when he realised the man *was* dead. As he would have been had Hofer not given him the Colt. He shoved the weapon back into the holster, bent down and heaved the man over on his back. Yes, he also wore the silver badge in his coat lapel. Martel ripped it free and dropped it in his pocket.

A ten-second search of the man's pockets revealed they were empty. No means of identification – except for the badge. He had no doubt all clothing identity such as maker's tabs had been removed. He straightened up and looked around, frustrated and dazed.

The tram was still hidden in the smoke but its silhouette was becoming clearer. No sign of the driver. Sensibly he had remained inside his cab. Martel felt sure he had kept the automatic doors closed to protect his passengers. Nearby was a pathetic sight – two cases standing on the pavement.

At any moment the tram driver was going to emerge from his cab. Martel scraped his shoes back and forth on the edge of the kerb to remove blood from the soles. Then he picked up the two suitcases and left the scene of the nightmare as he heard the distant scream of a patrol-car siren.

The blast from the explosion sent a shock wave down the funnel of Bahnhofstrasse which thumped Martel in the back. He turned down a side street towards the Old Town, taking a roundabout route to the Hauptbahnhof. He didn't think anyone aboard the tram had seen him but a man carrying two suitcases at that hour was conspicuous.

What had caused the explosion he had no idea. He wasn't too interested. At that moment he had three objectives. To hide Hofer's suitcase in a left-luggage locker at the station. Next, to book himself temporarily into a hotel near the station – if he returned to the Baur au Lac he could walk straight into the arms of the opposition. Finally, to phone Ferdy Arnold's headquarters in Berne.

Martel felt he was on the edge of a whirlpool. He could hardly credit what had happened in Bahnhofstrasse. And Swiss security was renowned for its ruthless efficiency. What the hell had gone so horribly wrong?

When a woman replied to his call to the Berne number Arnold had given him he opened with the identification phrase and she didn't react.

'What was that you said? Who are you calling? You know what time of night it is . . .'

'I'm sorry,' Martel replied. 'I was calling . . .' He repeated the number Arnold had provided him and risked it: after all, Arnold was a common name.

'No one here of that name – you have the wrong number. This is the number you said you were calling but – for the second time – there is no one here of that name. *Good night!*'

Martel sat staring at the receiver and replaced it. He was inside a third-floor bedroom he had booked at the Schweizerhof – which faced the Hauptbahnhof. Hofer's suitcase was parked in one of the station lockers, the key for which he had in his pocket. Why had Ferdy Arnold given him a meaningless phone number when he visited the apartment in Centralhof? The obvious conclusion was that *he was not the real Ferdy Arnold* – whom Martel had never met.

If this same man had organised the savage onslaught on himself and Hofer it explained his anxiety to leave the apartment urgently. *He had known what was waiting for them outside*. So he had to be well clear of the place when Martel came out with Hofer. But in that case why had Hofer accepted him as Arnold? Martel felt the sensation of being swept inside a whirlpool growing.

Leaving his room, he went down the staircase, again instinctively ignoring the lift. Crossing the street to the station he found a row of phone booths, went inside one and dialled the

Ferdy Arnold number Tweed had given him in London.

He *had* realised 'Arnold' had provided a different number, but he had assumed it was a security precaution and Tweed had not been immediately informed of the change. This time the reaction at the Berne number was different. He used the code-phrase, a girl asked him to wait just a moment.

'Who is this?'

The voice was crisp, almost curt, and had a ring of competence, of no nonsense about it. Martel identified himself.

'Where are you calling from?' Arnold demanded.

'That doesn't matter at the moment,' Martel replied. 'I have regretfully to report that your assistant, Claire Hofer, has been kidnapped by Delta ...'

'You were part of that massacre in Bahnhofstrasse in Zürich?'

'Massacre?'

'Delta – if it was Delta – bungled a major bank raid. A limpet mine was attached to the main door of a certain bank. It detonated and some people alighting from a tram which had been stopped were badly injured. What was that about Claire Hofer? And I'd still like to know where you're calling from ...'

'Skip that. This call is going through your switchboard ...'

'That's crazy.' Ferdy Arnold's voice reflected indignation and disbelief. 'Our security ...'

'You said something about a bungled bank raid.' Martel was bewildered. 'I'm limiting this call to two minutes so talk ...'

'I've just told you – a bomb, presumably with a quick-acting timer, was attached to the entrance to a bank. It blew the door but no one followed it up. The driver of the tram which was stopped saw nothing because smoke bombs were used ...'

'What about the Rolls Royce that stopped him by driving across his bows?'

'I don't know anything about that. On the pavement we found a small silver badge shaped like a triangle – or a delta ...'

'Send out an all points bulletin alarm for Claire Hofer.' Martel was checking the length of the call by the second-hand on his watch. 'I'm very worried about her ...'

44

'You can stop worrying.' Arnold paused and there was something in his tone Martel didn't like. 'We know what happened to her – part of the story anyway.'

'Then for Christ's sake tell me – and fast. In the short time we were together I came to like – admire – the girl . . .'

'Her body was discovered floating down the Limmat less than half an hour ago. She had been brutally and professionally tortured before they dumped her in the river. I want you to come in, Martel. I want you to come to an address in Berne . . .'

Arnold stopped speaking. Martel had broken the connection.

CHAPTER 5

Wednesday May 27

If Arnold had kept the conversation going so his tracers could locate the source of the call Martel was confident he had rung off in time. He was no happier about the real Arnold knowing his whereabouts than he was for the fake Arnold to obtain the same information. And the news of Claire Hofer had hit him hard.

Leaving the booth he walked round the huge Hauptbahnhof, stopping to study the departure board like a man waiting for his train. This great station – along with its counterpart in Münich – had fascinated the murdered Warner. Why?

Martel made a swift inventory of the place. *Gleise* 1–16: sixteen platforms, all of the tracks ending here. The long row of phone booths for communication and, he realised as he strolled round the hushed concourse, numerous exits. There was a *kino* – cinema – the *Cine-Rex*, and a Snack-Buffet.

He walked down one of the broad aisles leading away from the platforms past a large luggage storage counter facing a door marked *Kanton-Polizei*. Two men emerged dressed in blue uniforms with berets, their trousers tucked into boots. They had the look of paratroopers.

He passed *Quick*, a first-class restaurant which provided two more exits and came out into the street. The Hauptbahnhof was a place you could get out of swiftly – a place you could linger inside for a long time unobtrusively. An idea formed at the back of his mind and receded. He crossed two roads and gazed down into the black water of the Limmat river. Dizzying reflections from street lamps danced in the night.

These were the waters which within the past hour had carried the mutilated body of poor Claire Hofer. Martel was not a sentimental man but he decided someone was going to pay for that barbaric act.

Glancing round he noticed the huge greystone bulk of a four-storey building to his right on the Bahnhofquai. The *Stadtpolizei* – police headquarters. The working quarters of a friend, David Nagel, Chief Inspector of Intelligence. He checked his watch. 2245 hours.

While at the Hotel Schweizerhof he had borrowed a rail time-table and found that the last train from the Hauptbahnhof left at 2339, reaching St. Gallen at 0049 hours. He had less than one hour to catch that train – to get out of Zürich which was becoming a death-trap.

He entered police headquarters through the double doors in Lindenhofstrasse. The receptionist, a stocky policeman in shirt sleeves, confirmed that Chief Inspector Nagel was in his office. He asked Martel to fill in a printed form.

'Just tell him I'm here, for God's sake,' Martel snapped. 'If you keep me waiting you won't be popular. This is an emergency.'

'Even so . . .'

'And he's expecting me,' the Englishman lied. 'My name is all he will need . . .'

Within minutes he was inside Nagel's third-floor office overlooking the Limmat. The windows were wide open, letting in dense clammy air. There were the usual heavy net curtains, the usual neon lighting, harsh and uninviting, the usual filing cabinets along one wall.

'I've been hoping you would contact me,' Nagel said when they had shaken hands. 'Tweed called from London and warned me you were coming in. He said you might need help . . .'

'I think I do . . .'

David Nagel was a well-built Swiss with a thick moustache, humorous eyes and a mass of dark hair he kept well-brushed. Some of his colleagues dismissed him as a bit of a dandy whose greatest interest in life was women.

47

'No, that is my second greatest interest,' he would correct them when they hinted as much. 'My first is my work – which is why I'm not married. What wife could stand the hours I keep? So, being normal, my second greatest interest is ... Now get the hell out of here.'

Martel liked him. Tweed said he had the most acute brain in the Swiss police and security system – and Intelligence had one foot in both camps. Nagel came straight to the point – as he always did.

'You didn't fill in a form before you came up here, I hope?' He looked worried as he asked the question, and Nagel rarely showed anxiety no matter how critical the situation. 'You were dressed like that?' the Swiss continued, speaking rapidly. 'And not using that blasted cigarette holder ...'

'No to all your questions – and yes I was wearing these glasses.' Martel removed a pair of horn-rimmed glasses fitted with plain lenses. 'I had to give my bloody name to get through to you. Are you going to nag about that ...'

'Please, please, Keith ...!' Nagel held up a restraining hand in a pacific gesture. 'But from *your* point of view your whereabouts might be best left unknown. Ferdy Arnold's security mob is moving heaven and earth to locate you.'

Martel lit a cigarette and indulged himself in the luxury of employing his holder. He knew that Nagel disliked Arnold, that he had once told Tweed it 'was purely a political appointment'. The Swiss continued talking.

'Your name doesn't matter. When you have gone I shall tell the man at reception you are one of my key informants, that you used a code-name – that officially you never entered these premises. With no written record you will be safe from Arnold's hard men.'

'That's reassuring at any rate ...' Martel was about to refer to the debacle in Bahnhofstrasse when Nagel again went on speaking.

'I have a number here you must phone urgently. She called

me only ten minutes ago – knowing we are good friends. Despite my reservations about her chief, I like and trust Claire Hofer . . .'

Martel felt himself spinning, the whirlpool whipping him round faster.

CHAPTER 6

Wednesday May 27

Stunned, Martel's teeth clenched tight on the cigarette-holder. To mask his reaction he took the holder out of his mouth and readjusted the position of cigarette in holder. *She called me only ten minutes ago.*

What the hell was wrong with the timing? Thirty minutes earlier Arnold had told him on the phone that 'less than half an hour ago' her body had been found in the Limmat. That meant Hofer had been found about one hour from this moment. And now Nagel – the most precise Swiss – had clearly stated the call from Claire Hofer had come through 'ten minutes ago'. On the scrap of paper Nagel had handed to him was written a St. Gallen phone number.

Nagel would know the girl's voice well. Being Nagel he would have wanted proof of the identity of his caller. *Irrevocable* proof. Martel began to consider whether he could be going out of his mind.

'Something wrong?' Nagel enquired softly.

'Yes, I'm tired.' Martel folded the scrap of paper and put it in his wallet. 'What sort of a night are you having?'

'Routine so far.'

Again Martel was stunned. David Nagel, chief of police Intelligence, *had no knowledge of the traumatic event which had taken place in Bahnhofstrasse.* There was no reason for him to conceal such knowledge – Martel felt certain of this. He had to tread damned carefully.

'Why do you mistrust Ferdy Arnold?' he asked.

'It was a political appointment – not a professional one . . .'

'And why does Claire Hofer – who works for Arnold – call *you* when she has a message for me?'

'Because she knows you and I are close friends.' The Swiss paused. 'I also employed her before she transferred to counter-espionage . . .'

'You said you've had a routine night so far,' Martel probed.

'Except for the explosion aboard some tourist's launch out on the lake. Some poor idiot who obviously knew nothing about engines or boats – so he had an accident and lost his life. We did hear the faint boom of the detonation . . .' He pointed towards the open windows behind curtains which hung motionless in the airless night. 'The sound came up the Limmat from the lake . . .'

No, it didn't, Martel thought. It came straight up the funnel of Bahnhofstrasse and then down Uraniastrasse, the side street leading towards police headquarters. He was watching Nagel and the extraordinary thing was he was convinced the Intelligence man was not lying. Someone was trying to cover up the incident, to pretend it had never happened.

'Good to see you, David,' Martel said and stood up. 'And I'll call Claire Hofer soon but there's something I have to attend to, and you don't want to know about it . . .'

'That is a direct line which bypasses the switchboard,' Nagel suggested, pointing to one of three phones on his desk. 'I can leave you on your own . . .'

'It isn't that, David. I'm just short of time.'

'Enjoy yourself while you're in Zürich . . .'

It was 2310 hours when Martel left police headquarters. He had half an hour to catch the 2339 train to St. Gallen, but he still had things to deal with. He walked past a patrol car parked outside, a cream Volvo with a red trim. Two uniformed men sat in the front with the windows open. Where the devil had they been when all hell broke loose in nearby Bahnhofstrasse?

And he *had* lied to Nagel he recalled as he hurried back to the Hauptbahnhof. He felt certain he could rely on the Swiss but he had mistrusted the offered phone which passed through no switchboard. He was now gripped by a feeling of insecurity and

51

determined to take no chances.

'Maybe I'm getting paranoid,' he told himself as he slipped inside one of the empty phone booths in the station. *These* were safe. Again he remembered the dead Warner who apparently had also haunted Hauptbahnhofs. As he dialled the number Nagel had given him he began to sympathise with Charles Warner. Martel himself felt *hunted*.

The receptionist at the Hotel Hecht in St. Gallen confirmed that Claire Hofer was staying with them. She asked him to hold while she tried her room. A girl's voice came on the line – decisive, sharp and wary.

'Who is this?'

'Our mutual friend, Nagel, passed on your message and I want you to take certain action very fast. Can you get to an outside payphone? Good. Get there immediately and call me at this number.' He read out the booth number from the dial. 'It's Zürich code,' he added tersely. 'I'm very short of time . . .'

'Goodbye!'

Martel found he was sweating. The atmosphere inside the booth was oppressive. He felt both exposed and trapped in the confined space. The phone rang in an astonishingly short time. He snatched up the receiver. The same voice asked the question crisply.

'Is that . . .? Please confirm name of our mutual friend . . .'

'Nagel. David Nagel . . .'

'Claire Hofer speaking . . .'

'Again do what I tell you without questioning my judgement – as fast as you can. Pay your bill at the Hotel Hecht – make up some plausible reason why you have to . . .'

'All right, I'm not stupid! What then?'

'Book in at another hotel in St. Gallen. Reserve a room for me. Warn them I'll arrive about one o'clock in the morning . . .'

'You need parking space for a car?'

'No. I'm coming in by train . . .'

'I'll call back in minutes. I have to find accommodation and tell you where to come. Goodbye!'

Martel was left staring at a dead receiver. More precious time was being consumed. But she sounded good, damned good. He had to give her that. The whirlpool was gyrating faster. He felt he had been talking to a ghost. Claire Hofer had just been dragged out of the Limmat – according to Arnold . . .

Despite the growing heat inside the kiosk he inserted a cigarette into his holder, cursed, removed the cigarette and placed it between his lips minus holder. While talking he had turned round with his back to the coin box so he could watch the deserted concourse. He took several deep drags and the phone was ringing a second time. Her voice . . .

'Is that . . .? Good. Our mutual friend . . .'

'Nagel. Martel here . . .'

'I got lucky. Two twin-bedded rooms on the first floor. Hotel Metropol. Faces the station exit. Staring at you as you come out. I'll leave a note at the desk with just my room number inside the envelope. O.K.?'

'Very . . .'

'Goodbye!'

In the next few minutes Martel moved very fast. He bought his rail ticket for St. Gallen. At the Hotel Schweizerhof he paid for the room he no longer needed. He did his best to make the cancellation seem normal.

'I'm a consultant – medical – and I'm urgently needed in Basle by a patient . . .' *Consultant* was the word he had filled in on the 'occupation' section of the registration form when he had arrived. The term was impressive and totally vague.

He had not unpacked his bag – a precaution he always took when arriving at a fresh destination – so all he had to do was to shove his shaving kit and toothbrush inside and snap the catches. Running down the stairs – the night clerk would see nothing odd now in his speedy departure – he hurried across to the first of the taxis waiting outside the station.

'I want you to take me to Paradeplatz. Can you then wait a few minutes by the tram stop while I deliver something? Then drive

53

me straight back here?'

'Please get in . . .'

He was using up his last few minutes before the St. Gallen train departed but – knowing Zürich and the quietness of the streets at this hour – he believed he could just manage it. *Because he had to check the state of Bahnhofstrasse where shots had been fired, blood spilt all over the sidewalk, and a bomb detonated against a bank.*

He began chatting to the driver. All over the world cabbies are plugged in to a city's grapevine.

'Did you hear that terrific explosion not so long ago? Sounded like a bomb going off.'

'I heard it.' The driver paused as though picking his words with care. 'Rumour is some fool of a tourist blew himself and his boat up on the lake . . .'

'It sounded closer . . .'

Martel left the query mark hanging in the air, wondering why the driver sounded so cautious. They were near Paradeplatz: soon all conversation would cease.

'Sounded closer to me,' the driver agreed. 'I was with a fare in Talstrasse and that was one hell of a bang. Now it could have come up the street from the lake . . .' He paused again. 'Anyway, that's what the police told us.'

'The police?'

'A patrol car stopped at the Hauptbahnhof rank. The driver got out to chat. He told us about this fool tourist blowing himself up on the lake.'

'Someone you knew? The policeman?' Martel asked casually.

'Funny you should say that.' Their eyes met in the rear-view mirror. 'I thought I knew every patrol car policeman in the city. I've been driving this cab for twenty years – but I never met him before . . .'

'Probably a new recruit fresh out of training school.'

'He was fifty if he was a day. All right if I wait here?'

It suited Martel admirably. The cabbie had parked well inside Paradeplatz – which meant he wouldn't be able to see where

54

Martel went after he turned down Bahnhofstrasse. He lit a fresh cigarette and walked quickly. He was going to catch – or lose – the train by a matter of seconds.

The street was deserted and the only sound was that of his own footfalls on the flagstones. He crossed over to the other side and then stopped in sheer bewilderment. The whirlpool was spinning again.

There was no sign of the bloody incident Martel had witnessed and participated in two hours earlier. And there was no mistaking the location. He could see the archway where he and the girl had come through into Bahnhofstrasse. And there *was* a large and important bank in just the right position – opposite where the tram had been stopped, a bank with double plate-glass doors. But *the glass was intact*.

There was not a sliver of shattered glass in the roadway that Martel could see. The Swiss were good at clearing up messes, at keeping their country neat and tidy – but this was completely insane.

Now he was checking the sidewalk for blood, the blood he had slipped in, the dried blood still staining the soles of his shoes. *The sidewalk was spotless*. He had almost given up when he saw it. The fresh scar marks where bark had been torn and burnt by explosive from a tree. Even the Swiss couldn't grow a new tree in two hours.

CHAPTER 7

Thursday May 28

It was just after midnight at the remote *schloss* in the Allgau district of Bavaria. Reinhard Dietrich stood by a window in his library, looking out at the lights reflected in the moat. In one hand he held a glass of Napoleon brandy, in the other a Havana cigar. A buzzer began ringing persistently.

Sitting down behind a huge desk he unlocked a drawer, took out the telephone concealed inside and lifted the receiver. His tone was curt when Erwin Vinz identified himself.

'Blau here,' Dietrich barked. 'Any news?'

'The Englishman has left Zürich. He caught a train departing at 2339 hours from the Hauptbahnhof.' The wording was precise, the voice hoarse. 'Our people just missed getting on board after he jumped inside a compartment ...'

'*Left Zürich!* What the hell do you mean? What happened at the Centralhof apartment?'

'The operation was not a complete success ...' Vinz was nervous. Dietrich's mouth tightened. Something had gone wildly wrong.

'Tell me exactly what happened,' he said coldly.

'The girl has taken a permanent holiday and she was unable to tell us anything about her job. We gained the impression she had no information to pass on. You don't have to worry about her ...'

'But I do have to worry about Martel! Goddamnit, where is he now? Which train?'

'Its final destination was St. Gallen ...'

Dietrich gripped the receiver more firmly, his expression choleric. In clipped, terse sentences he issued instructions, slammed down the receiver and replaced the instrument inside the drawer. He emptied his glass and pressed a bell.

A hunchback padded into the room. His pointed ears were flat against the side of his head so they almost merged with his skull. He wore a green beize overall and smelt of cleaning fluid. His master handed him the glass.

'More brandy! Oscar, Vinz and his special cell bungled the job. It looks as though Martel has arrived in St. Gallen, for God's sake . . .'

'We dealt with the previous English,' Oscar reminded him.

Reinhard Dietrich, a man of sixty, had a thatch of thick silver hair and a matching moustache. Six feet tall, he was well-built without an ounce of excess fat. He was dressed in the outfit he preferred when at his country *schloss* – a London-tailored leather jacket and cavalry twill jodphurs tucked inside hand-tooled riding boots. Dietrich looked every inch the man he was as he stood savouring the Havana – one of post-war Germany's richest and most powerful industrialists.

He had entered the electronics field in its infancy, shrewdly judging this to be the product with the greatest development potential. His headquarters was in Stuttgart and he had a second large factory complex at Phoenix, Arizona. He sipped at his refilled glass, watching Oscar's unblinking eyes.

'We shall certainly deal with this fresh meddler from London. Vinz is flooding St. Gallen with our people. Martel will be tracked down by nightfall. They have eliminated that Swiss bitch, Claire Hofer.' His voice rose, his florid face reddened. 'Nothing must interfere with Operation Crocodile! On June 3 the Summit Express will be crossing Germany. On June 4 the Bavarian state elections will be held – Delta will sweep into power!'

'And Martel . . .'

'The order is – kill him!'

Martel left the night train at St. Gallen confident that no one had followed him. At Zürich he had caught the train seconds before it departed. Once aboard he had waited by the window to see if there were any other last-minute passengers. No one appeared and he made his way through an almost-empty train to a first-class compartment. With an overwhelming sense of relief he sank into a corner seat.

At St. Gallen he took his time getting off the train. As he carried his suitcase slowly towards the exit the platform was deserted. There is no more depressing place than a station in the early hours. As Claire Hofer had told him, the Hotel Metropol faced the station.

The night porter confirmed his reservation and Martel asked him the room rate. He counted out banknotes, talking as he did so to distract the man, adding a generous tip to keep him distracted.

'That's payment for two nights – this is for you. I'm so tired I can hardly stand up. I'll register in the morning. Are there any messages for me?' he asked quickly.

'Just this envelope . . .'

It had worked – the delay in filling in the registration form which is obligatory for a guest to complete on arrival at any Swiss hostelry. The form is in triplicate. During the night the police tour the hotels to collect their copy. By not filling in the form immediately Martel had delayed knowledge of his presence in St. Gallen by twenty-four hours.

Inside his twin-bedded room he opened the sealed envelope. In a neat feminine script were written the words 'Room 12'. It was the room next to his own. He knocked very lightly on the door and she opened it immediately. She didn't say a word until she had closed and locked it. Over her right hand was draped a towel.

'The mutual friend?'

'David Nagel, for God's sake . . .'

'I saw you from my window which looks across to the station – but you can't blame me for checking . . .

'I'm sorry. I *want* you to be careful. It's just that I last ate before noon on the plane. I'm tired . . .'

'You look exhausted.' She removed the towel, exposing a 9-mm pistol she had been concealing and which she slipped under her pillow. 'You must be thirsty. It's a hot night. I'm afraid I only have Perrier water ...'

'I'll take it from the bottle.'

He sank on to the bed furthest from the window and forced himself to study her as he drank. She was the right height, correct weight, and her dark hair was cut with a heavy fringe over her forehead and shoulder length at the back. In the glow from a bedside light her eyes were a deep blue. 'You'll want proof of my identity ...' He hauled out his passport, gave it to her and finished off the Perrier.

She tried to show him her own identity card but he was so weary he waved it aside. What bloody difference did it make? Delta had put in a substitute – Gisela Zobel – in Zürich. He had rescued another girl – whose description also matched – trussed up in a cupboard at the Centralhof apartment. The whirlpool began spinning in his head again ...

But this girl *felt* right. It was his last thought before he lay back on the pillow and fell fast asleep.

He woke with a sensation of alarm. It was dark, the air heavy like a blanket pressing down. He wasn't sure where he was – so much had happened in so short a period of time. He was lying on his back on a bed. Then he remembered.

He was just relaxing when he experienced a second tremor. He kept his breathing regular. Someone had taken off his tie, undone the top buttons of his shirt, taken off his shoes. What alerted him was the lack of weight under his left armpit. The shoulder holster was still strapped to him but *his Colt had been removed*. He turned his head carefully, not making a sound, and reached out with his right hand. The fingers of another hand touched his own, grasped his hand. A girl's voice whispered before the bedside light came on.

'You're all right. You're in St. Gallen at the Hotel Metropol. I'm Claire Hofer. It's four o'clock in the morning so you've only

59

had two hours' sleep . . .'

'I can get by on that.'

Martel was wide awake now, his throat feeling like sandpaper. He sat up and propped the pillow behind him. Claire Hofer was still wearing her pale grey two-piece suit and like himself, sat propped against a pillow. In the light glow he noticed she had made herself up afresh. No blood-red nail varnish, thank God!

'Your Colt is in your bedside table,' she told him. 'Not very comfortable sleeping with that. The door is double-locked – and as you see I've tipped a chair under the handle . . .'

'You seem to have thought of everything . . .'

Martel, who never accepted anyone at face value, set about discovering every facet of Claire Hofer. She was remarkably like the second girl he had encountered in the Zürich apartment, the girl he had rescued – only to let her be kidnapped and . . . Martel found it hard to push the atrocity to the back of his mind.

'What are you thinking about?' she asked.

'This . . .'

He extracted from his jacket pocket the silver Delta badge he had ripped from the lapel of a dead would-be assassin in Bahnhofstrasse. Casually, he tossed it on her bed. She moved away from it as though it were alive, staring at him, her eyes wide with fear.

'Where did you get that?'

She was quick and clever. During the few seconds while she was talking her right hand, which was furthest away from him and in shadow, slipped under her pillow and reappeared holding the 9-mm pistol which she aimed point-blank at his stomach.

'The badge frightens you?' he asked.

'*You* frighten me now. I shan't hestitate to shoot . . .'

'I believe you.'

He was careful to keep his hands folded in his lap, well away from the bedside table drawer. There was no softness in her voice now, in her expression, in the posture of her well-developed body. If he miscalculated the Swiss girl would pull the trigger.

60

'I took that badge off the body of a man I shot in Bahnhof-strasse last night. They were waiting for us when we came out of the apartment – Delta. None of your men with stocking masks or Balaclava hoods. Men in business suits! And each wearing a badge in his lapel. There was a lot of blood spilt – but an hour later the place was nice and tidy for tomorrow's tourists . . .'

'You said blood was spilt. You said "us" . . .'

'Why didn't *you* keep our appointment at Centralhof?' he snapped.

'Arnold was going to take me off the Delta investigation after Warner's murder – so I went underground. Lisbeth was sup-posed to bring you here, to make sure you weren't followed. Unlike you, she knows some of Arnold's trackers . . .'

'And she knows Ferdy Arnold himself?'

'No, she has never met him. Why?'

'Let me describe Arnold,' he suggested. 'A thin, wiry man in his late thirties. Brown hair brushed back without a parting. Slate-grey eyes . . .'

'That's not a bit like him . . .'

'I thought so. Someone impersonating him turned up while we were at the apartment. I was even suspicious of Lisbeth because she had to look up his number in her notebook – she should have known that backwards if she had been you. The fake Arnold must have phoned her before I arrived and made some excuse as to why she should use that number if the need arose. Who is . . .' He was very careful still with his use of tenses. '. . . the girl who impersonated *you*?'

'Before she got married we both worked for David Nagel in police Intelligence. We once played a joke on him – we dressed in exactly the same clothes and went into his office separately, one after the other within the space of ten minutes. He didn't grasp there was any difference and was furious when we told him. It's no wonder you were fooled.'

She showed her renewed confidence in him by slipping her pistol back under the pillow. Smiling by way of apology, she leaned forward and asked the question he had been dreading.

61

'Where is Lisbeth? Did she wait in the station here to catch a train back to Zürich? As you'll have gathered, she does look terribly like me – although we aren't twins. You realise she is my sister?'

In London Tweed was still at his desk studying a file when he received the frightening news. Rubbing his eyes, he glanced wistfully at the camp-bed he had had set up 'for the duration' as he termed it. Miss McNeil, his faithful assistant, brought in the signal.

A handsome, erect, grey-haired woman – men in the street turned their heads when she passed them – no one knew her age or even her first name, except Tweed, who had forgotten. She was just McNeil – who was always on hand when needed at any hour of the day or night. She also possessed a shrewd brain, a caustic tongue and an encyclopaedic memory.

'This just came in from Bayreuth ...'

Bayreuth. Alarm bells began ringing. Tweed unlocked the steel-lined drawer containing his code-book. At the moment the signal read like a perfectly normal business enquiry about the despatch of certain goods.

Bayreuth was in *Bavaria.* Lindau, the last place Charles Warner had set foot in before being murdered, was in Bavaria. Delta, the neo-Nazi Party, had its power base in Bavaria. He busied himself with the decoding, using a piece of thick paper clipped to a metal sheet so there could be no imprint of what he was writing.

'Would you prefer me to leave you alone?' McNeil suggested.

'Of course not! Just let me concentrate, woman ...'

It was a compliment – that she should be asked to stay, because Tweed felt that when the decoding was completed he might welcome company. She sat down, crossed her shapely legs and watched. It was fortunate that – like Martel – she could manage on two or three hours' sleep. As he finished his task Tweed's expression became blank – which told McNeil a great deal.

'Bad news?'

'The worst, the very worst.'

'You will cope. You always do ...'

'I'm not the one who has to cope. Manfred has just crossed the border into Bavaria from East Germany. Oh, Christ ...'

Manfred!

Tweed was appalled as he re-read the signal. It had travelled to him along a most devious route he could see in his mind's eye. First, his agent planted inside the Ministry for State Security in Leipzig, East Germany, had radioed the message from his mobile transmitter. The message had then been picked up by Tweed's station in Bayreuth.

From Bayreuth a courier had driven at breakneck speed to the British Embassy in Bonn. There the signal would have been handed personally to the security officer. He, in his turn, had radioed it to Park Crescent. The decoded signal was deadly and un-nerving in its implications.

Manfred today Wednesday May 27 crossed East German border near Hof into West Germany. Ultimate destination unknown.

He handed the signal to McNeil without a word, stood up and went to examine the wall-map of Central Europe he had pinned up when Martel had left for the airport. Tweed was quite familiar with the map. In his head he carried a clear picture of the geography of the whole of western Europe. But he wanted to verify which route Manfred might have taken.

From the Hof area an autobahn ran due south via Nuremberg to the Bavarian capital of München. That was the most likely route. And Warner had spent a lot of time in München, paying special attention to the Hauptbahnhof for some unknown reason. He went back to his swivel chair, adjusted his glasses and sagged into his cushion.

'We don't know much about Manfred, do we?' McNeil ventured.

'We know nothing – and we know too much,' Tweed growled. He tapped a file. 'I must be getting psychic in my old age – I was

63

looking at his dossier when you brought that signal.'

'He's a top East German agent, isn't he? Some query about his nationality and origins. A top-flight assassin – and a first-rate planner. An unusual combination ...'

'But Carlos is an unusual man,' Tweed said and pushed his spectacles back over his forehead.

'You really think he is Carlos? Nothing has been heard of him for ages ...'

'The Americans assume so. But there is something very peculiar going on which I don't understand. Delta is the neo-Nazis. Manfred is a free-lance Communist expert on major subversive operations. So who is behind Operation Crocodile – whatever that might be? And *Crocodile* – that reminds me of something I have seen ...'

'You look really worried. Shall I make coffee?'

Tweed stared at the silent phone on his desk. He spoke half to himself. 'Come in, Martel, for God's sake! I must warn you – before it's too late. You're up against both Nazis and Communists. It's double jeopardy ...'

In a darkened apartment in a large building near München police headquarters in Ettstrasse a gloved hand lifted a telephone. The man wearing nylon gloves was the sole occupant. The only illumination came from a shaded desk light. He dialled a number. It was 4 a.m.

'Who the bloody hell is this? Don't you know the time ...'

Reinhard Dietrich had been woken at the *schloss* from a deep sleep and his voice reflected his fury. If it was Erwin Vinz again he would blast him to ...

'Manfred speaking.' The tone of voice was creepily soft and controlled. 'We hear you have a problem and that we find most disturbing.'

Dietrich woke up very quickly, thrown off balance by the identity of the caller, by his words which suggested he knew something about the Zürich débacle. He sat up in bed and his tone of voice became polite and cooperative.

'Nothing we can't handle, I assure you ...'

'But in Zürich, it was *mis*handled, so what may we expect next in St. Gallen?'

Dietrich, a man accustomed all his life to issuing commands, dreaded the sound of Manfred's sleepy voice. When Manfred had first approached him at his Stuttgart office with his offer to supply arms and uniforms at cut-rate prices he had jumped at the chance. Now he half-regretted the decision – when it was too late.

'You don't have to worry about St. Gallen.' He spoke in a bluff confident tone. 'I have already made arrangements to deal with the situation ...'

'We are very pleased to hear it. More arms and uniforms are available for immediate collection at the same warehouse. Where and when will you store this consignment?'

Dietrich told him. There was a click and the industrialist realised Manfred had gone off the line. Arrogant bastard! And he detested his caller's habit of using the plural 'we' – as though Dietrich was taking orders from some all-powerful committee. At least more arms were on the way – God knows they had lost enough. How Erich Stoller of the BND tracked down the locations he had no idea.

In München Manfred switched off the desk light. Wherever he was staying in the West he always wore gloves – there would be no fingerprints to trace when he left the apartment. There was a thin smile on his face. Operation Crocodile was proceeding according to plan.

In the bedroom at the Hotel Metropol Claire Hofer was enduring a state of delayed shock after Martel told her of Lisbeth's murder. He omitted reference to the fact that she had been tortured. When she reacted she caught him off guard.

'And you let them take her? *Bastard!*' She hit him across the side of the face with the flat of her hand. When she raised her hand a second time he grabbed her wrist and pushed her down on the bed, his face inches from hers as she glared up at him.

65

Their position reminded him of when he had pinned his would-be assassin, Gisela Zobel, down on the sofa in the Centralhof apartment and she had attempted to distract him with sexual games.

But this girl was different. Tough as whipcord, but vulnerable, a vulnerability she covered up with an outwardly controlled manner. The deep blue eyes seemed larger than ever in the light from the bedside lamp. He kissed her gently on the forehead and felt her whipcord muscles relax.

'There were at least a dozen armed Delta soldiers in the assault,' he told her softly, still gripping her wrist. 'They piled out of two cars. I shot three men. I saw them hauling Lisbeth inside a large Mercedes which drove straight off. I blew it . . .'

'A dozen armed men!' Her eyes gazed into his. 'But how could you have saved Lisbeth against such odds? And why did they do this thing – take her away?' Her body had gone limp. He relaxed his grip on her wrist.

'They thought they were taking you . . .'

'Me? Why me?'

'Something big is coming up.' He perched on the edge of her bed and lit a cigarette. 'So Delta is eliminating every agent who might get in their way. First Warner, then the attempt on yourself. I'm their next target. Incidentally, why didn't Warner use the train to get from Lindau to Switzerland – why that business of the boat?'

'He was an ex-Navy man and mistrusted confined spaces – a train could be a trap he'd say. There was nowhere to run. Can't we hit back at these people?'

'We're going to. That's why I'm in St. Gallen. There's a rare embroidery museum here, isn't there? The receptionist at the Baur au Lac said so . . .'

'There is.' She was sitting up now, using a hand-mirror and a brush to tidy her dishevelled hair. 'And that's the place Charles used as a rendezvous to meet his contact inside Delta. How do you know about it?'

'We'll come back to that. Do you know how far Warner had

gone with his attempt to infiltrate Delta?'

'He had this contact I've just mentioned. I've no idea what he looks like. Charles went to great lengths to protect his identity, but his code-name is Stahl. Incidentally, you've seen the latest news about Delta?'

She reached for a newspaper and handed it to him. It was dated the previous day. The headline jumped out at him and beneath it was the main article.

New Cache of neo-Nazi Arms and Uniforms Found in Allgau.

The text was padded out but the message was simple. Acting on information received the Bavarian police had raided an isolated farmhouse just before dawn and found the arms dump. The farmhouse had shown traces of recent occupation but was deserted at the time of the raid ...

'That's the seventh Delta arms dump they've found in the past four weeks,' Claire remarked. 'They don't seem to be all that efficient ...'

'Odd, isn't it?'

'What are you thinking about?' she asked. 'You've got that look again ...'

He was staring at the wall, recalling his conversation with Tweed. Fragments of that conversation kept beavering away at the back of his mind.

The badge was found under Warner's body. The killer must have dropped it without realising ... And they completed the job by carving their trademark on his naked back – the Delta symbol ...

'I think there's something we're missing – it's just too damned obvious.' He checked his watch. 0430 hours. 'But we can trap the bastards. In the Embroidery Museum here in St. Gallen. In less than eight hours from now.'

CHAPTER 8

Thursday May 28

'This is what we're talking about – I hope . . .'

They were sitting at a secluded breakfast table in the hotel dining-room. Martel produced from his wallet an orange-coloured ticket and handed it to Claire. The ticket bore a number, several words printed in German and no indication of a town. *Industrie und Gewerbemuseum . . . Eintritt: Fr. 2.50.*

'Warner had that in his own wallet when he was killed,' Martel continued. 'I have my fingers crossed . . .'

'You can uncross them,' she said cheerfully. 'It *is* an entrance ticket to the St. Gallen Embroidery Museum. The building is in Vadianstrasse – near the Old Town. Not ten minutes' walk away . . .'

'Look at the back.'

Claire turned over the ticket and saw words written in a script she recognised. Charles Warner's. She was probably looking at the last words he wrote before he had embarked on his fatal boat trip from Lindau.

St. 11.50. May 28.

She looked at Martel and he detected a hint of excitement in her expression as he drank his eighth cup of coffee. He had already consumed seven croissants, three slices of ham and a large piece of cheese. He was beginning to feel better.

'May 28 – that's today,' she said and checked her watch. 'Nine o'clock. *St.* must stand for Stahl. In less than three hours we shall be talking to him . . .'

'*I* shall be talking to him,' Martel corrected her.

'I thought I was part of the team . . .'

'You told me Warner never let you attend these meetings. And if whoever turns up sees you he may take fright . . .'

'He won't recognise *you*,' she persisted stubbornly.

Martel quietly blew up. 'Now listen to me, Claire Hofer. You're not going to like this but there's no nice way to get the message across. I work alone – because then the only person I have to worry about is me. And me is all I've got – so I worry about me quite a lot.'

'I don't have to come inside the museum . . .'

'I haven't finished yet, so kindly shut up! Ever since I landed in Zürich nothing has been what it seemed. At the Centralhof apartment Delta had put in a girl to take me out. I find another girl in a cupboard – sorry about this, but it's necessary – and I'm led to think she's Claire Hofer . . .'

'I told you why we arranged it like that, damn it!'

Her face flushed with rage and her eyes blazed. He admired her spirit – he might even be able to use it – but he had to get his point across.

'Next thing,' he went on patiently, 'is a holocaust in Bahnhofstrasse – and within one hour all signs of it disappear . . .'

'Ferdy Arnold's wash-and-brush-up squad,' she said shortly.

'Come again?'

'You said yourself earlier you thought they had cleaned up the carnage to keep it quiet – to avoid worrying tourists. Arnold has this special team of engineers, glaziers, builders – you name it – standing by in case of a riot or terrorist outrage. They seal off the area temporarily and their motto is "as good as new within thirty minutes". They even have experts who fob off the press with some phoney story if necessary . . .'

'That's what I mean,' Martel said as he buttered another croissant. 'Nothing is what it seems. Delta – for some reason I have yet to fathom – advertises its outrages. Arnold pretends nothing has happened. He even spreads some lying story which fools Nagel of Intelligence. You really expect my meeting with this Stahl will turn out to be straightforward? Damned if I do.'

'And yet you're walking headlong into it?'

'I'll arrive at exactly 11.45. After breakfast you show me the place . . .'

'The rendezvous time is 11.50,' she reminded him.

'So I arrive five minutes early and wait to see who does come into that room. Warner could have been followed.'

'He was always extremely careful,' she observed.

'He is now extremely dead . . .'

In München the wide avenue of Maximilanstrasse leads straight as a ruler from Max-Joseph-Platz to the Bavarian state Parliament on an eminence overlooking the river Isar. To reach the east bank it passes over two bridges as it crosses a large island. The body was found trapped on the brink of one of the giant sluices below the first bridge.

It was discovered about two hours before Martel sat down to fortify himself at the Metropol in St. Gallen with a considerable breakfast. A lawyer on his way to work glanced over the parapet as he crossed the bridge. In the river a series of giant steps like four great weirs carried the swift flow of the water. At each step there is a series of square cement pillars at intervals. The corpse was folded round one of these pillars, snagged by chance.

The *Kriminalpolizei* arrived with a doctor to supervise retrieval of their evidence when a frogman had reported the man had been shot in the head. A preliminary examination was carried out inside an ambulance by the riverside. Chief-Inspector Kruger looked at the doctor after a few minutes.

'Surely you can tell me something? I have a pile of work on my desk a mile high and my wife is beginning to ask questions about my secretary when I arrive home.'

'Get a less attractive secretary,' the doctor suggested. 'Shot three times in the head. Powder burns visible. Likely time of death – but don't hold me to it – within past twelve hours. And no signs of rope abrasions on the wrists so they didn't tie him up to murder him . . .'

'I can at least check through his clothes for identification? That really is most kind of you, Doctor . . .

Kruger searched quickly with expert fingers while his deputy,

Weil, carefully said nothing. He could tell from his chief's expression that he was not pleased. He completed the search without producing one single item from the waterlogged body's pockets.

'No means of identification,' Kruger announced. 'That's just what I need. I can see what kind of a day this is going to be . . .'

'His watch,' replied Weil.

He lifted the corpse's left arm which seemed to weigh a ton and unstrapped the watch which had stopped at 0200 hours. He showed Kruger the back plate of the watch which was made of steel and had a single word engraved on it.

'One hell of a lot of help,' commented Kruger.

The word engraved in the plate was *Stahl*.

On their way to the Embroidery Museum Martel and Claire walked arm in arm. It was Martel who had made the suggestion. 'A couple is far less conspicuous,' he commented.

'If you say so . . .'

He bridled. 'Use your head. Two groups may be hunting for us. Delta for me – so they will search for a single man. Arnold's mob for you – so they'll look for a single girl . . .'

'Logical, I suppose, she said indifferently.

'And never let emotion cloud your judgement. I make it 11.30, fifteen minutes before I have to be inside that museum. That wallplate says Vadianstrasse . . .'

'The Embroidery Museum is at the far end on the left-hand side – and I've decided, I'm coming with you . . .'

'Not inside the place. I'll find somewhere nearby to park you.'

'I'm not a bloody car!' she flared up. She played her part well, hugging his arm and staring up at him with lover's eyes as she hissed the words. 'You're expecting trouble – you brought a silencer for your Colt.'

'I told you – nothing so far has been what it seemed and I have an idea the trend will continue.'

During their walk Martel had observed that St. Gallen was located inside a deep notch or gulch. Hemmed in on two sides by

71

vertical hill-slopes, the shopping area had been built on the floor of the gorge. Stepped up on the hillsides, one above another, were large solid-looking villas erected in the previous century.

The weather was again clammy with a heavy overcast and there was a hint of a storm in the air. Martel walked more slowly as they came closer to the entrance, his eyes scanning the area for signs of danger. He stopped again to look in a shop window but no one followed his example. On the surface the area was clean – only women shoppers, smartly dressed, strolling along the street.

'The police station isn't near, is it?' he murmured.

'As a matter of fact it is. *Stadtpolizei* is at Neugasse 5 – the first turning off to the left from that street over there . . .'

'Great! How far away on foot – walking fast? The Swiss police can walk fast.'

'Less than five minutes – two if they use a car. Why?'

'I like to know where all the pieces on the board are – in case of emergency.'

They had left the shop and walked the full length of the building containing the museum. Claire pointed to where the Old Town started while Martel searched for a convenient café to leave her. They should have allowed more time.

'Looking for somewhere to park the car?' she enquired. 'Well I've found the ideal place – and I can watch the entrance to the museum without anyone seeing me . . .'

She was pointing across the wide street to an orange booth with a black curtain pulled back revealing a metal stool. In large letters over the booth were the words PRONTOPHOT PASS-FOTOS.

'I'd better grab the seat before someone else decides they want a passport picture,' she said. 'Good luck. Don't forget to collect me on your way out. I don't want to sit there all day taking my picture – the results are lousy . . .'

Martel took one final look-round. He couldn't rid himself of the feeling something was wrong about the atmosphere. Shrugging his shoulders, he crossed Vadianstrasse, opened the door and went inside.

It was exactly as Claire had described: a wide flight of steps leading up into a large entrance hall. At a ticket window he paid a woman two francs fifty for a ticket like the one he had in his pocket, the one Warner had purchased. While buying it he held a handkerchief over his face and blew his nose incessantly. The woman behind the window would never be able to identify him later.

A notice indicated that the museum was on the first floor. He climbed two longer flights of steps. There was no one else about, the atmosphere was hushed. He could see why Warner had chosen this place and this time for meeting his Delta contact. On the wall outside the front entrance a plate had given the opening hours. *10.00. – 12.00.* and *14.00. – 17.00.* When the place closed at midday who else would arrive at 11.50?

To his left along the wide landing were a pair of double doors leading to the library. Very quietly, his soft-soled shoes making no noise, he walked to the library and tried the door. It was locked. He crossed back over the landing quickly and tried the Embroidery Museum door. It gave way under his pressure. He stepped inside, closed it and scanned the silent room.

The exhibits were in glass cases standing in various positions in a large room with windows overlooking Vadianstrasse. Before he was convinced the place was empty he checked several alcoves. Then he extracted the Colt from his shoulder holster and screwed on the silencer. His watch registered precisely 11.50 when he saw the handle of the door turning slowly.

He watched, fascinated, the Colt held behind his back, as the turning handle completed its revolution and then remained in that position without the door opening. It was a good ten seconds before the door began moving slowly inwards. Martel stepped back out of sight.

Because his hearing was acute he heard the slight click – the release of the door-handle after closing. He controlled his breathing. The silence in the museum room was so complete the patter of a mouse across the wood-block floor would have been heard.

Soon the new arrival, Stahl, would come into view. Was he checking to make sure he was alone? Or did he – as Martel would have done in his place – sense a presence in that silent archive of the ages, the repository of craftwork by people who had died centuries earlier . . .?

It was a man in a light overcoat and smart trilby. Very like a businessman. Like the men who had flooded out of the Rolls and the Mercedes in Bahnhofstrasse. Under the hat a bleak white bony face. In his lapel a silver triangular badge, the symbol of Delta.

In his right hand he held an object like a felt-tip pen – the needle-blade was already projecting ready for action. The click Martel had assumed to be the door-handle had been the pressing of the button which projected the blade.

When he appeared the bony-faced man was only a few feet from Martel. Stiffening his hand, he lunged forward, the needle-point aimed at Martel's stomach. The Englishman remained exactly where he was, jerked up the Colt and fired twice in rapid succession. The *phut-phut* of the silenced gun sounded unnaturally loud in the hushed atmosphere.

The bony-faced man dropped his hypodermic weapon and reeled backwards. He slammed into one of the display cases, flopped sideways and his head crashed down through the glass lid. As his legs gave way he slithered to the floor, his heels making runnels across the polished surface. A stream of blood gushed from his torn face.

Martel left the museum without being seen. As he slipped past the ticket window he glimpsed a woman's back. She was drinking from a cup. The Colt was rammed inside his belt. They closed in less than five minutes. He had to get out on to the street. But they were waiting for him out there. *Delta*.

They had sent in a single man to do the job but they would have people outside as back-up. It was that kind of thorough organisation. Martel had not forgotten the nightmare in Bahn-hofstrasse. The audacity, the ferocity. He opened the door and stepped out into Vadianstrasse.

Everything seemed normal. Housewives out shopping, singly or in couples. A man wearing yellow oil-skins and a cap, carrying some kind of bag, leaned against a wall on the opposite side. He was trying to light a cigarette: the lighter seemed to be defective.

Claire! He had to protect Claire, to lead them away from her. Already one Hofer – Lisbeth – had been killed. And they were out here somewhere. He could see Claire's legs below the closed curtain inside the photo booth. He began walking.

He timed it carefully. Taking out his holder to make himself conspicuous he inserted a cigarette. He stopped alongside the booth and cupped his hand to use the lighter, to conceal the fact that he was talking. The curtain was open a fraction of an inch. He didn't look towards the booth as he spoke.

'They sent a Delta operative. He's dead inside the museum. I am giving you an order. Stay there, give me two minutes to lead anyone out here away, then get to hell back to the Metropol and wait till I contact you ...'

Then he was moving away, heading into the Old Town where the road surfaces were cobbled, the buildings ancient, the shops new. He turned into Neugasse and followed the curve of the street.

Neugasse 5, Claire had said. Police headquarters. Five minutes' walk, two or less by car. He had to pinpoint the oppo-sition and this should give him more time. The bastards could hardly start something in close proximity to a police station. He stopped to look in a window.

He had no idea what the shop sold. He was concentrating on a reflection. The man in yellow oil-skins had stopped on the other side of the narrow street. He was staring into another window, holding a large carrier bag and puffing at his cigarette. His lighter had conveniently worked as soon as Martel began moving.

The Englishman sucked at his holder. Something was wrong. Something more than the fact that it appeared he was being shadowed by Yellow Oil-skins. He resumed his walk. *Stadt-polizei.* Walls a muddy grey roughcast, grey shutters almost merging into the walls. An archway entrance wide enough for a single car. He walked on.

He was approaching an intersection, a more spacious area which, he remembered from the street map Claire had shown him, was the Markt-Gasse. He turned left and stopped to drop his half-smoked cigarette which he stubbed under his heel. The possibility of a coincidence ended. Yellow Oil-skins was looking in yet another shop window. Something was very wrong indeed.

It was too damned obvious: using as a shadow a man clad in an outfit which could be picked out hundreds of yards away. It was as though he were making his presence as conspicuous as possible – to divert Martel's attention from someone else. *The danger was going to come from another quarter.*

He stood on the kerb gazing at a curious spectacle. In the middle of the street stood a small train for children made up of wooden, open-sided coaches with canvas canopies. At the front was a black railway engine with a gold trim and the driver, a man, was operating a whistle to signal imminent departure. Each of the coaches carried four children, two facing each other. A couple of coaches were occupied by mothers sitting with their offspring. The trolley-car train was large enough to carry adults.

Yellow Oil-skins remained staring into a window displaying ladies' underwear, for God's sake! Martel moved quickly, leaving the train still stationary. If there was to be havoc – Zürich-style – it must not happen near those children. Ahead he saw a buff-coloured building which was the Hotel Hecht – where Claire had originally been staying. Crossing the road, he concentrated his attention on everyone except Yellow Oil-skins.

The attack came from the least-expected quarter at a moment

when his alertness was briefly distracted by an astonishing sight. He was walking past the Hecht when he heard a piercing shriek, the train's whistle. It had followed him as it proceeded confidently amid the traffic to pass alongside the Hecht. In the last coach on the side nearest to him sat Claire Hofer.

The seat next to her was occupied by a small girl and two more children faced them. They were all looking away from the Hecht while Claire stared straight at him. Under cover of her handbag, the flap open, she was holding her pistol, the barrel aimed towards him.

He sensed rather than felt someone close to his left. Glancing away from the train he saw a tall woman wearing a dark hat with a veil concealing her face. Her shoulder-bag was supported by her left arm. In her right hand she held a familiar object – the needle-pointed hypodermic weapon.

This was the back-up Yellow Oil-skins had tried so very hard to conceal from him. Martel had a vague memory of seeing this veiled, elegantly-dressed woman in Neugasse and for a second he was taken off guard. He almost put out a hand to ward her off, which would have been his last movement since she would have jabbed the weapon into his hand and injected its contents.

Somewhere close by a car backfired, a sound cut off by the blare of a car's horn. The elegant woman wore a dress with a deep V-cut which exposed a generous portion of her bosom. Another distraction? Then she leaned back against the wall of the hotel. A small hole had appeared in the V of her bosom, as though drilled by a surgeon. The hole began to well redness as she sagged to the ground.

In falling her hat had tipped sideways, removing the veil from her face. Martel forced himself to walk on, threading his way among the morning shoppers. The face now exposed to view was not unfamiliar. It was the dead face of Gisela Zobel.

He saw the train moving on towards an ancient gateway in a wall which had probably once protected the town. Claire was still on board, clasping her closed handbag as she chatted to the girl next to her. The Swiss girl had shot his would-be killer from a moving vehicle. Marksmanship of that order he had never encountered before. And Yellow Oil-skins had now vanished as a crowd began to gather in front of the Hecht, huddled over something lying on the ground.

CHAPTER 9

Thursday May 28

In her bedroom at the Metropol Claire was shaking with fright. She held herself in check until Martel arrived back a few minutes after she had returned. Now reaction set in and she broke down. He sat on the bed beside her and she pressed her face into his chest and quietly sobbed. He stroked her soft black hair, saying nothing until he felt the tremors easing.

'You disobeyed orders,' he said harshly. 'While you were in the photo booth I told you get to hell back here. The next thing I see is you riding on that kids' train . . .'

'A bloody good job for you I did!' she flared up, then her expression changed to one of consternation. 'Oh, my God – are you saying that woman wasn't trying to kill you – I distinctly saw a knife in her hand . . .'

'It wasn't a knife – it was one of those hypodermic weapons Delta favour. You saved my life,' he went on in his normal blank monotone to help quieten her. 'How the devil did you follow me? I never saw you . . .'

'I wouldn't be much good if you had done,' she snapped back and blew her nose. 'Sorry if I fouled it up.'

'If shooting an assassin accurately from a moving vehicle comes under the heading fouling it up then please make a habit of it.'

'Did I kill her?'

'You killed the bitch,' he said shortly. 'It was Gisela Zobel, the girl who impersonated Lisbeth at Centralhof. There seems to be no end to the ruthless ingenuity of Delta. First they send in a man to keep the appointment inside the museum – a man wearing the Delta symbol in his lapel . . .'

'You left him there – with the badge?'

'Yes. Odd, isn't it, the way they flaunt that badge. Almost as though someone wants to advertise their role as murderers. I am beginning to get an idea about that. Then they have a back-up team. A very obvious man in yellow oil-skins follows me while a very unobvious woman in hat and veil waits her chance to finish me off . . .'

'I spotted both of them through the gap in the booth curtain. That's why I came after you . . .'

'And thank God you did,' Martel replied as he stood up. 'You haven't unpacked your case?'

'You told me not to – so only my toilet things are in the bathroom . . .'

'Pack them. We're catching the first train out of St. Gallen.'

'Why? I'm exhausted . . .' she protested.

'You can rest on the train. We're heading east for Bavaria . . .'

'What's the Goddamn rush?'

'The Goddamn rush is the police. They'll soon realise they have two murders on their hands. *Two*! The man I killed in the museum, the woman you shot outside the Hecht. Then they'll be watching every train leaving St. Gallen . . .'

Martel concealed one fact from Claire as they sat in a first-class compartment which they had to themselves aboard the Münich express. He was convinced they were moving into the zone of maximum danger – Bavaria. Somewhere in that scenically glorious part of Germany Delta had its headquarters.

Switzerland, the most neutral, stable country in Europe had almost been a death-trap. But the risks encountered in Zürich and St. Gallen were nothing compared with what lay ahead of them.

While waiting for the train in St. Gallen station Martel had called Tweed in London. This was one of the many advantages of Switzerland: its superb telephone system enabled you to dial abroad from a payphone where no one could intercept the call.

Martel had used his usual technique when speaking to Tweed – knowing his call would be tape-recorded. He had spoken in a kind of shorthand – shooting random facts at Tweed, every scrap of information he had picked up. Later Tweed, remote from the battlefield, would try to fit the fragments of data into some kind of pattern.

'Thursday calling,' he said as Tweed came on the line and waited for the answering code identification.

'Two–Eight here ...'

It was Thursday May 28. Martel used the *day* of the week while Tweed responded with the *date* of the month. Martel began to pour out data.

'*Delta very active inside Switzerland ... agents wear business-men suits ... Delta symbol openly displayed in lapels ... strange lack of cooperation from locals ... dummy Claire waiting Centralhof tried to kill me ... arrested by fake Arnold ... imprisoned Hofer waiting Lisbeth Hofer ... Claire's twin-like sister ... Lisbeth kidnapped during bloodbath in Bahnhofstrasse ... repeat in Bahnhof-strasse ... Ferdy Arnold later reported her body found in Limmat ... Nagel denied all knowledge events in Bahnhofstrasse ... now with genuine Claire Hofer St. Gallen ... leaving immediately with her to investigate scene Warner murder ... Claire reports Warner made three mentions Operation Crocodile ... something phoney about Delta neo-Nazis ... must go ...*'

'Wait!' Tweed's tone was urgent. 'Bayreuth reports Manfred has crossed the border near Hof into West Germany. Manfred – got it?'

'Christ!'

Martel had slammed down the receiver, grabbed his suitcase and run across the platform to the compartment door Claire had left open. Boarding the express, he hauled the door closed behind him as the train began moving east, dumped his case on a seat and sat down.

Even in the early afternoon the third-floor apartment in the sombre Münich apartment block was so dim the occupant had turned on the shaded desk-lamp. He had entered the apartment to find the phone ringing. His gloved hand lifted the receiver.

'Vinz – calling from Lindau ...'

'We are here,' Manfred replied in his soft, calm voice. 'You are calling to confirm that a successful deal was concluded in St. Gallen?'

'Regrettably it was not possible to conclude the deal ...' Erwin Vinz forced himself to go on. 'Kohler has reported from there ...'

'And why was the deal not concluded?'

'The opposition's negotiator proved uncooperative ...' Vinz was sweating, his armpits felt damp. 'And the services of two of our people were terminated ...'

'T–e–r–m–i–n–a–t–e–d?'

Manfred repeated the word with great deliberation as though he were sure he had misheard. There was a pause and the light from the desk-lamp was reflected in the lenses of the large dark-tinted glasses Manfred wore. In Lindau Vinz made the effort to continue.

'The Englishman is now aboard an express bound for München. It is due here in about half an hour ...'

'So,' Manfred interjected smoothly, 'you have made all preparations to board the express at Lindau to continue negotiations with this gentleman.' Now it was Manfred's turn to pause. 'You do, of course, realise it is imperative you conclude the deal with him before the train reaches München?'

'Everything has been arranged by me personally. I just thought I should check with you ...'

'Always check with me, Vinz. Always. Then, as a matter of courtesy, you keep Mr Reinhard Dietrich informed ...'

'I will report progress ...'

'Passengers have been known to fall out of trains,' Manfred purred. 'You will report *success* ...'

Cooped up inside his payphone on the Bavarian mainland Erwin Vinz realised the connection had been broken. Swearing, he pushed open the door and hurried away through a drift of grey mist.

The medieval town of Lindau – once an Imperial city – was blotted out in the fog coming in off the lake. The Old Town is a network of cobbled streets and alleyways which at night only the most intrepid venture down. Not that there is normally any danger – Lindau is a most law-abiding place.

Shortly after Manfred received his phone call three cars proceeded over the road bridge and headed for the Hauptbahnhof. The station is another curious feature of Lindau. Main-line expresses on their way from Zürich to München make a diversion at this point. The line takes them across the embankment to the west on to the island. They stop at the Hauptbahnhof next to the harbour.

If you alight from an express at Lindau you pass through *Zoll* – the customs and passport control post – because you have crossed the border from Austria into Germany. But boarding a train at Lindau for München you do not pass through *Zoll* – since you are already in Germany.

This factor was important to the eight men led by Vinz alighting from the three cars at the Hauptbahnhof. The drivers took the cars away immediately. Dressed like businessmen, two of the eight passengers carried suitcases containing uniforms. These would be donned aboard the München express as soon as it began moving out of Lindau.

The uniforms were those of a German State Railways ticket inspector and a German Passport Control official. It was the latter – travelling rapidly through the train and explaining there was a double-check on passports – who expected to locate Keith Martel. The plan was simple. Erwin Vinz, thirty-eight years old, small, thin and with hooded eyelids, was in charge of the execution squad.

Vinz would wear the Passport Control uniform. Vinz would locate the target. If Martel were travelling alone in a compartment it would be invaded when the express was travelling at

83

speed by four men. The outer door would be opened and the Englishman would be hurled from the train. The whole operation, Vinz calculated, would take less than twenty seconds.

If Martel had fellow-passengers in his compartment Vinz would ask him to accompany him because there was a query on his passport. He would be guided to an empty compartment and the same procedure would be followed. Vinz knew that this particular express was always half-empty on this day of the week.

The platform marked for the arrival of the express was deserted as the eight men arrived separately from the concourse. The fog created a hushed atmosphere and the men moved in it like ghosts. Vinz checked his watch. They were in good time. The express was due in twenty minutes.

CHAPTER 10

Thursday May 28

'You'll like Lindau, Keith,' Claire said as Martel peered out of the window from the fast-moving express. 'It is one of the most beautiful old towns in Germany ...'

'I know it.' He had his mind on something else. 'I shall want to contact Erich Stoller of the BND as soon as we can – to let him have a look at this ...'

Unlocking his case, he produced something rolled up in a handkerchief. A blue, shiny cylinder like a large felt-tip pen. There were two press-buttons: one on the casing, the second at the base.

'I rescued this little Delta toy from the floor of the Embroidery Museum where the killer dropped it. This button half-way along the casing ejects and retracts the needle. I imagine the one at the base injects the poison. Ingenious – you can use the full force of the palm of your hand to operate the injection mechanism. Stoller's forensic people will tell us what fluid it contains ...'

'That woman I shot outside the Hecht ...'

'Was going to use the duplicate of this. Intriguing that Reinhard Dietrich runs an electronics complex – which involves fine instrumentation ...'

'You mean *he* manufactures that horrible thing?'

'Damned sure of it.' He replaced the weapon inside his case and looked again out of the window. Up to now the view had been one of green cultivated fields and rolling hills – one of the most attractive and least-known parts of Switzerland. Well clear of the tourist belt.

The landscape was changing. They were crossing flatlands

dimly visible in swirling mist which hid nearby Lake Konstanz. They saw few signs of human habitation and there was something desolate in the atmosphere. Martel concentrated on the view as though he might miss something important.

'This is the Rhine delta, isn't it?' he queried.

'Yes. We cross the river soon just before it runs into the lake.'

Delta. Was there significance in this geographical curiosity at the extreme eastern end of the lake? The southern shore was Swiss except for a weird enclave of land occupied by the German town of Konstanz away to the west. The northern shore was German. But at this eastern tip a few miles of lake frontage was *Austrian*.

Martel adjusted the horn-rimmed spectacles with plain glass he wore to change his appearance. He lit a fresh cigarette, being careful not to use his holder. He seemed to have relapsed into a dream.

'We shall soon be in Lindau,' Claire said exuberantly, trying to drag him out of his dark mood. 'Surely we must find something – it was ...' Her voice wavered and then she had herself under control. 'It was the last place Warner was seen alive.'

'Except that we are getting off at the stop before – Bregenz in Austria.'

'Why?'

'Bregenz could be important. And it will be the last place Delta will expect us to leave the train ...'

Hauptbahnhof, Münich ... Hauptbahnhof, Zürich ... Delta ... Centralhof ... Bregenz ... Washington, DC, Clint Loomis ... Pullach, BND ... Operation Crocodile.

These were the references the dead Charles Warner had written in the tiny black notebook hidden in a secret pocket, the notebook Erich Stoller of the BND had discovered on the body and flown to Tweed in London.

Bregenz.

As the express slowed down Claire caught a glimpse of Lake Konstanz through the corridor windows – a sheet of calm grey water. The express stopped and when Martel opened the door at the end of the coach he found no platform – they stepped down on to the track. He dumped his suitcase, took Claire's and held her elbow while she descended the steep drop. She shivered as she picked up her case and they made their way across rail tracks to the station, an old single-storey building.

'You shivered ...'

'It's the mist,' she said shortly.

A cold clammy dampness moistened her face and she felt it penetrating her light raincoat. She had lied. It *was* the mist partly – but mainly it was the atmosphere created by the drift of greyish vapour. You saw things, then they were gone.

Behind Bregenz looms the massive heights of the Pfänder, a ridge whose sides are densely forested. As they crossed to the station Claire saw a gap appear in the mist pall exposing the dripping wall of limestone, then it too was gone. There was no ticket barrier to pass through – tickets had been checked aboard the express. They deposited their cases in the self-locking metal compartments for luggage and walked into Bregenz.

The place seemed deserted, as though it were a Sunday. A line of old block-like buildings faced the station. Martel paused, puffing his cigarette as he glanced round searching for anything out of place. Claire gazed at him.

'Those glasses make you look studious – they change your whole personality. And you're walking more ponderously. You're just like a chameleon. Incidentally, what are we going to do here?'

He extracted two photos of Charles Warner obtained from Tweed before leaving Park Crescent and handed her one of the prints. She looked at the picture of the man she had worked with for over six months, the man who had been brutally murdered on the lake behind them – only a short distance from where they stood.

'The story is we're looking for a friend – Warner,' Martel told her. 'His wife is seriously ill and we think he's somewhere here.

We'll buy a street map, divide up the place into sections – then meet up at an agreed place in two hours' time ...'

'It sounds a hopeless task,' she commented when they were studying a street plan bought at a kiosk.

'Warner was here – he made a reference to the place in his notebook. Concentrate on anywhere selling cigarettes – he smoked like a chimney. He had a strong personality, made an impression on anyone he talked to. Now, we'll decide which district each of us is going to tackle. Half this job is legwork ...'

In the Münich apartment the phone began ringing and Manfred, who was expecting the call, picked up the receiver with his gloved hand. It was Erwin Vinz. Manfred, a teetotaller, poured Perrier water as he listened intently.

'I am speaking from Münich Hauptbahnhof,' Vinz began after giving the identification code. 'I got off the train a few minutes ago ...'

Manfred knew immediately something was wrong. Vinz was rambling, reluctant to come to the point. Manfred introduced into the conversation his often-used ploy.

'Excellent! We assume all went well. Appointment kept and deal concluded?'

'The Englishman was not on the train. There is no doubt – I can vouch for the fact personally. *If* he got aboard at St. Gallen he must have got off at Romanshorn or St. Margarethen in Switzerland.'

'Kohler saw him closing the compartment door after he boarded the express at St. Gallen ...'

Manfred's voice was gentle and deliberate, concealing his livid rage. Vinz's insolence in emphasising *If* cast doubt on Kohler's competence. Not that Manfred cared a damn about Kohler – but Vinz was trying to shift the blame and that he would not tolerate.

'Kohler would have known,' Manfred continued, 'if our friend left the train while it was moving through Switzerland ...' Manfred saw no reason to explain that Kohler would have had men with a clear description of Keith Martel waiting at each

88

Swiss stop. He continued to make Vinz sweat.

'Your sector began at the Swiss border. You got on the train at Lindau ...'

'The bastard must have got off at Bregenz,' Vinz interjected. 'It was the only place left uncovered ...'

'Left uncovered by *you* ...'

Bregenz! Manfred's hand gripped the receiver tightly. The one town he did not want Martel poking around in was Bregenz. He felt like screaming at Vinz, but the sensitivity of the situation must at all costs be hidden.

'I can have a team in Bregenz in one hour,' Vinz volunteered, disturbed by the silence at the other end of the line.

'We would like your team to keep its appointment with the client in half an hour. I hold you personally responsible for bringing about a successful conclusion to this transaction ...'

Inside the payphone at München Hauptbahnhof Vinz swore again. Once more Manfred had abruptly terminated the conversation. And now he had to fly his bloody team back from München to the airstrip nearest Bregenz. This time they had to eliminate the Englishman.

In London Tweed had left his office for his flat in Maida Vale after receiving the St. Gallen call from Martel. Mason, Howard's new deputy, had tried to delay him. Looking leaner and hungrier than ever, he arrived as Tweed was leaving.

'The chief would like to see you in his office, sir. He says it is extremely urgent ...'

'It always is – to him. I'll see him when I get back.'

Tweed took a cab to the flat. He also took Miss McNeil and she carried the Martel tape concealed in a hold-all. While in the cab he asked his question.

'That new recruit, Mason. Is he any good at anything?'

'He'd make a good bodyguard,' McNeill replied in her crisp Scots accent. 'He's an expert at judo, karate. A marksman with handguns. Special Branch were happy for Howard to take him.'

'Why?'

McNeil had a finely-tuned ear on the grapevine. Probably due to her gift for listening with attentive concentration and unlimited patience.

'He was too physical – always resorted to heavy handling of any suspect at the drop of a hat. A lot of hats – and clangers – were dropped, I gather.'

At the flat McNeil played back the tape of Martel's conversation on the machine kept there permanently, making notes in neat loops and curls. She had offered to make the tea but Tweed insisted only he could make it the way he liked it. You would imagine he had been a lifetime bachelor, McNeil thought, as she went on making her notes. Tweed arrived with the tray of tea as the tape came to the end of the recording.

The block of flats Tweed lived in was self-service. He had a Sicilian woman who came in to clean the place and often complained she was 'illiterate in three languages'. There was a restaurant on the ground floor. Here Tweed, now on his own, led a self-contained existence. He poured the tea as he asked the question.

'Anything strike you about Martel's data?'

'Two things. Delta seems to be acting in a frenzy – as though they're working against a deadline. *Bloodbath*. That's strong language from Martel in a report. And another reference – *something phoney about Delta neo-Nazis*. I don't understand what he's driving at . . .'

'McNeil, you're a treasure. You always spot the salient facts. Makes me feel redundant. I'm pretty sure the deadline is June 2 when the Summit Express leaves Paris – because by morning it will be crossing Bavaria . . .'

'You're thinking about the Bavarian state elections?'

'Exactly. Three main parties are competing for power – to take over the state government. Dietrich's Delta – the neo-Nazis – the government party under Chancellor Kurt Langer, and the left-wing lot under Tofler, the alleged ex-Communist. If something dramatic happens on June 3, the day before the election, it might swing the election result – into Tofler's hands. For the

West it would be a major disaster.'

'What dramatic event could happen?'

'I only wish I knew.' Tweed sipped his tea. 'I'm convinced Delta has some secret plan – hence the frenzy to eliminate anyone digging into their affairs.'

'What about the reference to *something phoney*?'

McNeil sat quite still, watching Tweed gazing owlishly through his spectacles into the distance. He was, she knew, capable of sudden flashes of intuition – a leap into the future he divined from just the sort of ragbag of facts Martel had provided.

'It has the feel of a separate cell operating secretly inside Delta,' Tweed said slowly. 'That's the only explanation for some of their actions which seem to be designed to ensure they *lose* the election . . .'

'Now you've *lost* me,' McNeil commented tartly.

'Where *have* you two been?'

Howard was waiting for them when McNeil and Tweed returned to the latter's office. Standing stiff-backed he had the window behind him – so his own face was in shadow while the new arrivals were caught in the full glare of the light from the curved window. He clasped his hands over his stomach which was decorated with the double loop of a gold watch-chain.

Very militant in mood as well as stance, Tweed observed as he sat behind his desk. He knew the type only too well. An inferiority complex as large as Everest – so they compensated by periodic assertions of authority, just to make sure they still held it.

'Went for a walk in Regent's Park,' Tweed lied blandly.

'You're working on a problem?' Howard pounced.

The SIS chief was in a nervous state of mind, McNeil decided. She was carrying the empty hold-all inside which she had smuggled out Martel's tape to the flat in Maida Vale.

'What's inside that hold-all?' Howard demanded.

'Cheese sandwiches – Cheddar, if you must know,' Tweed interjected. 'It's better than the Cheshire – more flavour . . .'

'Could you very kindly find something to do elsewhere?' Howard asked McNeil, who promptly left the room, still carrying the hold-all.

'Have you heard from Keith Martel?' Howard barked as soon as they were alone.

'I thought you were concentrating on security for the PM on her trip to the forthcoming Summit Conference in Vienna. So why interest yourself in Martel ...'

'It's a waste of personnel. Just when I need every man ...'

'So you told me. If you want it on record send me a minute and I can show it to the Minister.' Tweed perched his glasses on the end of his nose and peered over the rims at his visitor, a mannerism which he knew infuriated Howard. 'By the way, I suppose the normal people are in charge of security for the others – the Presidents of America and France, and the German Chancellor?'

'Tim O'Meara in Washington, Alain Flandres in Paris and Erich Stoller in Bonn. Does it really concern you?'

'Not really. I just wondered if all my old friends were still in their jobs.' Tweed looked at his chief. 'These days so many get the chop just when they least expect it ...'

Howard left the room, his mouth tight, his stride almost that of an officer route-marching. He would be incensed for days over the exchange which had taken place – and would therefore keep well away from Tweed, which was what the latter intended. McNeil peered round the door.

'Has he gone?'

'Yes, my dear, the British lion has roared. It is now safe to return.' He opened a copy of *The Times* atlas. 'Crocodile – I'm sure the meaning of that codeword is under my nose ...'

Erwin Vinz took his execution squad back into the new search area – Bregenz – by the fastest possible route. Flying from a private airstrip outside München he landed his men at another airstrip close to Lindau. From here the eight men piled into three waiting cars and were driven at speed to the border and Bregenz beyond. It was three o'clock when they pulled up in front of the station.

'I think Martel got off the train here,' Vinz told the two men in the rear of his car. 'He may well still be in Bregenz. You stay here. The rest of us will quarter the town and drive round until we locate him ...'

'And if we do see him board a train?' one of the two men asked as he alighted from the car.

'He has a fatal accident, of course!' Vinz was irritated by the man's stupidity. 'Whatever happens he must not reach Münich ...'

Vinz held a brief conference with the other five men. 'There are twenty thousand deutschemarks for the man who locates Martel. You have his description. You tell people he escaped from a home for the mentally disturbed, that he is dangerous. Rendez-vous here two hours from now. Turn over this backwater!'

Martel picked up the spoor Charles Warner had left behind in Bregenz at his twelfth attempt. The contact was a bookseller, an Austrian in his early forties with a shop at the end of Kaiser-strasse. Outside was the pedestrian underpass where Martel had arranged to meet Claire in half an hour's time. He told his tale, showed Warner's photo and the reaction was positive.

'I know your friend. Grief seems to be his companion ...'

'Grief?' Martel queried cautiously and waited.

'Yes. His closest friend died here while on a visit. It was during the French military occupation of the Vorarlberg and the Tyrol after the war. His friend was buried here so he thought he would pay his respects.'

'I see ...'

Martel did not see at all and was careful to say as little as possible. The bookseller broke off to serve a customer and then continued.

'There are two Catholic cemeteries in Bregenz and one Protestant. This man's friend had a curious religious history. Born a Protestant, he was converted to the Catholic faith. Later

93

he appeared to lose his faith. Under the peculiar circumstances the man who came into my shop asked for the location of all three cemeteries. I showed them to him on a street map.'

'How recent was his visit to you?'

'Less than a week ago. Last Saturday ...'

'Can you sell me a street map and mark the three cemeteries?'

The bookseller fetched a map and ringed the areas. 'There is the Blumenstrasse, the Vorkloster – both are Catholic. And here is the Protestant burial-ground ...'

Claire was waiting when Martel descended the steps into the otherwise deserted subway. She stood gazing at a scene behind an illuminated window set into the wall. The glass protected relics of an archeological dig which had unearthed the ancient Roman town which once stood on the site of present-day Bregenz.

'Spooky, isn't it?' Claire remarked and gave a little shudder. 'All that time ago. And today in this mist the whole place seems creepy – and I haven't found a trace of Warner ...'

'Last Saturday he was standing not a hundred feet from where we are standing now ...'

She listened while he summed up his interview with the helpful bookseller. As he completed his résumé she was frowning. 'I'm not grasping the significance ...'

'Join the club – except that one thing's almost frighteningly certain. He was here last Saturday. Sunday he's murdered out on the lake. Whatever he found in Bregenz probably triggered off that murder ...'

'But how long ago was the French military occupation of Austria, for God's sake? This goes back to just after the war ...'

'Not necessarily. The Allied occupation of Austria ended May 15 1955 – so whatever Warner dug up could have happened close to that date ...'

'It's still over a quarter of a century ago,' she objected, 'so what could have happened then that's relevant to today?'

'Damned if I know – that's what we have to find out. That

yarn Warner spun about his closest friend dying here was eye-wash, but he had his teeth into something. The period – the time of the French occupation might mean something . . .'

'So how do we find out, where do we start?'

'We hire a car first at a place I saw near here. Then we visit the three cemeteries Warner was enquiring about. The secret has to lie in one of them. Literally . . .'

Erwin Vinz walked into the bookseller's shop in Kaiserstrasse. Despite his later arrival in Bregenz he had, without knowing, an advantage over Martel: six men were scouring the town. He spoke first to a girl assistant and asked for the manager. She went upstairs to find the proprietor who had talked to Martel.

'I'd better go down and see this man myself,' the bookseller decided.

On the ground floor he listened while Vinz told his story. The verbal description Vinz gave was graphic. Take away the glasses and add a cigarette holder and the bookseller recognised that this man was describing his earlier visitor. The Austrian studied Vinz and was careful not to interrupt.

'You say that this man has escaped from a mental asylum?' he enquired eventually.

'Yes. A very violent patient. Unfortunately he can give the impression he is completely normal and this makes him even more dangerous. You have seen this man?'

CHAPTER 11

Thursday May 28

IN GOTTES FRIEDEN ALOIS STOHR 1930–1953

In God We Trust ... Inside the mist-bound cemetery known as the Blumenstrasse three people stared at the headstone. Martel and Claire were bewildered. Alois Stohr? The name meant nothing to either of them. Martel turned to the gravedigger who had brought them to this spot. Again he showed him Warner's photo.

'Look, you're quite certain this was the man who asked to see this particular grave?'

The old gravedigger wore an ancient cap and his moustache dripped moisture globules from the grey vapour swirling amid the headstones. So far as Martel could see – which was not very far – they were the only visitors. It was not a day to encourage sentimental journeys.

'This is the man.'

The gravedigger, Martel noted, spoke with the same conviction of recognition as had the bookseller when viewing the photo. And he had identified Warner previously before Martel gave him a sheaf of schilling notes.

'When did he come here?' Martel asked.

'Last week. Saturday.'

The same story that the bookseller had told. It was maddening. Martel no longer had any doubt that Charles Warner had visited this particular grave only a short time before he was murdered. But where was the link-up – what made Alois Stohr so important he must remain undisturbed at all cost?

'Did he say anything else, anything at all?' Martel demanded.

'Simply asked me to show him the grave of Alois Stohr ...'

Watching on the sidelines Claire had an overpowering impression the gravedigger was withdrawing into his shell under the impact of Martel's interrogation. The Englishman continued.

'Did he give the date of Stohr's death?'

'Only said it was near the end of the French occupation ...'

Warner had used a similar phrase while talking to the bookseller in Kaiserstrasse. *It was during the French military occupation* ... Why pinpoint the time like that instead of giving an approximate year?

Claire had remained silent, studying the gravedigger, and she spoke suddenly, her voice confident as though she knew the reply and was interested only in confirmation?

'Who else visits this grave?'

'I don't know as I should talk about such things,' the old boy said after a long pause. Martel almost held his breath: Claire, by a flash of intuition had put her finger on something they would otherwise not have been told. She kept up the pressure.

'My friend gave you a generous sum so we expect complete frankness. Who comes here?'

'I don't know her name. She comes every week. Always on a Wednesday and always at eight in the morning. She lays a bunch of flowers, waits a few minutes and then goes ...'

'How does she get here?' Claire persisted. 'By car? By cab?'

'She comes in a cab – and keeps it waiting till she leaves ...'

'Her description? Colour of hair? Her age – roughly. How is she dressed? Modestly? Expensively?'

The barrage of questions reinforced the gravedigger's obvious reluctance to say more. He handed Warner's photo back to Martel and picked up his shovel, prior to departure.

'Expensive – her clothes ...'

'Colour of hair?' Claire went on relentlessly.

'Can't say – she always wears a head-scarf ...'

'And you passed on this same information to the man in this photo when he came here?' Martel asked.

The gravedigger, shouldering his shovel like a soldier, was moving away, vanishing into the mist shrouding the headstones. His voice came back like that of a ghost.

'Yes. And I think he found out where she lived. While she was here I saw him talking to her cab-driver. Money exchanged hands ...'

Have you seen this man?

The bookseller who had talked to Martel adjusted his glasses and gazed at Erwin Vinz. He took his time before replying.

'You have some form of identification?' he enquired.

'You *have* seen the escaped patient then?' Vinz pressed eagerly. 'As to identification – we're not police, we don't carry cards ...'

'Your description means nothing to me. I have never had anyone in my shop remotely resembling this man. If you will excuse me, I have a shop to run ...'

He watched Vinz leave, shoulders hunched, his mouth a thin line. He climbed into a car outside, said something to the driver and the vehicle disappeared. The girl assistant spoke tentatively.

'I thought we did have a man in here earlier ...'

'You think that man who just called had anything to do with an asylum?' There was a note of contempt in the Austrian's voice.

'For one thing he was a German so he would have approached the authorities if his story were true ...'

'You think he was ...'

'Lying in his teeth. You have just met a neo-Nazi – I can smell the breed, to say nothing of the badge he flaunts in his coat lapel. If he returns, tell me and I will call the police ...'

The sun had burnt off the mist and it was now a brilliant afternoon. When Vinz arrived and left two men to watch the railway station there remained a team of six – including himself – and he had divided them up into pairs. Each couple took one of the three cars to explore the district allocated to them.

One couple was driving up Gallus-strasse, a prosperous residential area, while Vinz was making his abortive visit to the bookshop. Vinz's men had just enquired at yet another hotel and again drawn a blank. The car descending Gallus-strasse towards them contained Martel and Claire. Both vehicles moved at a sedate pace as they closed the gap between them.

Vinz's men, in a BMW, were keeping down their speed so they could check the sidewalks for any sign of Martel. Behind the wheel of the Audi they had hired, Claire drove slowly through the unfamiliar district while Martel, beside her, gave directions as he studied the town plan.

'At the bottom – to avoid going past the railway station – we turn . . .'

'Oh, my God! Keith – inside that BMW coming towards us. I saw the sun flash off something shiny in the lapel of that man beside the driver. I'm sure it's a badge. It's Delta . . .'

'Don't speed up, don't look at them, don't change anything – just keep going as you are doing . . .'

'They'll have your description . . .'

'Good luck to them!'

Inside the BMW the man in the front passenger seat carried a Luger inside his shoulder holster. He studied the two people in the oncoming Audi. It was second nature for him to overlook no-one. Imprinted in his memory was the detailed description of Martel every member of the squad had been provided with.

Gallus-strasse was exceptionally quiet at this hour. Claire was suddenly aware she was gripping the wheel tightly and forced herself to relax – *not to look at the BMW driver who had lowered his window which would allow his passenger to fire at her point-blank*.

'Steady now . . .!'

Martel spoke softly, his lips scarcely moving as he studied the street map spread out on his lap. The two cars, still slow-moving, drew level. The passenger inside the BMW stared hard at the man next to the girl driver. Then the cars were moving away from each other.

'Something about that Audi?' asked the man behind the wheel.

'Just checking. Not a bit like him ...'

At the bottom of Gallus-strasse Martel directed Claire to keep them away from the lake front – and the railway station. She gave a sigh of relief.

'Not to worry,' he remarked. 'I wonder how they got here while we were still in town ...'

'They were Delta ...'

'I saw the badges out of the corner of my eye as they passed us. In any case, I was prepared ...' He lifted a corner of the street plan and she saw his right hand gripping the butt of his .45 Colt. 'Any sign of hostile action and I could have blown them both away. There was no one else about. And how did you expect them to recognise me?'

She glanced at him. He wore a Tyrolean hat with a feather in the band purchased while she arranged the hire of the Audi. Clamped between his teeth was a large, ugly-looking pipe he had bought in another shop. On the bridge of his Roman nose perch- ed horn-rimmed glasses. The transformation from his normal hatless appearance with cigarette-holder at jaunty angle was total.

'God,' she said, 'I'm a fool not to have your confidence ...'

'Your reaction was correct,' he rapped back. 'The day you're not nervous in a situation like that is likely to be your last. Now, let's head for the border and the whirlpool – Lindau.'

In the late afternoon Vinz phoned Reinhard Dietrich from Bregenz. He was exhausted. So were his men. By phoning the *schloss* he also avoided reporting to the man he most feared. Manfred.

'Vinz speaking. We were asked to undertake a commission ...'

'I know.' Dietrich sounded irritable. 'I was informed by the agent who placed the commission. I take it you have earned your keep?'

In the payphone near Bregenz station Vinz gazed out at the

dense fog rolling in from the lake. 'From the beginning it was an impossible task,' he said. 'We ran ourselves into the ground. The Englishman is not here ...'

'What! He must have got off that express at Bregenz. Don't you see – he chose that stop because he guessed the competition might be waiting for him at Lindau. And Bregenz is a small town ...'

'Not all that small,' Vinz snapped. He was so tired he answered back. 'The layout is complex – and the fog has returned. The whole place is blotted out ...'

'Get back here at once! All of you! We'll discuss our next move the moment you arrive. And don't stop anywhere for a drink or anything to eat ...'

'We haven't eaten all day ...'

'I should bloody well hope not! Straight back here! You understand?'

Dietrich slammed down the receiver. He was red in the face. He ran his hands through his silver hair and gazed round the library. Vinz would never know his outburst had been prompted not by rage but by *fear*. He rang for Oscar and when the hunchback arrived told him to pour a large brandy.

'They haven't found the Englishman,' he said savagely.

'He must be clever. The first spy, Warner, was clever – but he revealed himself in due course. This new Englishman will make the same mistake ...' He handed the brandy to Dietrich who took a large gulp and shook his head.

'He eludes every trap. He has been on the continent less than two days and is getting closer to Bavaria, to Operation Crocodile, every moment. In six days' time the Summit Express will be crossing Bavaria!'

'So we have six days to find him,' Oscar said reassuringly, refilling his master's glass.

'God in heaven, Oscar! Don't you see you can turn that round? *He has six days to find us!*'

Close to the main entrance to Dietrich's walled estate there was a small forest by the roadside. The entrance was guarded by wrought-iron gates and a sentry lodge. It was early evening when a large bird swooped over the gates and all hell broke loose.

Behind the gates ferocious German shepherd dogs appeared, huge brutes which leapt at the gates, barking and snarling, eager to tear any intruder to pieces.

Inside a Mercedes parked out of sight on the edge of the trees Erich Stoller, chief of the BND, listened to the sound of the dogs, his slim hands lightly tapping the wheel. Forty-three years old, Stoller was six feet tall and very thin, his face lean and sensitive.

His chief assistant, Otto Wilde, sat beside him clasping a cine-camera equipped with a telephoto lens. Small and plump, Wilde was terrified of fierce dogs. He glanced at his chief.

'Supposing they open the gates . . .'

'Oh, we can deal with that.' Stoller opened the glove compartment, extracted the gas-pistol nestling inside and handed it to his companion. 'A whiff of tear-gas up their nostrils should discourage their ardour . . .'

'They know we're here – they have picked up our scent . . .'

'Nonsense! They were startled by that large bird which swooped past the entrance. When we develop your film it will be interesting to see if any old friends are present. I think I recognised one – the driver of the first car . . .'

Parked out of sight they had witnessed the recent return to the *schloss* of a cavalcade of three cars. Erwin Vinz had been driving the leading vehicle. What Vinz did not know was that when they pulled up at the entrance – waiting while the dogs were locked up in their compound – Otto Wilde had been busy with his camera.

This was Stoller's first visit to the area of the *schloss* owned by Dietrich. By chance Vinz's team, returning from its fruitless search for Keith Martel, arrived while the BND chief was surveying the target area. Stoller was persisting in his efforts to locate Delta's main base.

'I'm convinced, Otto,' he remarked as he reached for the

ignition, 'that Delta could have its headquarters here.'

'Why?'

'Because it is the home of Reinhard Dietrich who has put himself forward in the state elections as the next Minister-President of Bavaria, because you say the estate is vast . . .'

'I showed you on the map. Look at the distance we drove round the perimeter to get here . . .'

'So, it could fit. You can't see the *schloss* from any point from the road. It is remote, secluded – ideal for concealing a horde of rabble-rousers. And God knows they are rousing – look at the riots recently. Almost as bad as in England . . .'

'They're opening the gates!'

Stoller had started the engine and was already driving into the open and on to the road leading past the entrance to the *schloss*. It was the direct route to München and Stoller was not prepared to go the other way for some millionaire thug who employed killer dogs.

'Raise your window,' he ordered Wilde, using one hand to shut his own. The dogs were out in the road, rushing towards the unmarked police car. Faces appeared at either window, fangs bared, mouths slavering, the heads huge, paws clawing desperately to get beyond the glass to ravage the men inside. Stoller put his foot down.

The car leapt forward. Two of the beasts appeared briefly in front of the radiator. The occupants felt the thuds of speeding metal colliding with animal bodies. Then they were hurtling past the open gates where men were pouring out led by a tall, well-built blond giant. Wilde looked back.

'They're going to follow us in a car . . .'

'That damned bird started it,' Stoller said calmly. 'The dogs kicked up, Dietrich's guards became suspicious – and sent out the hounds. Did you notice the blond Adonis who appeared to be their leader? That was Werner Hagen – a keen wind-surfer. We have to evade them – on no account must they know they're under surveillance . . .'

'Evade them? How?'

They moved at manic speed round bends in the country road and Wilde braced himself. He was almost as terrified of Stoller's driving as he was of fierce dogs: his chief had the reputation of being the fastest driver in Bavaria. Stoller gave a fresh order.

'When I stop at the next intersection stay in the car – and get well down out of sight. I'll need the gas-pistol – I'm going to block the road. Look, this will do . . .'

Wilde glanced over his shoulder and saw only deserted roadway. Stoller had gained a temporary lead – but Wilde knew the road ahead would be empty and for miles there were long straight sections. It couldn't be done . . .

Ahead a farm-track led off to the right. Stoller jammed on the brakes, there was a screech of rubber and he turned through ninety degrees, ending up a short distance along the track. Wilde was saved from being hurled through the windscreen by Stoller's insistence that he always wore his seat-belt. It was not over yet.

Stoller was now backing rapidly until his vehicle blocked the road. Grabbing the gas-pistol handed to him by Wilde who was already hunching himself below window level, he left the car, slamming the door shut. He ran towards a large tree near the roadside and hid behind the massive trunk.

The pursuing car – driven by Werner Hagen with two men accompanying him – came round a nearby bend. Hagen found himself confronted by a Mercedes broadside on and which appeared to be empty. He braked, stopped, reached for the gun under his armpit and told the two men to wait in the car.

Leaving his door open he looked cautiously round while the man in the back lowered his window to see what was going on. Stoller used the tree trunk to steady himself, aimed the gas-pistol and pulled the trigger. The missile exploded on the driver's seat – a bull's-eye which spread fumes in all directions, smothering Hagen who dropped his gun and staggered, coughing, unable to see anything.

The man in the front passenger seat was choking, his vision blurred. In a matter of seconds Stoller reloaded and took fresh aim. The second missile passed through the open rear window and exploded in the rear of the car. Stoller ran back to his own vehicle.

Minutes later he was miles away, driving along one of the endless stretches with no sign of any other vehicle in his rearview mirror. Wilde saw that his chief was frowning.

'You pulled that off beautifully. Why the scowl?'

'I was thinking about Martel. Tweed warned me he was coming – but he's a loner . . .'

'So, like Warner, no cooperation?'

'On the contrary, he'll contact me when he needs me. Excellent judgement. I just wonder where he is at this moment . . .'

CHAPTER 12

Thursday May 28

Martel drove the hired Audi across the road bridge linking the mainland of Bavaria with the island of Lindau. He no longer wore the Tyrolean hat nor was he smoking the pipe used to disguise his appearance in Bregenz.

Hatless, his profile prominent with its strong Roman nose, the Englishman smoked a cigarette in his holder at a jaunty angle. It was as though he wished to draw attention to his arrival to any watchers who might be stationed in Lindau.

'What do you think you are doing?' Claire had demanded when he discarded his disguise as soon as they had crossed the border into Germany.

'Showing the British flag,' replied Martel. 'If I had a Union Jack pennant I'd be flying it ...'

'Delta will spot us soon enough ...'

'Sooner, I hope.'

'You're setting yourself up as a target?' she protested. 'You must be mad – have you forgotten Zürich, St. Gallen ...'

'The point is I have remembered them – and we're working to a time limit. You said the Bayerischer Hof is the top hotel on the island?'

'Yes, and it's next to the Hauptbahnhof ...'

'Then we must rig it so it looks as though you've arrived on your own by train. We'll register separately, eat separately in the dining-room. We don't know each other. That way you can guard my back. And put on those dark glasses which transform your appearance ...'

'Would sir like anything else?'

'Yes, guide me to the hotel,' he said. 'This place is a rabbit warren and I've forgotten the burrows. Use the map.'

They had a taste of the beauty of the island when they drove over the bridge and past a green park which ran to the lake edge. The mist had lifted temporarily and the sun was a luminous glow. She checked the map and gave directions. Within minutes she laid a hand on his arm.

'We're almost there. Better drop me here. Turn left at the end. The Bayerischer Hof is on your left, the Hauptbahnhof on your right, the harbour straight ahead. Where do we meet?'

'At the terrace elevated above the harbour, the Romerschanze – the place where a tourist looking through binoculars witnessed the killing of Warner without realising it . . .'

She left the vehicle, carrying her suitcase. Only two or three tourists were in this quiet section of the old street but she took no chances, calling out in German.

'Thank you so much for the lift. Now I shall catch my train.'

'My pleasure . . .'

The pavement artist, Braun, spotted Martel as soon as he drove round the corner.

Today Braun's picture drawn in crayon on the flagstones was an impression of the amphitheatre at Verona. The small cardboard box for coins lay beside the picture. Again wearing a windcheater and jeans he was patrolling back and forth, hands clasped behind his back as though taking a rest from his labours.

He was actually watching the exit doors from the Hauptbahnhof. A main-line express from Switzerland was due. He turned round at the precise moment Keith Martel appeared and recognised him immediately. It was no great feat of observation.

Thick black hair, early thirties, tall, well-built, clean-shaven, prominent Semitic-like nose, habitually smokes cigarettes in holder at slanting angle . . .

The pavement artist was so thrown off-balance by Martel's sudden appearance, by the accuracy of the description provided, that he almost stopped in mid-stride – which would have been a blunder since it might have drawn the target's attention to

107

himself. He strolled on as the Audi passed him and he heard it pull up. He sneaked a glance over his shoulder so he would be able to recognise the Englishman *from behind*.

'I wonder, you curious sod . . .'

Martel muttered the words to himself as he stared in his wing mirror, still seated behind the wheel. It had been a reflex action – to make one final check before he got out of the car with his suitcase. The swift glance of the pavement artist over his shoulder showed clearly in the mirror.

He got out of the car and saw the mist beginning to roll in from the lake, invading the harbour. He walked inside the hotel's spacious, well-furnished reception hall and up a few steps to the desk. The girl behind the counter was helpful and brisk. Yes, they had an excellent double bedroom on the third floor over-looking the lake. Certainly it would be acceptable for him to pay for his room in advance as he might have to make a sudden departure on business.

'And if you would fill in the registration form, sir?'

The conversation had been carried on in English – Martel was booking in under his own name and nationality. Under the heading *Occupation* he wrote *Consultant*.

Escorted upstairs in the lift by the porter, he was shown into a huge room with a large bathroom. Martel liked to travel well and Erich Stoller was paying. As soon as he was alone he went to the side window which, as he expected, overlooked the Haupt-bahnhof and hotel entrance. He saw Claire coming out of the station.

Her performance had been a model of skilled evasion. Wear-ing her dark glasses and a head-scarf, she had crossed the road immediately Martel had turned the corner. The pavement artist had not even seen her. He was not *looking* for a girl, only a man, Martel . . .

Once inside the Hauptbahnhof Claire had waited for someone else to walk out. A couple staying at the hotel had gone across to check the timetable board. Claire emerged with them, having heard a brief snatch of their conversation in German.

'I'm looking for the Bayerischer Hof,' she said to the elderly man who was beside her. It was his wife beyond who answered.

'My dear, it is just across the road. We're staying there ourselves. You'll find it an excellent hotel . . .'

'Let me have your case,' the German said and took it, grasping the handle.

It was perfect cover for anyone who might be watching. Claire appeared to belong to the couple who had gone to the Hauptbahnhof to meet her. The pavement artist never even noticed her as the trio vanished inside the hotel entrance.

From the open third floor window in his bedroom Martel stared at the sidewalk immediately below where his car was still parked. The pavement artist held a tiny notepad in the palm of his hand and he was noting down the vehicle's registration number.

Seen from street level, the pavement artist's action was carried out with such skill no one noticed what he was doing. He never gave a thought to the possibility that he might be observed from above.

'Got you, you bastard . . .'

Martel muttered the words as he ran to his case, snapped open the locks and pulled out from under neatly folded clothes a small instrument. He shoved it inside his jacket pocket, left the room and descended in the waiting lift.

At ground floor level he ignored Claire who was completing the registration form after reserving a single room with bath. Walking to the exit, Martel peered out and strolled into the street. As he expected, the pavement artist was casually crossing the road on his way to the Hauptbahnhof.

The watcher had to have some quick means of communication with his employers – what could be more convenient than the public telephone booths he would undoubtedly find inside? The double doors closed in Martel's face as the pavement artist entered ahead of him. The Englishman pushed a door open slowly and walked into a large booking-hall. The row of phone booths was to his left.

The pavement artist had entered a booth in the middle of the row, the only one now occupied. Martel paused. Shoving his hand into his jacket pocket he waited until his quarry picked up the receiver and commenced dialling. Then Martel entered the booth to the right and slammed the door shut.

The noise attracted the pavement artist's attention. Out of the corner of his eye, his head bent over a notebook he appeared to be consulting, Martel sensed the man's shocked disbelief. For the next few seconds he held his breath. It was a question of psychology.

The pavement artist turned his back on Martel and continued making his call. It was the reaction Martel had prayed for. The man was *not* a top-flight professional. Had Martel been in his place he would have continued dialling the first figures which came into his head, listened for a moment as though getting the wrong signal, slammed down the receiver and left the booth.

He knew exactly what had happened instead. Startled to find his target in the next booth, the man had experienced seconds of indecision. *But because he had started dialling – and because he was certain Martel could not possibly suspect him –* he continued what he had been doing.

Martel raised his own receiver with one hand while the other performed a quite different action. Extracting the instrument taken from his suitcase, he pressed the rubber sucker at waist-level on the glass window separating his booth from the next one. He then inserted the hearing-aid in place, using his upper left forearm to conceal the wire from the sucker to the ear-piece.

The Englishman was gambling on the second-rate calibre of the pavement artist – that he would keep his back to Martel to hide his features. The instrument was working perfectly. Every word of the conversation in the next booth was transmitted to him with great clarity.

'Is that Stuttgart . . .?'

Martel memorised the number, although unable to hear the other end of the conversation.

'Edgar Braun speaking,' the pavement artist said formally. 'Is that Klara . . .'

'*Cretin!* You have already made *two* mistakes!' the girl told him venemously. 'No number or name at this end to be transmitted. You want someone to keep an appointment with you?'

'S-orry . . .' Braun mumbled the words. He had been badly thrown off balance by Martel's sudden appearance in the next booth. His fervent wish now was that he had broken off the call – but he dare not do that at this stage because Klara would guess something was wrong, that he had blundered. The only thing was to press on.

'The second consignment you were expecting has arrived,' Braun continued. 'It has been delivered safely to the Hotel Baye-rischer Hof a few minutes ago . . .'

'Where exactly is that ?' Klara demanded, her tone icy.

'Facing both Hauptbahnhof and harbour. The following car registration number is linked with the consignment . . . I stay on duty?'

'Yes! We shall react at once. And I shall have to report your indiscretion . . .'

'Please . . .'

But the Stuttgart connection had gone dead. Behind Braun's back Martel had pulled the rubber sucker from the glass, hauled the earpiece free and thrust the whole contraption in his jacket pocket. The change in Braun's tone had warned him the conversation was ending.

Martel performed a pantomime as Braun sneaked out of the booth without a glance in his direction. He spoke loudly in English about nothing into the receiver. When Braun disappeared through the exit he left the booth. He now had solid data for Stoller to check.

Inside the luxurious tenth-floor apartment in a building less than a mile from the headquarters of Dietrich GmbH, Klara Beck slammed down the receiver. Tearing open a fresh pack with nails painted like red talons she lit her forty-first cigarette of the day.

'Braun must be losing his marbles,' she said to herself.

The cigarette was necessary to calm her nerves – and her voice – before she phoned Reinhard Dietrich. Although sexually attractive she knew it was her outward coolness which most appealed to the Bavarian millionaire, which made her his mistress. Her apparent calm in all situations was such a contrast to Dietrich's choleric temperament – and to that of his whining wife.

Taking several deep drags, she expelled smoke from her lungs, her bosom heaving with the relaxation afforded by the nicotine. It was time to make the call. She dialled the number of the *schloss*. Dietrich himself answered.

'Yes!'

Just the single, curt word.

'Klara calling. It is convenient to talk?'

'Yes! You received the emerald ring? Good!'

They had performed the ritual of positive identification. During alternate calls Dietrich would refer to sending her a fur or some item of jewellery – which secretly infuriated her since few of these desirable gifts were ever given to her. She hurried on.

'The second consignment has been delivered. I have just heard – it has arrived at the Hotel Bayerischer Hof in Lindau . . .'

'Meet me there this evening!' Dietrich responded instantly. 'Get the executive jet to fly you to the airstrip nearest Lindau. Then take a hired car. A room will be reserved for you. Your help may be needed . . .'

'There is a car registration number. Here it is . . .'

Dietrich repeated the number and broke the connection without a goodbye. Klara Beck replaced the receiver slowly, preserving her self-control. Despite her annoyance she was impressed. She had just told Dietrich in an oblique manner that Keith Martel – the man they had scoured Switzerland, Austria and Bavaria to track down – had been located. Dietrich had reacted decisively to the news, taking only seconds to plan his next move.

One phrase intrigued her. *Your help may be needed* ... It conjured up one possibility – Dietrich was considering asking her to seduce Martel. She went into the bedroom, slipped out of her dress, the only item of clothing she was wearing in the clammy atmosphere, and studied her full-bodied nude form in a full-length mirror.

It could be fun – playing with the Englishman. Before – at the appropriate moment – she rammed the needle between his ribs and pressed the button which released the lethal injection.

At the *schloss* Dietrich had ordered Oscar to bring one of his packed suitcases for an overnight stay. A series of cases were packed and unpacked daily by the attentive Oscar.

There were cases for a short trip, cases for more prolonged journeys, cases for hot climates and cases for countries like Norway in the depths of winter. The system meant Dietrich was ready for departure anywhere at a moment's notice. On the intercom he summoned Erwin Vinz who had recently returned with his team from Bregenz. He did not mince his words.

'Someone else has done the job for you! A woman at that! I am leaving at once for the Bayerischer Hof in Lindau – Martel has just arrived there. Choose your best men, follow me and book in at the same hotel ...'

'This time we should get him ...' Vinz began.

'This time you *will* get him, for God's sake! Before morning – he will be tired after his recent activities ...'

'Peter has the car waiting,' reported Oscar who had returned with a Gucci suitcase.

Wearing a suit of Savile Row country tweeds Dietrich left the library, crossed the large hall and Oscar held open one of the two huge entrance doors. Dietrich ran down the steps and climbed into the rear of a black, six-seater Mercedes. The uniformed chauffeur closed the door as his master pressed a button and lowered the window to give the order.

'Lindau. Drive like hell ...!'

*

Inside Lindau Hauptbahnhof Martel paused outside the phone booth, inserted a cigarette into his holder and lit it. Braun had vanished through the exit doors but Martel waited to see whether the German was smarter than he appeared to be – whether he would dodge back into the station to check up on the Englishman. He did not reappear.

Martel strolled towards the exit doors, opened one a fraction and peered out. On the sidewalk outside the Bayerischer Hof, Braun was on his knees with his back towards Martel, adding to his drawing. The Englishman walked out and got inside one of the taxis waiting under a huge tree.

'The Post Office,' he said. 'Quickly, please – before it closes.'

'It is no distance . . .'

'So you get a good tip for taking me there . . .'

At the post office Martel explained he wanted to call London and gave the girl behind the counter the Park Crescent number. He was gambling that Tweed was waiting for his call. Within two minutes the girl directed him to a booth.

'Thursday calling,' he said quickly as Tweed came on the line.

'Two-Eight here . . .' the familiar voice replied.

Martel began pouring out data to be fed into the recording machine.

'Warner seen in Bregenz . . . visited cemetery, grave of Alois Stohr . . . headstone 1930–1953 . . . references to time of French occupation . . . expensively dressed woman, identity unknown, visits grave each Wednesday morning . . . Warner contacted her . . . Delta active everywhere . . . two men in car in Bregenz . . .'

'Did they see either of you?' Tweed interrupted urgently.

'We sighted them . . . no reverse sighting . . . now staying Bayerischer Hof Lindau . . . Delta watcher pavement artist Braun sighted and reported me – repeat me . . . Stoller should check Stuttgart phone number . . . Stuttgart contact woman named Klara . . . closing down . . .'

'Wait! Wait! Damn! He's rung off . . .'

Tweed replaced the receiver and stared at McNeil who switched off the recording machine. A very thrifty, Scots type,

McNeil. Tweed was certain she had never taken a taxi in her whole life. Buses and the Underground were her sole means of transportation.

'The maniac is setting himself up as bait to flush Delta into the open,' he snapped. 'I know him . . .'

'He's a loner. He gets results,' McNeil said placidly.

'He's in the zone of maximum danger,' Tweed replied grimly. 'Get me Stoller on the phone. Quickly, please. I sense an emergency.'

CHAPTER 13

Thursday May 28

The signal had been arranged between Martel and Claire before they made separate entrances into the magnificent dining-room as though strangers. The Englishman had a single table next to a picture window which looked out on to the fog-bound harbour.

The signal was that if anyone significant entered the dining-room while they ate their separate meals Claire would light a cigarette. In the middle of her dessert she was doing just that, lighting a cigarette.

A most dominant personality had made his entrance – and he came into the room in precisely this fashion, like an accomplished actor making his entrance on stage. There was a sudden hush in the conversation: eyes turned and stared towards the entrance. The new arrival paused and surveyed the people at their tables.

He ran a hand through his thick, silver-coloured hair, tugged gently at his moustache, his ice-blue eyes sweeping the assembled guests. Other eyes dropped as they met his gaze. His skin was tanned and leathery. He had changed into an immaculate blue bird's-eye lounge suit.

The maître d'hotel escorted Reinhard Dietrich to another window table at the opposite end of the room from Martel. And since his arrival there had been a subtle change in the atmosphere. The conversation was now carried on in murmurs. Handsome women glanced at the table where the millionaire sat, which amused Martel.

There's no glamour like a lot of money, he thought.

Two or three minutes after Claire had vacated her table he left the room. Wandering along a wide corridor he found her standing at the reception desk, waiting her turn while a fresh arrival – (an attractive brunette in her late twenties with a full-bodied figure) – was completing the registration form.

The reception hall opened out into a well-furnished and spacious lounge area with comfortable armchairs. Martel chose one of these chairs, settled himself and picked up a magazine. He inserted a cigarette into his holder, lit it and waited.

The attractive new guest had gone up in the lift to her room with the porter. Claire was asking the receptionist about train times to Kempten – the first thing which came into her head. The receptionist was being very helpful, checking a rail timetable and noting times on a slip of paper.

'Thank you.' She turned away and then turned back. 'I thought I recognised the girl who just arrived. She stays here often?'

'Her first visit as far as I know, Madame ...'

Claire had her handbag open, slipping the piece of paper inside as she wandered into the lounge area. As she passed Martel's arm-chair she deliberately tipped her bag and the contents spilt over the floor. Her 9-mm pistol remained safely inside the special zipped-up compartment.

'Let me help you,' Martel said, gathering up objects.

'I'm so sorry ...'

Their heads were close together. The receptionist was a distance from where Martel sat. They carried on their brief conversation in whispers.

'That girl who just arrived,' Claire told him. 'I saw the name on the registration form. *Klara* Beck – from *Stuttgart* ...'

'The hyenas are gathering. And the man in the dining-room who arrived as though he owned the damned world – Reinhard Dietrich?'

'Yes – I've seen pictures in the paper ...'

The spilt contents had been collected up. Claire, who had been crouching with her knees bent, her back to the receptionist, stood up and raised her voice.

'That really was most kind of you – and most clumsy of me ...'

Claire wandered to the far side of the room and chose a chair where she could see everything and had her back to the wall. She opened her handbag, unzipped the compartment, slid out the pistol and left it inside the bag where she could reach it swiftly. She had just completed this precaution when Erwin Vinz and his associate, Rolf Gross, walked into the reception hall, each carrying a small case.

Claire *froze* – then slid the gun out of her handbag and covered it on her lap with a newspaper. *Rolf Gross had been the driver of the Delta car they had encountered in Gallus-strasse in Bregenz.*

Both men glanced into the lounge area as they crossed to the steps leading to the reception counter. Claire thought Gross stared at Martel who was reading a newspaper and smoking a cigarette in his holder. Vinz appeared to notice nothing and neither man showed any interest in the girl at the back of the room.

Slipping the gun inside her handbag, she closed it, stood up and wandered over to the reception desk where both men were filling in their registration forms. She waited patiently, looking at a picture on the wall.

'We require two single rooms with baths,' Vinz said in the tone of voice used for addressing serfs. 'If you haven't singles, two doubles will do. And we want dinner ...'

'I have two single rooms ...' The receptionist was not looking at Vinz although his tone of voice remained polite. 'And I would suggest you hurry to the dining-room which stops serving ...'

'Inform them of our arrival! We both require steaks, plenty of potatoes. The steaks rare – and a very good bottle of red wine. We'll be down as soon as *we* are ready ...'

'Understood, sir. The porter here will show you your rooms.'

With obvious relief he turned to Claire with a smile. She asked for a street plan of Lindau and he explained that a section of the Old Town was a 'walking-only' zone. At that moment Reinhard Dietrich, smoking a large cigar, came down the corridor from the

impression he was staying the night and now he has left in a chauffeur-driven limousine. Something is going to happen ...'

'What do we do?' she asked calmly.

'One trump card is they don't know there are two of us – they think I'm on my own ...'

'So?'

'Slip back to your own room – be careful no one sees you.'

'And what are you going to be doing?'

'Contacting the local police. It's late but I want to talk with Sergeant Dorner. My guess is he's the only man in Lindau we can trust ...'

'You're going out in this fog? It is still foggy?'

'Thicker than ever. Which is helpful. More difficult for anyone to see me leaving and where I go. It's only a short distance – you showed me on the map ...'

'I'm coming with you!' She sat up in bed and felt for her shoes on the floor. 'I can watch your back ...'

'Go to your room before I belt you ...'

'You are a very stupid man and I don't like you much. Bloody well take care ...'

He waited until she had gone before venturing out. And he had deliberately not mentioned the creaking door. If she had known about that he would never have got rid of her.

The atmosphere of menace hit Martel the moment he walked out into the night. Mist globules settled on his face. The damp chill penetrated his thin coat. He could just make out the bulk of the Hauptbahnhof as he turned right and headed for Ludwigstrasse, a narrow, cobbled street which was the direct route to police headquarters.

There was no one visible but he heard it again, the sound he had detected from his bedroom window three floors up – the *creak* of one of the station doors being opened. He was careful not to glance in that direction as he turned right again and proceeded along the centre of Ludwigstrasse – as far away as possible from the darkened alcoves of doorway recesses.

123

His rubber-soled shoes made no sound on the cobbles although he had to place his feet firmly on their surface – the street was slimy with dampness. He wore his grey-coloured raincoat, which merged with the atmosphere, unbuttoned. Anyone grabbing him would find themselves holding only the fabric of the coat. And he had easy access to the Colt in his shoulder holster. He stopped.

The sound of the foghorn out on the lake. But his acute hearing had caught a second sound – the whispering slither of a padded sleeve moving against a coat, something like Gannex material. Behind him.

The watcher waiting inside the Hauptbahnhof had heard nothing, he was convinced. But even in the mist he could have seen Martel's silhouette outlined for a few seconds against the glow of lights in the lounge as he left the hotel.

He stood motionless in a shadowed area and the whispering stopped. Somewhere behind him his follower realised that Martel had also paused. The trouble was the bastards probably knew every inch of Lindau. *Their* problem was they could not be sure of his destination.

He started walking again suddenly, sensing there were several men somewhere in the mist. There *would* be several: Delta operated in strength. He had not forgotten Zürich where men had poured out of the two cars. He had been counting side-turnings and came to a street light, a milky globe supported by a wall-bracket. *Krummgasse.*

Martel had no option. To reach the main street, Maximilian-strasse, he had to leave the dubious safety of the narrow Ludwig-strasse and make his way along the even narrower alley of Krummgasse. Moving away from the blurred glow of the light he stared into the well of darkness. Once he negotiated Krummgasse he was within shouting distance of the police station.

Behind him he heard again the slither of sleeve against cloth. They were moving in. Reinhard Dietrich would be miles away – his previous presence totally unlinked with the murder of a second Englishman in the Lindau area. Martel went inside

Krummgasse – taking longer strides to confuse the man behind him, accustomed to his earlier, slower pace.

Martel's night vision was exceptional and he was peering ahead. For the moment he had out-distanced the follower behind. He stopped again and heard no whispering slither. His tactic was to get to the more open Maximilianstrasse and then sprint for police headquarters. *Ahead of him* he heard the squeak of a shoe.

The mouse in the trap. Himself. A man – men? – coming up behind. And the enemy also in front just when he was close to the end of Krummgasse. Delta had planned well. The moment he entered Ludwigstrasse they had guessed his destination – or assumed the one place he must never be allowed to reach. The police station.

So at the end of each alley leading from Ludwigstrasse to the parallel street, Maximilianstrasse, they had positioned a soldier. The squeaking shoe suggested the man in front was advancing down Krummgasse towards him, closing the pincer movement. Martel darted into the shadowed recess of a doorway and prayed that Squeaky Shoe would arrive quickly.

Something solid emerged from the swirling mist, right hand projected forward like a fencer about to lunge. With his left hand Martel extracted a Swiss five-franc coin from his pocket and tossed it across the street. *Clunk!*

In the hushed silence the sound was surprisingly loud and the man, who seemed familiar – something about his marionette-like movements – stopped next to the Englishman's doorway, glancing the other way. There was still no repetition of the slither – so the follower behind was a distance away. Martel moved.

The man sensed danger, turned and held his right hand ready to ram it forward. The barrel of Martel's Colt crashed down on the would-be assassin's head with tremendous force. Martel felt the barrel hammer through a hat, strike the skull and reverberate off it. The attacker slumped and lay in a twisted heap on the cobbles like a pile of old clothes.

Martel ran. Reaching the end of the alley he turned right and by the glow of a street lantern read the legend *Stadtpolizei* on a wall-plate. The entrance was round the corner in Bismarckplatz. He shoved open the door and stopped in front of a counter behind which a startled policeman gazed at him.

He slammed down a piece of plastic like a credit card on to the counter and slipped the Colt back inside its holster as the policeman surreptitiously unbuttoned his hip holster. Still short of breath, he gasped out the words.

'Sergeant Dorner! And bloody quick! If he's at home get him out of bed. There's my identification. And send a couple of men to Krummgasse. There should be a body for them to trip over ...'

'We've had an alert out for you, Martel – they should have seen you when you crossed the Bavarian border ...'

Martel was impressed by Sergeant Dorner. A short, burly man in his early forties, he had sandy hair, shrewd grey eyes with a hint of humour, and a general air of a man who knew what he was doing, a man not frightened to take decisions.

Martel was seated across a table from the police officer on the second floor of the building overlooking Bismarckplatz, drinking a cup of strong coffee. It was very good coffee.

They had found the body lying in Krummgasse, the body Martel had identified as Rolf Gross, the second man who had arrived late at the Bayerischer Hof. They had found more than that. Underneath the corpse – Martel's powerful blow had split Gross's skull – was lying what Dorner called a 'flick hypodermic'. He held up the weapon with the needle projecting inside a plastic bag.

'You were lucky,' Dorner commented. 'And this clears you. The fingerprint boys checked Gross's against those on the handle. It must look like a felt-tip pen before this button is pressed and the needle shoots out. Forensic were dragged out of bed to tell me what it contains ...'

'And what is inside it?'

'Potassium cyanide in solution. It's the kind of weapon you'd

126

expect the Soviets to have dreamt up . . .'

'Maybe they did . . .'

'But these people are Delta – neo-Nazis. I've never seen any weapon like it before . . .'

'I have. It's a Delta special,' Martel replied with grim humour. 'So how do you account for the fact that neo-Nazis are using it?'

'I don't,' Dorner admitted. 'Nothing makes sense about what is going on. We're finding the caches of their weapons and uniforms with Delta badges too easily . . .'

'*Too easily?*'

'Yes. Erich Stoller of the BND is on his way here. I got him out of bed, too . . .' Dorner lowered his voice. 'When Stoller flew here after Warner's body was found he told me he has an informant who regularly passes on the location of these arms dumps. Always in an uninhabited place – an abandoned farm building, an empty villa.'

'In other words you get the arms, the uniforms – the *news* in the press – but you never grab a single person?'

'Weird, isn't it?' Dorner stood up and lit a cheroot, staring out of the window he had closed against the mist. 'We get no individual, no record of a property owner we can trace. Just as we've been unable to locate any colleague of Gross's . . .'

'I told you Erwin Vinz is staying at the Bayerischer Hof . . .'

'Paid for his room and left ten minutes before my men got there. Said an urgent business message had called him away. I've put my best man on guard outside Claire Hofer's room – dressed as a porter, he's whiling away the night cleaning shoes.'

'Thanks.' Martel, almost dropping from lack of sleep, was beginning to approve of Sergeant Dorner more and more. 'And as I told you, Reinhard Dietrich was staying at the same hotel . . .'

'Not *staying*,' Dorner corrected him. 'He arrives in that bloody great Mercedes, has a leisurely dinner, a chat with you – and then leaves. What do I charge him with? Eating too large a dinner and smoking Havana cigars?' He eased his large buttock on to the edge of his desk. 'Bloody frustrating . . .'

'So we set a trap – make them an offer they can't refuse.'

Dorner took the cheroot out of his mouth and frowned. 'Just what are you proposing?'

It took Martel one hour, the arrival of Erich Stoller, eight cups of coffee and four cheroots to obtain their backing for his plan.

CHAPTER 15

Friday May 29

Claire reports Warner made three mentions Operation Crocodile . . .

While Martel was finally catching up on his sleep at the Baye-rischer Hof after the key meeting with Stoller and Dorner, Tweed – in his Maida Vale flat – was playing the same section of the tape-recording of Martel's report from St. Gallen over and over. It was the fifth time he had listened to the recording, he was alone and tired.

During the day there had been another row with Howard who was about to fly to Paris. There he was attending a meeting of the four security chiefs responsible for the security of the VIP's who – in only five days' time – would start their journey from Paris aboard the Summit Express bound for Vienna.

The British Prime Minister would fly to Charles de Gaulle Airport and from there would be driven direct to the Gare de l'Est. At about the same time the French President's motorcade would be on its way to the same destination.

The head of the French Secret Service in control of security for his President was Alain Flandres, an old friend of Tweed's. And the American President, flying the Atlantic direct to Orly Airport in Air Force One, would be driven from there at high speed to join the others.

The security chief – head of the American Secret Service – responsible for his chief of state was Tim O'Meara, a man Tweed had met only once. It was a recent appointment. The fourth VIP – Chancellor Kurt Langer of West Germany – was scheduled to board the express the following morning at München. Erich Stoller of the BND would lose sleep watching over his master.

'Why this bloody train lark?' Tweed had asked Howard

during the confrontation in his office. 'They could all fly direct to Vienna to meet the Soviet First Secretary. It would be a damned sight safer ...'

'The French President,' Howard had explained tersely. 'Hates flying. The excuse given is they'll all take the opportunity to coordinate policy at leisure before the train reaches Vienna. I do need every man possible and Martel ...'

'What's the route?'

'The direct one,' Howard had replied stiffly. He implied Tweed's knowledge of geography was limited. 'Paris to Strasbourg ...'

'Ulm, Stuttgart, München, Salzburg – then Vienna ...'

'Then why ask?' Howard rasped.

'To check no diversion is planned ...'

'Why the hell should there be one?'

'You tell me,' Tweed had replied, watching with some satisfaction as Howard stormed out of the office.

But Howard had cause to worry, Tweed thought later in the early hours in his flat. *The Times* atlas was open in front of him with the double-page spread of Plate 64 – South-West Germany including the northern tip of Switzerland. On it he followed a large section of the route from Strasbourg across Bavaria to Salzburg.

Operation Crocodile ...

What the hell could that be? He took off his glasses, rubbing his eyes. Without them everything – including the map – was blurred. You saw everything in simplified shapes. He raised a hand to close the atlas and then stopped, rigid, like a man unable to move. *He could see the crocodile!*

In the morning after breakfast Martel made an elaborate pantomime about hiring a launch from a man in Lindau harbour – the same harbour from which Charles Warner, also in a hired launch, started out on his last journey.

There was a lot of waving of hands. There were discussions about the merits of one vessel compared with another. There was debate as to how long he wanted to hire the craft for. Finally, there was lengthy argument about the price.

From a distance two women watched this carefully staged charade. Perched on a seat on the Romerschanze terrace overlooking the harbour, Claire played the rôle of tourist. And Martel had warned her again there must be no sign to tell a watcher that they knew each other.

She swivelled her field-glasses at apparent random. Lake Konstanz was living up to its unpredictable reputation. Fog-bound the previous evening, the new day was crystal clear with a vault of Mediterranean-like sky. To the south across the placid lake was a superb panorama of snow-tipped mountain peaks including the Three Sisters of Liechtenstein. A handful of tourists trudging round the waterfront added to the peaceful scene.

Klara Beck, also equipped with binoculars, sat on a seat on the front with the hotel behind her. She had not been forgotten by Martel who had reported her presence to Sergeant Dorner and Stoller the previous night.

'My men report Klara Beck is apparently staying the night at the hotel,' Dorner relayed to Martel after receiving a phone call.

'That I would expect,' Martel had commented.

'Why, may I ask?' enquired Stoller.

'Because Delta don't realise I know she belongs to them. She's had no contact with Dietrich since she arrived, no contact with Erwin Vinz or Rolf Gross – so she's the ideal person to leave behind as a spy. And in the morning I can use her ...'

Martel was using Beck now, Claire decided as she trained her lenses on the girl. Like Claire, Beck was using her binoculars and they were aimed in the direction of Martel.

'I think, dear, you're going to move soon,' Claire said to herself.

She left her seat, strolled down the steps to the harbour front and wandered slowly towards the hotel in the warming glow of the sun. Her timing was perfect. She was close to Beck's seat when the German girl got up and began walking rapidly back towards the Bayerischer Hof entrance. On the mole Martel had just ostentatiously shaken hands with the man he was hiring the launch from.

But when she turned the corner it was not the hotel Beck headed for. Instead she crossed the road, passed under the large tree where taxis waited and disappeared inside the Hauptbahnhof. Her shadow followed.

Pushing open a door, Claire glanced to her left and saw what she had expected. Beck was inside one of the telephone booths, making a call. Claire drifted over to a bookstall and started to look at paperbacks. The new development worried her.

Inside the phone booth Beck dialled a local number, cradled the receiver on her shoulder and looked towards the station exit. No one was there. At the other end of the line a man's voice responded as though waiting for her call.

'Hagen here . . .'

'Werner, this is Klara . . .'

'We are ready. Any joy?'

'The goods are aboard a grey launch. Departure imminent . . .'

She broke the connection and left the station, crossing over to the hotel at a leisurely pace, drinking in the delight of the sun's warmth. On the steps she paused close to a pavement artist as he began drawing a fresh picture, taking out her cigarette pack.

'Watch for the police bringing back that grey launch,' she murmured.

She lit the cigarette and went into the lounge. She had just triggered off the execution of the second Englishman.

Sergeant Dorner was not looking where he was going as he walked down Ludwigstrasse towards the harbour. He crashed into the girl and would have knocked her over except for his swift grab round her shoulders with both hands. Claire Hofer, who had timed her arrival as agreed earlier, stood quite still. Dorner, wearing civilian clothes, spoke loudly.

'I do apologise. My own clumsy fault . . .' His voice dropped, his lips scarcely moved. 'Everything is organised. Fifteen minutes from now the island is sealed ...'

Dorner left Claire who walked rapidly after checking her watch. Minutes – seconds – counted if the trap were to be successfully sprung. She turned down a short cut to the harbour front. Martel was aboard his launch, reached by climbing down a steep ladder attached to the side of the mole.

Claire glanced to her right, saw the pavement artist, Braun, as he strolled into view, hands clasped behind his back. Taking a brilliant red head-scarf out of her shoulder-bag she wrapped the covering round her head.

Aboard the launch Martel saw the flash of brilliant red cloth – the signal that everyone was in position. He caught a glimpse of Sergeant Dorner strolling round the harbour to where the large police launch was berthed. Lighting a cigarette, he watched Claire out of the corner of his eye. She was hurrying now towards the open-air bathing-pool walled off from the lake below the Romerschanze terrace.

Reaching the pool, she used the entrance ticket purchased earlier and entered one of the changing cubicles. With the door locked she stripped off her synthetic jersey dress, revealing the bikini she wore underneath. Slipping the rolled-up dress and her pistol inside a water-proof bag, she attached the bag to her wrist with a leather thong.

She left the shoulder-bag which was now empty inside the cubicle, locked the door, checked her waterproof watch and walked along the outer wall. At that time of day there was hardly anyone about. She dived off the wall into the lake.

Slipping loose the mooring rope, Martel went inside the cramped-ed wheel-house of the launch and checked his watch – which earlier he had synchronised with Claire and Sergeant Dorner. Two minutes to go. He inserted a cigarette into his holder and lit it.

The only lingering traces of the mist which had shrouded Lake Konstanz the previous day covered the Austrian shore. The forecast promised a warm sunny day. It was a major factor

Martel had taken into account when finalising his plan with Dorner and Stoller. And at this moment the BND chief was controlling operations from an office at *Stadtpolizei*.

Martel was careful not to look towards the eastern side of the harbour. Moored to its berth by the Lion Mole lay the two-decker launch of the Water Police commanded by Sergeant Dorner. The German was already below-decks, changing into official uniform after slipping aboard unnoticed. Martel double-checked his watch, took a deep breath and began to leave harbour.

Inside his office at *Stadtpolizei* Erich Stoller stood looking out of the window into the main street. It was just another day for the townspeople. Tourists sat at tables outside Hauser's drinking coffee and consuming cream cakes. Behind him on a heavy table was the transceiver and its operator – the key to Stoller's control.

With the use of the transceiver he could instantly communicate with police cars discreetly stationed near the road bridge, with other vehicles strategically placed on the mainland near the end of the rail embankment.

The transceiver also kept him in direct touch with Sergeant Dorner aboard the police launch still berthed in the harbour. A signal came over the transceiver.

'Siefried is riding . . .'

Dorner had reported that Martel was on his way.

At a remote point on the misty shore five wind-surfers ran down the shallow beach to board their waiting craft. They were stationed midway between Lindau and the Austrian town of Bregenz. Their leader, Werner Hagen, a six-foot blond giant, was running towards them, gesturing at the lake. He had been waiting by a telephone inside a deserted warehouse, waiting for the call from Klara Beck.

'He's leaving Lindau harbour,' he shouted as he ran to his own sail. 'A grey launch. Martel alone is aboard . . .'

They wore swimming trunks as they manoeuvred their sails into the gentle breeze. Round each man's wrist was a belt from

134

which hung a sheath encasing a large throwing knife. A silver triangle, the Delta symbol, was attached to the side of their trunks. The team of executioners, led by Werner Hagen, headed for a position about half a mile outside Lindau harbour.

'Thank God I found you – it was difficult in this mist . . .'

Claire leaned against the hull of the launch where Martel had hauled her aboard. With her legs stretched out and her bosom heaving with the recent effort she let Martel untie the leather thong and place the waterproof bag beside her.

The launch was stationary. Martel had taken it out through the harbour exit moving slowly, sounding his siren – according to regulations for ships entering or leaving – for longer than necessary to help Claire locate him. A wind was blowing up, making a low whining sound which got on Claire's nerves.

'You think they'll come?' she asked.

'Damned sure of it . . .'

She extracted from the bag her dress and the 9-mm pistol. He looked at the dress and picked it up to take it inside the wheel-house. 'This won't be much good for you to wear . . .' He came out checking the action of his .45 Colt and slipped it back inside the shoulder holster.

'It's synthetic jersey cloth,' she told him. 'I chose it since it's practically crease-proof . . .'

She broke off, realising his attention was elsewhere. He still had the engine switched off as he peered eastward into the grey, thinning mist. The light wind was dispersing it slowly.

'You think they're coming from over there?' Claire asked.

'It's the shortest distance from a shoreline where they're least likely to be detected. In a minute you put on this face-mask – if one of them gets away I don't want you recognised . . .'

'And that thing?' She pointed to a bulky instrument on the small chart-table in the wheelhouse. 'Is it radar?'

'It's a tape-recorded signal which does two things – it signals Stoller at his headquarters when I press a button – warning him we're under attack. It also sends out a continuous signal which

Dorner in his police launch can pick up to home in on where we are.'

'You worked this out pretty well,' Claire commented.

'Because from the Warner killing I know we're up against a first-class brain who thinks out *his* plans well . . .'

'Reinhard Dietrich?'

'No. An international anarchist called Manfred.' Martel was inside the wheelhouse, about to start up the engine. 'And I should never have agreed to your coming . . .'

'But you did!'

'So put on your face-mask and shut up,' he told her brusquely, then fired the engine.

The mist had cleared in the west where the vast waters of the lake stretched away like an oily blue sheet. On the eastern mole of Lindau harbour the Lion of Bavaria was a massive silhouette as they got under way.

Claire had adjusted the face-mask and after checking her pistol tucked the weapon inside the top of her pants. Martel's instructions – given to her earlier in his room at the hotel – had been precise.

'If they come – as they came for Warner – I need one man alive so I can work on him. After what they did to Warner, the rest can drown . . .'

Martel kept down the launch's speed, heading out direct across the lake towards the distant Rhine delta. That, he was convinced, was the lonely country where Warner had intended to make his landfall.

One thing bothered him. The grey pall to the east between the launch and the Austrian shoreline was persisting. How could anyone moving in from that direction locate him? And if they did they would be on top of the launch almost before he saw them. Looking again towards Austria he saw movement in the mist.

Werner Hagen gripped his sail with one hand while he checked the compact device attached to the mast. It was a miniature radar set designed at Dietrich's electronics factory in Arizona. Martel's launch showed clearly on the screen.

He's following Warner's route, Hagen thought.

He made a gesture to the other five wind-surfers who were closer together than would be their normal tactic: it was vital they did not lose sight of each other. The gesture told them the target had been sighted. And the mist was lifting as they glided across the rippled waters of the lake.

Hagen timed it nicely, keeping one eye on the radar screen, the other on the dispersing wall of vapour ahead. He held on to the sail with his left hand and dropped his right, unsheathing the razor-edge knife which had carved out of Warner's back the crude outline of Delta's symbol. Then he saw the launch, made a fresh gesture and the team curved in a semi-circle to force Martel to stop.

It happened too fast for comfort. One moment the view from the wheelhouse showed a vague disturbance in the wall of mist, shapes which could have been a mirage. Then six wind-surfers appeared, three of them steering their sails across the course Martel was following, compelling him to stop the engine.

'They're here,' he yelled to Claire and pushed the signal button.

'I've seen them!'

She knelt with her back to the wheelhouse, holding the pistol out of sight, gripping the butt with both hands.

'They're under attack!'

Crouched inside the wheelhouse of the police launch Sergeant Dorner watched the winking bleep which had suddenly appeared on his specially adapted radar screen. Standing up in full view, he switched on the powerful engine which flared with a roar.

Dorner knew that at this moment there would be no lake steamer approaching the entrance but he obeyed regulations, sounding his siren as the launch rushed from its berth – the mooring rope had been surreptitiously slipped free when he sneaked on board.

Parallel to the exit, he stopped the forward rush and swung his wheel well over, turning the craft through ninety degrees, thrashing up a wake which transformed the harbour into a turmoil of waves and froth. With his bow aimed between the two moles he opened the throttle, his siren screaming non-stop. The launch shot forward as he increased speed, checking the blip on his screen.

'Get me there in time,' Dorner prayed.

Klara Beck had decided not to leave the excitement to Braun so she had occupied the same seat on the front. Confident, now that she had made her vital telephone call, she had been relaxing and gazing round like a tourist. The sudden departure of the police launch appalled her.

She hurried along the promenade, dashed across the street and into the Hauptbahnhof. She was half-way to the row of telephone booths when she stopped. Across the window of each booth a gummed sticker carried the legend *Out of Order*. A uniformed policeman strolled up to her and she fought down a moment of panic.

'You wished to use the phone?' he enquired.

'They can't *all* be out of order,' she protested.

'The notice is clear enough,' he replied less politely. 'They are working on the fault now.'

'Thank you . . .'

She made herself walk out of the Hauptbahnhof slowly. Her pace quickened as she went across to the Bayerischer Hof. Once in her room she picked up the receiver to dial a number. A girl's voice came on the line.

'I am very sorry but there is a temporary breakdown in the phone system. Would you like to give me a number and I will call you as soon as . . .'

'It's not important . . .'

Exerting her exceptional self-control Klara Beck put down the

138

receiver and lit a cigarette. God, would she be blamed for not warning Dietrich. What the bloody hell was going on?

'Cut all the lines to the mainland ...'

At the police station Erich Stoller gave the order immediately he received Martel's signal. In the same room with him a policeman sat with the phone to his ear – the line held open to the exchange where they were waiting for precisely this order. The turning of three switches isolated Lindau island from all telephonic communication with the outside world.

On hearing the order a second policeman left the room and ran to the radio-control office. A signal went out to patrol-cars strategically placed in advance. The road bridge to the mainland was blocked. Other patrol-cars appeared at the mainland end of the rail embankment, closing off the cycle track and footpath.

A 'fault' developed in the signal box controlling rail traffic to Lindau, stopping all trains. Only a man with Stoller's authority could have achieved this result. Now his main worry was what might be happening out on the lake.

Werner Hagen was supremely confident as he led his team of wind-surfers to encircle and engulf the launch. The element of surprise was everything. The blond giant was the first to reach the port side of the stationary launch and he placed one bare foot over the side prior to temporarily abandoning his sail. His right hand held the large-bladed knife ready for the first lunge.

He was surprised to see a girl, her features concealed behind a face-mask, and then he was otherwise occupied. Martel came out of the wheelhouse wielding a boat-hook. He had guessed Hagen was the leader – it was written all over him.

The swing of the boat-hook ended as it struck Hagen a vicious blow at the side of the head. He sprawled full-length inside the launch, lifting his head in time to meet the carefully calculated thud of Martel's gun barrel. He collapsed unconscious.

A second man was coming aboard, knife in hand, when Claire aimed her pistol and shot him three times in the chest. Blood spurted and formed a pool below the deck-planks. Martel looked round and summed up the situation. Four killers left. Three still forming a crescent round his bow, another coming up behind the stern. He heaved Claire's target overboard, dashed back inside the wheelhouse and opened up full throttle.

The trio blocking his passage could not react in time. The launch moved too suddenly, too fast. One moment it was stationary, then it was a projectile hurtling towards them, its bow smashing their frail craft, weathered wood hammering into pliable flesh.

One man, giving a final scream, was literally keel-hauled as the launch beat his already-broken body to pulp. The other two men lay floating close together in a patch of lake which suddenly became red, their bodies crumpled like the relics of their sails.

'There's the man behind us,' Claire called out.

Martel was already taking appropriate action as he put the engine into reverse and moved backwards at speed, steering by glancing over his shoulder. The stern of the launch struck the surviving killer, he fell and the propeller passed over him.

'We'll run for it,' he told Claire. 'I think I see Dorner on the way ...'

CHAPTER 16

Friday May 29

It was a sunny, hot, sweaty day in Paris when Howard flew in
to Charles de Gaulle. He was attending the conference to finalise
security aboard the Summit Express. Typically he travelled
alone. Typically he wore country tweeds.

From the airport a car sent by Alain Flandres drove him to
No. 11, rue des Saussaies, official headquarters of the Sûreté.
This narrow, twisting street, only a few minutes' walk from the
Elysée, is rarely noticed by tourists. Inside an archway unifor-
med policemen watch the entrance.

Flandres often chose the complex of sombre old buildings for
a clandestine meeting. The place was well-guarded, there was
much coming and going by plain-clothes detectives – so the
arrival of three civilians in separate cars was unlikely to attract
attention. The head of the French Secret Service was waiting to
greet Howard in a second-floor room equipped with a table,
chairs and little else.

'Good to see you, Alain,' Howard said tersely.

'I am delighted to welcome you to Paris, my friend,' Flandres
replied enthusiastically as he shook hands and turned to a man
already seated at the table.

'You know Tim O'Meara, of course? Just in from
Washington . . .'

'We had the pleasure of meeting once,' the American interjected. He shook hands without rising from his chair and resumed
smoking his cigar.

They sat round the highly polished table while Flandres
poured drinks. Howard fiddled with the new pad and pencil in
front of him, sitting stiff-backed. O'Meara did not improve on

further acquaintance he was thinking. Heavily built, in his early fifties, the American had a large head, was clean-shaven, wore rimless glasses and exuded self-confidence. He did not behave as the 'new boy'.

The fact was Tim O'Meara had only been chief of the American Secret Service detachment which guarded his President for a year. In his loud check sports jacket – he also was obviously playing the tourist – he settled his bulk in his chair as though he had been a member of the club for a decade.

As he poured the drinks Alain Flandres observed all this with a hint of Gallic amusement. Short and of slim build, Flandres was impeccably dressed in a lounge suit despite the heat. Also in his early fifties, the Frenchman's features were finely chiselled and he sported a trim, pencil-style moustache the same colour as his well-brushed dark hair.

'Erich Stoller from Germany is due any moment,' he announced as he settled in his own chair and lifted his glass. 'Gentlemen – welcome!'

He sipped at his cognac, noted that Howard took a big gulp while O'Meara swallowed half his glass of neat Scotch. There was tension under the surface, Flandres observed. This was a gathering of nervous men. Who was the catalyst?

The door opened and Erich Stoller was ushered into the room. His tall, thin figure was in extreme contrast to the other three, as was his manner. He tended to listen, to say very little. He apologised for his late arrival.

'An unexpected problem required my urgent attention . . .'

He left it at that. It was mid-afternoon and he had no wish to reveal that in the morning he had been in Lindau, sealing off the island while Martel took his launch on to the lake. He'd had the devil of a rush to reach Paris – involving a helicopter flight to Münich airport where a plane had waited for him.

'Only some beer,' he told Flandres, sitting bolt upright in his chair. An excellent psychologist, he proceeded to throw Howard completely off Martel's scent by irritatng him. 'And how is my friend, Tweed?' he enquired. 'I expected to see him here . . .'

'Tweed is home-based these days,' Howard said curtly, his face very bony. 'Getting on in years, you know ...'

'Really? I thought you were both the same age,' Stoller remarked blandly and drank some beer.

'This isn't his territory,' Howard snapped. 'Maybe we can get on with the subject which brought us to Paris?'

'But, of course!' Flandres agreed, even more amused by this exchange. 'I have the route of the Summit Express ...' He proceeded to unroll a large-scale map of Northern Europe with the route marked in red. He sat back in his chair and lit a cigarette watching the others study the sheet.

Alain Flandres, whose handsome features and easy charm proved so irresistible to women, also had a flair for the dramatic. He made the remark casually and three heads bent over the map jerked up.

'A sighting of Carlos – Manfred – call him what you like, was reported in London this morning – in Piccadilly to be precise ...'

'*Manfred!* How the hell do *you* know what's happening in London? And will someone tell me whether he really is Carlos?'

It was Howard who had exploded. Flandres noted he was edgier than he had realised. Why, he wondered? In a casual tone of voice the Frenchman explained.

'A girl operative of mine, Renée Duval, is working at the French Embassy for the moment. This telex just came in from her with an extract from your midday paper.' While Howard read the strip the Frenchman handed him, Erich Stoller commented on Carlos.

'Carlos has no known base. Manfred has no known base. No one is sure of the real appearance of Carlos. The same applies to Manfred. Carlos has been known to take temporary refuge behind the Iron Curtain – as has Manfred. Both are independents who cooperate with the KGB only when it suits them ...'

'So there *are* two of them?' Howard broke in.

'Or,' O'Meara intervened in his gravelly voice, 'has Carlos *invented* two of them – if so, which is the real one? You omitted, Erich, to add that both men – *if* two exist – are brilliant assassins . . .'

Flandres studied the American more closely. That is a most telling point you have made, my friend, he was thinking. Howard coloured with annoyance at Stoller's next question.

'Could you be more precise about this sighting in London? How was he dressed? Why was he recognised so easily?'

'His usual "uniform",' Howard murmured reluctantly. 'Windcheater, jeans, his dark beret and very large tinted glasses.'

'Can you elaborate on this incident?' the German persisted.

'He was recognised by a policeman patrolling on foot. Carlos – if it was Carlos – vanished up Swallow Street leading to Regent Street. The policeman pursued him and lost him in the crowds. Later, one of the assistants in Austin Reed, a nearby man's outfitter, found on a chair the windcheater with the beret and glasses on top. Underneath the windcheater was a loaded .38 Smith & Wesson . . .'

'A *patrolling* policeman,' Stoller continued. 'He was walking up and down a particular section of this street?'

'I imagine so, yes. Probably keeping an eye open for IRA suspects. Where is all this leading to?' Howard demanded.

'Someone dressed in this manner could have made sure the policeman did see him and then disappeared?'

'I suppose so, although I hardly see the point . . .'

O'Meara relit his cigar. 'A Havana,' he explained. 'I have to get through this box before I return to the States where, as you must know, they are contraband.'

Stoller, after his unusual burst of conversation, lapsed into silence and Flandres had the eerie impression the German was studying one particular person. But he could not identify which man had for some unknown reason aroused the BND chief's interest.

They proceeded with the main business in hand – planning security for their respective political heads attending the Vienna Summit. The rail journey was broken down into sectors. The division into sectors was marked on the map.

Paris to Strasbourg – French. From Strasbourg via Stuttgart

and Münich to Salzburg – German. The last stage, Salzburg to Vienna – American, with nominal cooperation from the Austrians. Alain Flandres, in sparkling good humour, did most of the talking.

Howard was allocated a 'mobile' role – his team would cover all three sectors. Flandres went over his sector in detail, pointing out potential danger points from terrorist attack – embankments, bridges. O'Meara, puffing his cigar, decided the Frenchman knew his job.

Then it was Erich Stoller's turn and again O'Meara was impressed. The German paused as he reached a certain point on the map and was silent for a short time. Something in his manner heightened the tension inside the airless room as he prodded with his finger.

'Here the express crosses into Bavaria. There is a certain instability in this area. It is unfortunate the state elections take place the day after the train crosses this sector ...'

'The neo-Nazi business? Delta?' Howard enquired.

'Tofler,' O'Meara said with great conviction. 'His support is growing with each fresh discovery of more Delta arms and uniforms. And Tofler is a near-Communist. His programme includes plans for detaching Bavaria from West Germany and making it a "neutral" province or state like Austria. That would smash NATO and hand Western Europe to the Soviets on a platter ...'

'Chancellor Langer is fully aware of the problem,' Stoller said quietly. 'His advisers tell him Tofler will not win ...'

Flandres arranged for excellent food and drink to be brought in and they continued going over the route until late in the evening. The Frenchman sipped at his glass of wine as he looked round at his colleagues, all of whom were now in shirt-sleeves. The evening was warm and clammy. The bombshell fell after he made his remark.

'I am beginning to think, gentlemen, that the main requirement for our job is stamina ...'

He broke off as an armed guard entered the room and handed

145

him a message. He read it, frowned and looked at Howard. 'This says the British ambassador is outside with an urgent signal which he must pass to you at once.'

'The *Ambassador?*' Howard was shaken but nothing showed in his expression. 'You mean he has sent a messenger . . .'

'I mean the Ambassador in person,' Flandres said firmly. 'And I understand he wishes to hand you the signal himself while you are present at this meeting.'

'Please ask him to come in,' Howard requested the guard.

A tall distinguished man with a white moustache entered the room holding a folded slip of paper. Everyone stood, brief introductions took place, and Sir Henry Crawford handed the folded slip to Howard.

'Came direct to me, Anthony – in my personal code. No one except myself knows about it. It was accompanied by a request that I came here myself. Reasonable enough – when you read the contents.' He looked round the room. 'A pleasure to meet you all and now, if you will excuse me . . .'

Howard had unfolded the slip and read it several times before he sat down and gazed round the table. His expression was unfathomable but the atmosphere had changed. The Englishman spoke quietly, without a trace of emotion.

'This signal is from Tweed in London. He makes an assertion – I emphasise he gives no clue as to his source. Only the gravity of the assertion compels me to pass it on to you under such circumstances . . .'

'If Tweed makes an assertion,' Flandres commented, 'then we can be sure he has grounds for doing so. The more serious the assertion the less likely he is to reveal the source. It might endanger the informant's life . . .'

'Quite so.' Howard was aware that his armpits were stained with dampness. He cleared his throat, glanced at each man and read out the contents of the signal.

Reliable source has just reported unknown assassin will attempt to eliminate one – repeat one – of four VIP's aboard Summit Express. No indication yet as to which of four will be target. Tweed.

CHAPTER 17

Friday May 29

On the morning of the day when the four security chiefs met in Paris for their afternoon conference, Martel's launch headed for a remote landing-stage on the eastern shore of Lake Konstanz.

Werner Hagen, sole survivor of the wind-surfer execution squad, lay helpless in the bottom of the launch. His mouth was gagged, wrists, knees and ankles were bound with strong rope and a band of cloth was tied round his eyes. All he could hear was the chugging of the engine, all he could feel was the compression of the ropes and the glow of the sun on his face.

Inside the wheelhouse Martel steered the craft closer to their objective, guided by Claire who stood alongside him. The mist had dispersed, the shoreline was clear, and he slowed down until they were almost drifting as he scanned the deserted stony beach, the crumbling relic of a wooden landing-stage.

'You're sure we won't run into someone – campers, people like that,' he checked as the momentum carried them forward in a glide.

'Stop fussing,' she chided. 'I told you – I know this area. I used to meet Warner here when he came down from München. And last night I parked the hired Audi among those trees before I walked to the nearest railway station to catch a train back to Lindau.'

'I don't see the Audi ...'

'You're not bloody meant to see it!' she exploded. 'When are you going to give me credit for being able to cope on my own? You know your trouble, Martel?'

'If I don't do a job myself I start worrying about it ...'

'Right! So have a little faith. And – before you ask me – I do know the way to that old water-mill I mentioned, which is another place where Warner and I used to meet. Although why we're driving there I don't understand ...'

'To interrogate Blond Boy ...'

He had carried Werner Hagen to the car and dumped him on the floor in the rear, folding him up like a huge doll so no part of him protruded above window level. Then he had relaxed while Claire took the wheel and drove them some distance to another crumbling relic – the water-mill, located at a remote spot in the Bavarian countryside.

Everything was exactly as Claire had described it. There was no way of guessing the purpose the mill had once served – but the huge wheel still turned ponderously as foaming water from the rapids behind the structure revolved the wheel. Martel studied the wheel, watching the blades dip below the surface before they emerged dripping to commence another revolution.

'Yes,' he decided, 'it will work ...'

'What will work?'

'My new version of the old Chinese water torture. Blond Boy has to talk ...'

It took their combined strength to manhandle the German into the required position. Before they started Martel told Claire to don her face-mask again. 'To scare the living daylights out of him he has to *see* – which means removing his blindfold. Tuck your hair up inside the back of your mask. You're wearing the slacks left in the car – he'll think you're a man ...'

With her face-mask adjusted she helped Martel as he stood on the platform above the slow-turning wheel. They spread-eagled Hagen over a part of the wheel clear of the water and moved rapidly – whipping more rope round his recently-freed ankles and attaching them to one of the huge blades.

To make it worse, Martel had laid the German with his head downwards so it submerged under the water first while the upper part of his body was still above the surface. It took them ten minutes to secure Hagen's splayed body to the wheel and then the blindfold was removed. He glared with hatred at Martel and then a look of doubt crossed his handsome face as he caught sight of the sinister figure of Claire.

Standing very erect, wearing Martel's jacket to conceal her bosom, she stared through the face-mask at the German with her arms crossed, her pistol in her right hand. She looked the epitome of a professional executioner.

Then the wheel dipped again and Hagen took a deep breath for when he went under the water. The trouble was the slow revolution of the wheel kept him submerged for longer than he could hold his breath. He surfaced spluttering water, his lungs heaving. He knew there was a limit to the period of time he could survive the ordeal.

There was another factor Hagen found increasingly difficult to combat. The circular rotation was disorientating and he was becoming dizzy. His great fear was he would lose consciousness, taking in a great draught of water while submerged.

Martel made a gesture and they retreated from the platform to the river bank. He inserted a cigarette into his holder and lit it as the wheel continued its endless revolutions. Away from the shade of the water-mill the sun beat down on them out of a sky like brass.

'We can talk now without him hearing us,' he remarked. 'He is, of course, slowly drowning . . .'

'Let him,' Claire said calmly, her face-mask eased up clear of her mouth. 'He's probably the one who carved up Charles . . .'

'The female of the species . . .'

'How long are you going to leave him?' she enquired.

'Until I gauge his resistance is broken. When we release him he has to talk immediately. I just hope he knows something . . .'

They waited until Hagen was on the verge of losing consciousness, until he was swallowing huge quantities of water each time he went under. Claire re-adjusted her face-mask and they ran to the platform. They had the devil of a job freeing Hagen: constant immersion in water had made the ropes impossible to untie. Martel used a knife he kept inside a sheath strapped to his left leg.

When he carried the water-logged man to the river bank Martel had to work on him, kneading his body to eject water. Claire sat on a rock a short distance away, her pistol aimed at the German. The first question Martel fired was an inspired guess.

'Who are you?'

'Reinhard Dietrich's nephew and heir . . .'

Only the face-mask concealed Claire's astonishment at the reply. They had hit pure gold. She remained still and menacing as Martel continued the interrogation.

'Name?'

'Werner Hagen – you know these things . . .'

'Just answer the questions.' He waited while Hagen coughed and cleared his lungs. 'What is the Delta deadline for Operation Crocodile?'

'June 3 – the day before the election . . .' He paused and Claire sensed his powers of resistance were returning. She raised her pistol in her right hand, used her left arm as a balance and took deliberate aim.

'Oh God, stop him!' Hagen pleaded with Martel. 'I'm answering your questions. I want out of the whole bloody business. Something's wrong. Vinz's . . .'

'You said June 3. You were going to add something,' Martel prodded.

'The key is the Summit Express will be moving across Bavaria . . .'

'All this we know,' Martel lied. 'Warner got the information to London.' He puffed at his cigarette to let his statement sink in. 'I simply want confirmation from you about Delta's flash-point for June 3 . . .'

'You know that!' The surprise was apparent in Hagen's tone. He was still in a state of disorientation.

'So why not tell us what is worrying you – something to do with the Summit Express? Yes?'

'One of the four western leaders aboard is going to be assassinated . . .'

150

The statement sent Martel into a state of shock although nothing in his expression betrayed the reaction. His teeth clenched on the holder a fraction tighter and he continued the interrogation.

'Who is the target?'

'I don't know! *God in heaven, I really don't know ...!*'

Hagen's shout – caused by Martel's glance towards the revolving wheel – was convincing.

'How do you know any of this? You – a mere lad,' Martel jibed, 'but a murderous thug at that ...'

'Because I'm Reinhard Dietrich's nephew!' Hagen flared. 'I'm regarded as his son, the son his wife never provided. He confides in me ...'

'You said earlier "I want out of the whole bloody business. Something's wrong." Don't think about it! Tell me quickly – what is wrong?'

'I'm not sure I know,' Hagen replied sulkily.

'I'm waiting for a reply,' Martel reminded him. 'The trouble is, I'm not a patient man.'

'My uncle is supposed to take over Bavaria in the coming election. The people are turning to us because they fear the party of Tofler, the Bolshevik.' He was recovering rapidly, sitting with a frown on his face. 'But as soon as we build up a store of uniforms and arms for the militia to be formed when we win, the BND discover them – as though someone is informing the BND ...'

'And who is going to assassinate one of the western leaders?'

Martel threw the question at him. Hagen stood up slowly. 'I have the cramp ...' He bent down and massaged the calf of his left leg, then straightened up, flexing his hands.

'I told you I'm not a patient man,' Martel snapped.

'The assassin – again I swear I do not know his identity – is one of the four security chiefs supposed to be guarding the western leaders ...'

The reply threw Martel completely off guard for the fraction of a second. It was all Hagen needed. He rushed forward, aiming a blow at Claire which knocked her off the rock she had perched on. She could have pulled the trigger but knew Martel wanted the German alive.

Hagen's headlong rush was intended to carry him to cover behind the water-mill before either captor could react. It carried him forward as he intended but he stumbled over a protruding outcrop of rock close to the water mill.

He screamed, hands outstretched to save himself. Claire heard the horrid sound of his skull striking one of the descending metal blades and the scream faded to a gurgle. He lay motionless, head and shoulders in the river. A gush of blood welled, mingling with the peaceful sound of tumbling water.

Claire ran forward, steadied herself on the slope and checked Hagen's neck pulse as Martel came up behind her. Standing up she looked at the Englishman, shaking her head.

'He's dead. What do we do now?'

'Get him back to civilisation and contact Stoller or Dorner at once. I have to find a safe phone to call Tweed.'

They reached police headquarters in Lindau with the body concealed in the back of the car under Martel's raincoat. Dorner gave them the news without preamble.

'Erich Stoller left a message strictly for your ears – he flew to Paris for a security conference. I will make arrangements about Hagen – Stoller will want him sent by special ambulance to a morgue in München. As to making a phone call to London which can't be intercepted, the answer is the Post Office ...'

Dorner drove them there himself. They were closing the doors when the German gently pushed them open and escorted his two companions inside.

A few words from Dorner persuaded the switchboard operator to call the London number. Martel first tried the Maida Vale flat and was relieved when he heard Tweed's voice which sounded weary. The voice changed pitch when Tweed realised who was calling. He activated the recording machine, rushed through the identification procedure and spoke before Martel could say any more.

'Operation *Crocodile*, Keith. You're standing in the middle of it. Look at a map of southern Germany through half-closed eyes – concentrate on the shape of Lake Konstanz. The damned thing is just like a crocodile – jaws open to the west with the two inlets, Uberlingersee and Untersee . . .'

'That confirms my data – something is scheduled to happen in Bavaria. Reinhard Dietrich's nephew, Werner Hagen, talked before he left us permanently . . .'

Crouched over the table in his flat Tweed gripped the receiver more tightly. Events were piling on top of each other – always the most delicate and dangerous phase in an operation. He listened as Martel continued.

'One of the four VIP's aboard the Summit Express is scheduled for assassination on the train. Do you read me . . .'

'Of course I do.' Tweed's voice and manner had never been calmer. 'Give them numbers – starting geographically from west to east. Which number is the target . . .'

'Informant didn't know . . .'

'At least we're alerted. Aboard the train – I've got that. Identity of assassin?'

The question Martel was dreading. Would Tweed think he had gone off his rocker? He took a deep breath, thankful that Dorner had stayed with the switchboard operator so no one could overhear this call.

'I'm convinced – and so is my colleague – that this next bit of information provided by Hagen is genuine. You have to trust my judgement . . .'

'Get on with it, man . . .'

'The killer is one of the four security chiefs who will be guarding the VIP's. And, before you ask, not a damned clue as to who is the rotten apple. I'd better get off the line, hadn't I?'

'I consider that a sensible suggestion . . .'

Tweed had the devil of a time, almost the worst few hours he could remember. He found a cab quickly to take him to Park

Crescent, but then his problems were only beginning. That supercilious careerist, Howard, had flown to the security meeting in Paris without telling anyone where the conference was being held. Supercilious *careerist?* It suddenly occurred to him that Howard was one of the four prime suspects ...

Never averse to using unorthodox methods, Tweed was careful to follow protocol on this occasion. He knew Sir Henry Crawford, the British Ambassador in Paris, but his first move was to call a friend at the Foreign Office.

'... an emergency,' Tweed explained. 'I have to send a signal and it must reach the Ambassador within two hours ...'

'Why not phone the Embassy first to make sure he will be there to receive the message,' his friend had suggested.

Had Tweed put forward this suggestion he had no doubt it would have been stiffly rejected as a breach of protocol – but it was all right providing the idea came from the Foreign Office.

He made the call, spoke to the Ambassador, who assured him there was no problem. He would wait for the arrival of Tweed's coded signal and, since the matter was so delicate, deliver the decoded message himself.

'Yes,' he concluded, 'I do know where the conference you are concerned with is taking place ...'

Crawford was cordial – and discreetly uninformative as to where the conference was being held. It was the reaction Tweed had anticipated. He took another cab to meet his contact at the Foreign Office.

'I have spoken to Sir William Crawford,' he announced when he was seated in an uncomfortable armchair. This statement formed a bridge between the Ambassador in Paris and his contact – across which the contact was compelled to walk.

'What is the message?' the other man in the room enquired.

'It was agreed I should present that in isolation to the cipher clerk on duty. I hope you don't mind?'

Tweed was at his meekest, most concerned with not offending the august institution inside whose portals he had been privileged to enter. This was unusual – for someone outside the

Foreign Office to use its private code. Tweed employed the weapon of silence, adjusting his glasses while the other decided whether he could see any way out. He couldn't.

'Come with me,' he said, a chilly note infusing his tone.

Ten minutes later the signal was on its way to Paris. Other than Tweed, the only person who knew its contents was the cipher clerk. *He* would reveal it to no one. Tweed sighed with relief as he hailed yet another cab in Whitehall, gave the Park Crescent address and sank back into the seat.

Low cunning had won the day. The Ambassador himself would know the contents – should any witness ever be needed that the signal had been sent. And the Ambassador was personally delivering the message to Howard *in the conference room.* That would force Howard to read out the warning to the other three security chiefs.

'I wish I could be there to study their faces when that message is read out,' Tweed reflected as the cab proceeded up Charing Cross Road. 'One of those four men will be shaken to the core ...'

'It could be any one of the four. You'll have to track through their dossiers back over the years ...'

Tweed gave the instruction to McNeil as they strolled together in Regent's Park after the clammy heat of the day. It was still light, the trees were in full foliage, the grass had a springy rebound which Tweed loved. Everything was perfect – except for the time-fuse problem he must solve.

'O'Meara, Stoller and Flandres ...'

'Don't forget Howard,' Tweed said quickly.

'What am I looking for?' NcNeil enquired with a note of sharp exasperation.

'A *gap*.' Tweed paused under a tree and surveyed the expanse of green. 'A gap in the life – in the records – of one of those four trusted men. Maybe as little as two months. Time unaccounted for. He will have been trained behind the Iron Curtain – I'm sure of that. This man was planted a long time ago ...'

'Checking Howard's dossier will be tricky ...'

'You'll need cover – a reason why you're consulting all these files from Central Registry. I'll think of something ...'

He resumed his walk, his shoulders hunched, a faraway look in his eyes. 'The funny thing, McNeil, is I'm certain we've already been given a clue – damned if I can put my finger on it ...'

'Tim O'Meara won't be any easier than Howard to check – he's only been head of the President's Secret Service detachment for a year.'

'Which is why I'm taking Concorde to Washington tomorrow if I can get a seat. I know somebody there who might help. He doesn't like O'Meara. A little prejudice opens many doors ...'

'Howard will want to know why,' she warned. 'The expense of the Concorde ticket will be recorded by Accounts ...'

'No, it won't. I'll buy the ticket out of my own pocket. There is still something left from my uncle's legacy. I'll be away before Howard returns. Tell him I've had a recurrence of my asthma – that I went down to my Devon cottage ...'

'He'll try and contact you ...'

'About my signal via the Ambassador?' Tweed was amused. 'I've no doubt when he returns his first job will be to storm into my office. Make it vague – about my trip to the cottage. I felt I just had to get out of London. It will all fit,' he remarked with an owlish expression. 'He'll think I'm dodging him for a few days. He'll never dream I've crossed the Atlantic.'

McNeil stared straight ahead. 'Don't look round – Mason is behind us. He's pretending to take that damned dog of his for a walk ...'

Tweed paused, took off his glasses, polished them and held them up as though checking his lenses. Reflected in the spect-acles was the image of Howard's lean and hungry-looking deputy recently recruited from Special Branch. He also had stopped by a convenient tree which his Scottie at the end of a leash was investigating.

'I prefer the dog to the man,' Tweed commented as he

replaced his glasses and started walking again. 'Add him to the list. If anyone can find the vital discrepancy in the dossiers you can ...'

Howard had reserved a room for the night at the discreet and well-appointed Hotel de France et Choiseul in rue St. Honoré. While he waited for his guest he put in a call to Park Crescent. When the night duty operator answered he identified himself and continued the conversation.

'I want a word with Tweed,' he said brusquely.

'Just a moment, sir. I will put you through to his office.'

Howard checked his watch which registered 2245 hours. He was disturbed: Tweed was still inside Park Crescent when the building would be empty. It was later than he had realised when he made the call. He had another surprise when McNeil's voice came on the line. He spoke quickly to warn her it was an open line.

'I'm talking from my hotel room. I'd like an urgent word with Tweed ...'

'I'm afraid Mr Tweed has been taken ill. Nothing serious – a bad attack of asthma. He's gone down to the country for a few days ...'

'It's not possible to get him on the phone?'

'I'm afraid not, sir. When can we expect you back?'

'Impossible to say. Goodnight!'

Howard ended the call on a stiff note: he never liked questions about his future movements. Sitting on his bed he frowned while he recalled the conversation. That was an odd departure from McNeil's normal behaviour – asking a question she knew he would disapprove of.

In the Park Crescent office Miss McNeil smiled as she replaced the receiver. She had been confident the final question would get Howard off the line before he probed too deeply. She returned to her examination of the dossier in front of her. It carried a red star – top classification – on the cover, and a name. Frederick Anthony Howard.

In the Paris bedroom Howard was pacing impatiently when there was an irregular knocking on his locked door, the signal he had agreed with Alain Flandres. Despite the signal he extracted from his case the 7.65-mm automatic Flandres had loaned him and slipped it inside his pocket before opening the door. Flandres walked into the room.

'*Chez Benoit, mon ami!*'

The slim, springy Flandres was a tonic; always optimistic, his personality *fizzed*. He walked round the room smiling, his dark eyes everywhere.

'Chez What?' Howard enquired.

'Benoit! Benoit! They serve some of the best food in all of Paris. The last serving is at 9.30 in the evening – but for me *le patron* makes the exception. The Police Prefect often eats there. You are ready? Good ...'

Flandres had a cab waiting at the entrance to the hotel. The journey took no more than ten minutes and the Englishman, sunk in thought, remained silent. Normally voluble, Flandres also said nothing but he studied his companion until they arrived and were ushered to a table. They were examining the menu when Flandres made his remark.

'My telex from London about the Carlos sighting this morning in Piccadilly has disturbed you? You wonder who he went there to meet? You were in London this morning?'

Howard closed the menu. 'What the bloody hell are you driving at, Alain?' he asked quietly.

'I have offended you?' Flandres was astonished. 'Always it is the same – I talk too much! And Renée Duval, the girl who sent me the telex – I have withdrawn her from London. She was only on routine assignment. Now, the really important subject is what we are to select for dinner ...'

Flandres chattered on, steering the conversation away from the topic of the telex. He was now convinced something else was disturbing the Englishman, something he was carefully concealing from his French opposite number.

CHAPTER 18

Saturday May 30

Washington, DC, Clint Loomis . . .

The extract from the secret notebook discovered on Warner's dead body had linked up with nothing so far, Tweed reflected.

Concorde landed on schedule at Dulles Airport. Tweed was not among the first passengers to alight, nor among the last. He did not believe in disguises but before disembarking he removed his glasses. This simple act transformed his appearance.

Clint Loomis was waiting outside. He ushered him straight into a nondescript blue sedan. The American, in his late fifties, had not changed since their last meeting. Serious-faced, his dark eyes penetrating and acutely observant, he wore an open-necked blue shirt and pale grey slacks. His hair had thinned somewhat.

'We can say "Hello" when we get there,' he remarked as he drove away from Dulles. 'Maybe you'd better take off your jacket . . .'

The sun was blazing, the humidity was appalling. It was like travelling inside a ship's boiler room.

'Is it always like this in May?' Tweed enquired as he wrestled himself out of his jacket, turned to cast it on the seat behind and looked through the rear window, studying the traffic.

'In Washington nothing is "always",' Loomis replied. 'In the US of A we're a restless lot – so we change the weather when we can't think of anything else to change. We'll talk when we get there – and no names. O.K.?'

'The car could be bugged?'

'They're bugging everything these days – even clapped-out old CIA personnel. Just to keep someone in a job. You have to file a report to show the boss you're still in business.'

'Why the rush at the airport? My bag slung on the back seat . . .'

'We could be followed, that's why. By the time we get where we're going we'll shake any tail . . .'

'Like arriving in Moscow,' Tweed said drily.

The signposts told him they were heading for Alexandria. Tweed looked through the rear window again and Loomis glanced at him with a frown of irritation.

'We're *not* being followed if that's what's bothering you . . .'

'When we get to a place where you can stop, could I take the wheel for awhile, Clint?'

'Sure. If that's the way you feel . . .'

This was one of the many things Tweed liked about Loomis – if he trusted you he never asked questions. He did whatever you requested and waited for explanations.

Later, as they stood outside the car prior to changing places, the Englishman glanced back up the highway. A green car had also pulled in to the side and one of the two male occupants got out to lift the bonnet. A blue car cruised past which also contained two men – neither of them spared the stationary sedan a glance, Tweed observed. He got in behind the wheel and began driving.

'What make is that green car behind us – the one behind the truck? You'll see it as we go round this curve . . .'

'A Chevvy,' Loomis replied. 'It pulled up when we did . . .'

'I know. And that blue car ahead of us – which was cruising and is now picking up speed to keep ahead. They have a sandwich on us, Clint. Those two cars have been with us since we left Dulles. They keep changing places – one in front, one behind . . .'

'Jesus Christ! I must be losing my grip . . .'

'Just the fresh eye,' Tweed assured him. 'Better lose our friends one at a time, don't you think?'

They were coming up to traffic lights at an intersection and the green Chevvy was still one vehicle behind them when Tweed performed. To his right was one of those damned great trailer trucks which transported half of America's freight coast to coast. He rammed his foot down ...

'*Look out – the lights ...!*' Loomis yelled.

There was a scream of rubber as Tweed shot forward like a torpedo. He swerved crazily to avoid the trailer which was coming out with the lights in its favour. A second scream – of air-brakes being jammed on. Loomis looked back and then at Tweed who had returned to his correct lane. To the American he looked so bloody unruffled.

'You nearly got us killed back there ...'

'I don't see the green Chevvy any more,' Tweed commented with a glance in his rear view mirror.

'Like hell you don't – it just rammed its snout into the side of that trailer. It was overtaking as you hit the lights ...'

'To change places with the blue job ahead of us. Now ...' Tweed tapped his fingers on the wheel. '... we lose him and we're on our own, which will be more comfortable ...'

'Not the same way. *Please!* I thought you Brits were sober, law-abiding types. You realise what would have happened had a patrol-car been nearby ...'

'There wasn't one. I checked.'

The meeting place was a white power cruiser moored to a buoy on the Potomac river. Tweed had followed signposts to Fredericksburg and then, guided by Loomis, turned off down a minor road to the east. By now he had lost the blue car in an equally hair-raising performance which had ended in their tail skidding off the highway. It was very quiet and deserted as Tweed switched off the engine, climbed out and savoured the breeze coming off the water.

'That's yours?' he asked, pointing at the cruiser.

'Bought it with my – severance pay, don't you call it? – when I left the Company. Plus a bank loan I'm damned if I'll ever pay off. It gives me safety – I hope ...'

'Safety?'

Tweed concealed his sense of shock. His trip to Washington was developing in a way he had never expected. First they had been followed from Dulles by an outfit which had money at its disposal. It cost a lot of dollars to employ *four* men to do a shadow job. And ever since he had arrived Clint Loomis, retired from the CIA, had shown signs of nervousness.

'The Company doesn't like people who leave it alive.'

Loomis was dragging a rubber dinghy equipped with an outboard which had been hidden among a clump of grasses down to the river's edge. He gave a lop-sided grin as the craft floated and he gestured to his visitor to get aboard. 'I suppose it comes from all those dumbos who got out and wrote books, revealing all as the publishers' blurbs say.'

'You're writing a book?' Tweed asked as he settled gingerly inside the vessel and Loomis started up the outboard.

'Not me,' Loomis said with a shake of his head. 'And when we get to the *Oasis* ...' He pointed towards the power cruiser, '... that's when we shake hands.'

'If you say so,' Tweed replied.

They crossed the smooth stretch of water and Loomis slowed the engine to a crawl as the hull loomed up. Aboard the *Oasis* a huge Alsatian dog appeared, running up and down the deck, barking its head off. Then it stopped at the head of the boarding ladder and stared down, jaws open, exposing teeth which reminded Tweed of a shark.

'Now we shake hands,' Loomis explained. 'That shows him you're a friend and you don't get chewed up.'

'I see,' said Tweed, careful to make a ceremony of the display of friendship. The dog backed off as he mounted the ladder without too much confidence while Loomis tied up the dinghy and followed him on deck.

'Over the side!' Loomis ordered.

The dog dived in, swimming all round the boat until it completed one circuit. Loomis stretched over the side down the ladder, hooked a hand in the dog's collar and hauled it aboard as the animal pawed and scrambled up the rungs. It stood on the deck and shook itself all over Tweed.

'Shows he likes you,' Loomis said. 'We'd better go below now that everything is safe. A beer?'

'That would be nice,' Tweed agreed, following his host down the companionway where the American handed him a towel to dry himself. He was beginning to have serious doubts as to whether he had been wise to cross the Atlantic.

'What was all that business about the dog?' he enquired.

'The swim in the river?' The American settled himself back on a bunk, his legs stretched out, his ankles crossed. For the first time he seemed genuinely relaxed. 'Waldo has been trained to sniff out explosives. So, we get back and find him alone on deck. Conclusion? No intruders *aboard* the cruiser – or one of two things would have happened. Waldo would be dead – or a man's body would be lying around with his throat torn out. O.K.?'

Tweed shuddered inwardly and drank more beer. 'O.K.,' he said.

'Next point. Waldo is trained to stay aboard no matter what. So the opposition uses frogmen who attach limpet mines with trembler or timer devices to the hull – devices which detonate with the vibration of a grown man's weight walking on deck. I send Waldo overboard and he swims round once without a pause. Conclusion? If there were mines Waldo would be yelping, kicking up one hell of a row when he gets the sniff of high-explosives. Now we know we're clean . . .'

'What a way to live. How long has this been going on? And who is going to attach the limpet mines?'

'A gun hired by Tim O'Meara who kicked my ass out of the Company when he was Director of Operations – before he transferred to become boss of the Secret Service.'

'And why would O'Meara do that?'

'Because I know he embezzled two hundred thousand dollars allocated for running guns into Afghanistan.'

*

In his Münich apartment Manfred concentrated on the long-distance call. His main concern was to detect any trace of strain in the voice of his caller. Code-names only had been used.

'Tweed knows there is a selected target,' the voice reported.

'He has identified the target?'

Manfred asked the question immediately, his voice calm, almost bored, but the news was hitting him like a hammerblow. He might have guessed that in the end it would be Tweed who ferreted out the truth. God damn his soul!

'No,' the voice replied. 'Only that there is one. You might wish to take some action.'

'Thank you for informing me,' Manfred replied neutrally. 'And please call me tomorrow. Same time ...'

Replacing the receiver, Manfred swore foully and then comforted himself with the thought that he had detected no breaking of nerve in the voice of the man who had called him. Checking in a small notebook, he began dialling a London number.

This incident took place on the day before Tweed departed for Washington, late in the evening on the day the four security chiefs attended the conference at the Sûreté building in Paris.

Tweed realised he had walked into a nightmare. The question he couldn't answer to his own satisfaction was whether Clint Loomis was paranoid, suffering from a persecution complex which made him see enemies everywhere. Hence the obsession with security aboard the *Oasis*.

Against that he had to weigh the fact that they *had* been followed by four unknown men in two cars when they left Dulles Airport. It was Loomis who changed the subject – much to Tweed's relief.

'Charles Warner came to see me two weeks ago – he was interested in O'Meara. Have you also flown to the States just to talk to me? I'd find that hard to believe ...'

'Believe it!' Tweed's manner was suddenly abrupt. 'When O'Meara was CIA Director of Operations he manipulated your retirement?'

'Bet your sweet life ...'

'You know his history. What is that history?'

'He was an operative in the field early on. I was the man back home who checked his reports ...'

'After a period of duty at Langley he was stationed in West Berlin for several years? Correct?' Tweed queried.

'Correct. I don't see where you're leading, Tweed. That always worries me ...'

'*Trust me!*' The Englishman's manner had a quiet, persuasive authority. He had to keep Loomis talking, to concentrate his mind on one topic. O'Meara's track record. 'You say you checked his reports from West Berlin. He speaks German?'

'Fluently. He can pass for a native ...'

'Did he go under cover – into East Berlin?'

'That was strictly forbidden.' There was a very positive note in Loomis' reply. 'It was written into his directive ...'

'Anyone else with him in this unit?'

'A guy called Lou Carson. He was subordinate to O'Meara ...'

'And all the time O'Meara was in West Berlin you're convinced he obeyed the directive – under no circumstances to go over the Wall?'

He was watching Loomis closely. The American had swung his legs off the bunk and was opening another can of beer. Tweed shook his head, his eyes fixed on Loomis who was staring into the distance.

'Maybe that was when the bastard first started to dislike me,' he said eventually.

Tweed sat quite still. He had experienced this before with interrogations – you *sensed* when pure chance had played into your lap. There was a time to speak, a time to preserve silence.

Loomis stood up and stared through a porthole across the peaceful waters. The craft rocked gently, scarcely moving. Tweed looked round the neat cabin. The American kept a tidy ship. He had kept a tidy desk at Langley, Tweed recalled – which was where he should still be. Loomis started talking.

'This particular unit in West Berlin was just these two guys – keeping tabs on the East German espionage set-up. It was one

165

time Carlos was reported as being in East Berlin ...'

'Really?'

'We had a system of identification codes,' Loomis continued, 'so I always knew when a signal came from O'Meara and when it was from Lou Carson – without either man knowing the other had his personal call-sign. We started playing it pretty close to the chest after the débacle ...'

'Let me get this clear. Each man had his own identification signal so you knew who was sending a report. But both O'Meara and Carson thought the system applied only to them – not to the other?'

'You've got it. You know, Tweed, you get a feeling when something is wrong. Signals were coming through from O'Meara but the wording didn't sound like O'Meara – although they carried his sign. So I hopped on a plane and arrived in West Berlin unannounced. Lou Carson was pretty embarrassed. I'd caught him with his pants down. He was on his own ...'

'And where was O'Meara?'

'He surfaced two days later. Swore he had gone underground to another base for a couple of months because our normal one had been blown to the East German security people ...'

'You believed him?' Tweed pressed.

'No, but that was only a gut feeling. You don't go to the Director with gut feelings. He likes solid evidence ...'

'How had O'Meara got round the identification system?'

'Simple – he'd handed Lou Carson his identification log book so Lou could send messages and it would look as though they came from O'Meara. Carson cooperated because O'Meara told him to ...'

'What happened next?' Tweed asked while Loomis was still wound up.

'Both men were recalled to Washington and others took their place. O'Meara had done a good job in West Berlin, he knew the right people, he can charm the birds out of the trees. Before I know it, he's promoted over my head and he's sending me to Bahrain with two hundred thousand dollars in a case aboard a special flight ...'

'You said he embezzled the money.'

'Let me finish, for Christ's sake! When the people with the guns for Afghanistan checked the money I handed over they said it was counterfeit. They had a bright Indian who had worked for currency printers ...'

'The counterfeit was good enough to deceive you?'

'I'd have accepted it without question. O'Meara had the case locked in his office safe, he took it out and handed it to me. He levered me out of the Company over that incident,' Loomis blazed. 'They let me go quietly because there had been too many scandals and they were worried about their image ...'

'O'Meara just cleaned you out? No one else?'

'Lou Carson went. There were others. He was bringing in his own people. When he'd wrecked half-a-dozen lives he joins the Secret Service and walks away from the wreckage. There are guys like that everywhere ...'

'It happens – but it's not pleasant,' Tweed murmured, then he changed the subject. Best to leave a pleasant atmosphere behind when he boarded Concorde for London the following day.

The second long-distance call to Manfred came duly at the agreed hour the following day while Tweed was aboard the *Oasis*. It was Manfred who opened the conversation.

'You have nothing to worry about. Tweed is in Washington.'

'The devil he is! How do you know that?'

'Because I have people everywhere. The problem is a small one. Measures have already been taken to deal with it ...'

'You mean you're going to have Tweed ...'

'*Enough!* And the answer to your question is no. It would be bad policy. Crocodile will proceed on schedule. Now I must go – I have matters to attend to ...'

It would be bad policy ... Manfred stood quite still, staring into space. He had not been quite frank with his caller, but Manfred was often anything but frank. He was certainly not going to admit that the killing of Tweed would be an extremely difficult operation. The Englishman was equipped with a sixth sense where danger was concerned.

Instead there was a better way of dealing with the problem. He picked up the phone again to call a Washington number.

It was Sunday May 31. Tweed had spent the night aboard *Oasis* – which the American had moved to a fresh mooring. This action confirmed the nervousness Tweed had detected on his arrival.

'Never stay in the same place for long,' Loomis remarked as he tied up the cruiser to a fresh buoy. 'And always move after dark without lights.'

'Illegal, isn't it?' Tweed enquired. 'To sail without navigation lights?'

'Bet your sweet life it is . . .'

Over a meal which the American cooked in the galley they talked about old times. Loomis remarked he had heard Tweed was being held in reserve for 'the time when Howard trips over his big feet. Then they bring you back to clean up the mess. No, don't protest,' he admonished, waving his spatula, 'my grapevine is good.'

Just prior to his departure for Dulles, it was Tweed who noticed two incidents which disturbed him. He was on deck with his suitcase, waiting for Loomis to climb down the ladder into the dinghy, when he observed movement onshore.

'Loan me your field-glasses, Clint,' he called out.

Something in his guest's tone made Loomis react quickly. Tweed raised the glasses to his eyes, adjusted the focus and studied the shoreline briefly. Then he handed them back, his lips compressed.

'Bird-watching?' Loomis enquired.

'There were two men in the trees over there. One of them had a camera with a telephoto lens – bloody great piece of equipment. I think he was photographing the *Oasis* . . .'

'Probably just a camera nut. They shoot anything.'

They had climbed down into the dinghy and the dog, Waldo,

stood at the top of the ladder keening, when a helicopter appeared, flying from the Chesapeake Bay direction down the centre
of the channel. As they left the cruiser Tweed craned his neck
to get a look at the machine.

'That's the third time that chopper has over-flown us since I
arrived,' Tweed commented.

'You see them all the time in this part of the world. Coastguard
machines, private jobs ...'

Loomis was concentrating on steering the dinghy to where
they had parked his car. Tweed, hunched in the stern, continued
staring up at the helicopter. The sun was reflecting off the
plexiglas, making it impossible to see inside the pilot's cabin.

'I think it was the same machine each time,' he insisted.

Loomis was unconcerned. 'It's O.K. – we left Waldo on
board.'

At Dulles they repeated their performance of the previous day
– wasting no time. Tweed got out of the car and walked rapidly
into the building without a glance back. Behind him he heard
Loomis already driving away.

Aboard Concorde after lift-off it seemed to Tweed he might
never have visited America – it had all happened so quickly. He
was so absorbed in his thoughts he never noticed when they
passed through the sound barrier. Fragments of conversation
with Loomis drifted back into his mind.

*... O'Meara ... surfaced two days later ... he had gone under-
ground to another base ... a couple of months ... he'd handed Lou
Carson his identification log book ...*

Tweed began to feel drowsy. He closed his eyes and fell asleep.
It was the steep angle of descent which woke him. They were
landing at London Airport. It had all been a dream. He had
never been away at all. When he arrived at Park Crescent
McNeil's expression prepared him for the shock.

CHAPTER 19

Sunday May 31

Clint Loomis parked his car in a different place when he returned from Dulles alone. He knew every inch of the shoreline on
both banks and this time he chose an abandoned shed at the end
of a dirt track to house the vehicle. Then he started the long walk
back to where the outboard was concealed.

It was another brilliant sunny day and the heat beat down on
the back of his neck as he dragged the dinghy to the water's edge,
got inside and fired the motor. In the distance the cruiser *Oasis*
was gleaming, the sun reflecting off the highly-polished brass.
For a moment he was reminded of Tweed when he heard the
sound of a helicopter and saw the machine disappearing in the
direction of Chesapeake Bay. Then he concentrated on navigat-
ing his small craft.

Waldo was waiting for him, barking his head off at the top of
the ladder. As he was tying up the dinghy Loomis vaguely
noticed a second power cruiser rather like his own heading on a
course towards him from Chesapeake Bay. He went through the
same security precaution – tipping Waldo overboard and waiting
while the dog swam round the boat before hauling him aboard.

The odd thing was Waldo only displayed signs of agitation
when he was back on deck. He was shaking himself dry – and
Loomis grinned as he recalled how Tweed had taken the brunt
of the water the previous day – when the dog stopped, still
dripping. His body tensed, his ears lay flat, his teeth were bared
and he stood rigid while he emitted a slow, drawn-out snarl.

'What's the matter, boy? Tweed got you nervy ...'

Loomis followed the direction of Waldo's stare and his expression changed. Waldo was gazing at the oncoming cruiser

which, unless it changed course, would pass close by them on its way upriver. Loomis could see no sign of anyone on board, which was odd. You would expect someone on deck on such a glorious day. He ran down into the cabin.

In a locked cupboard the ex-CIA man kept a small armoury. Opening it, he looked at the machine-pistol, the double-barrelled shotgun, the three hand-guns. He chose the shotgun.

It was like a ghost ship, the oncoming cruiser, Loomis thought as he came up on deck. Tinted glass in the wheelhouse windows which masked the presence of men who *must* be inside. Damnit, one man must be at the wheel. Chugging slowly and ominously, a cloth over the side concealing the name painted on its bow, it closed with *Oasis*.

Waldo was a coiled spring, hairs bristling, the softness of the growl from deep in his throat infinitely more menacing than his normal barking. Loomis glanced round to see if help was near at hand. Only a vast expanse of empty water greeted him.

He crouched low, his shotgun out of sight. If this was trouble one blast through the wheelhouse window was liable to take out anyone inside. The helmsman certainly – which meant the vessel would no longer stay on its remorseless course.

It was due to pass within yards on the port side, the side where Loomis waited. The hell of it was he couldn't initiate any action in case they were peaceful sailors going about their lawful occasions as the Brits would phrase it. The thought made him wish he had Tweed on board. He had a feeling Tweed would not just have sat and waited. But what the hell else could he do?

Stand up and address them through his loud-hailer? And present someone with a perfect target. Already he was working on the premise that the approaching cruiser was hostile – without one shred of evidence. Yes! Waldo was evidence – his reaction to the vessel was unusually violent . . .

They set about the task in a way Loomis had not foreseen. They were almost alongside *Oasis* when a flutter of dark, pineapple-shaped missiles sailed across the water separating the two vessels and landed in various places. On deck. On the foredeck. At the foot of the companionway. *Grenades!* Jesus Christ ...!

They had slightly different time fuses. One landed underneath Waldo and detonated on impact. The dog disintegrated into a flying mass of bloody meat and bone, smearing the woodwork. Loomis went crazy. He stood up.

'*Bastards!*'

His shotgun was levelled point-blank at the tinted glass of the other vessel but before he could pull the trigger a grenade which had landed just behind him exploded. All feeling suddenly left his legs and he found himself floating backwards, falling down the companionway. He landed at the bottom just as one of the grenades which had ended up in the cabin also detonated. It sliced away half his head.

A boathook grappled *Oasis*'s side when ten separate explosions had been counted. The man holding it wore a frogman's suit. The engine of the killer cruiser had been stopped and another man, also wearing a frogman's suit, leapt nimbly aboard holding a sub-machine gun.

He took only two minutes to search *Oasis*, to note that Loomis was dead, that no one else was hiding aboard. Then with the same agile movements he returned to his own cruiser, the engine started up and the vessel set on a new course which took it far away from *Oasis* as swiftly as possible.

In the burning-glass blue of the sky the pilot of a helicopter turned his machine and headed it away from Washington. Over his radio he spoke one word repeatedly.

Extinction ... extinction ... extinction ...

CHAPTER 20

Sunday May 31

The headquarters of *Bundesnachrichtendienst* – the BND, the German Federal Intelligence Service located at Pullach – is six miles south of München. Erich Stoller's nerve centre was surrounded by a wall of trees and an inner wall comprising an electrified fence. Stoller, with his dry humour, referred to it as 'my own Berlin Wall'. He had just made this remark over coffee to Martel.

Tweed, due to catch the 13.05 flight back to London, was still fast asleep aboard the *Oasis* owing to the difference in the time zones. They sat in Stoller's office inside a single-storey concrete blockhouse of a building. Through the armour plate-glass window a stretch of bare earth showed where armed guards patrolled. Beyond was the electrified fence and beyond that dense pine trees. It was another hot morning and the temperature was rising rapidly.

'I spent four years in Wiesbaden with the Kriminalpolizei,' the German told Martel. 'Then I transferred to the BND.'

'And after that?'

Martel watched Stoller's dark eyes as he drank some more of the strong coffee, his manner relaxed, his voice expressing friendly interest.

'A year here and then two inside the Zone ...' Stoller's tone became sombre at the recollection of his time in East Germany. 'You know what it's like – going underground. It felt like ten years. Every hour of your waking day on the alert, every waking minute expecting a hand to drop on your shoulder. And you don't sleep, too well,' he concluded with a wry smile. 'I thought you knew about that period ...'

'Tweed doesn't tell me everything,' Martel lied easily. 'How long have you been back in civilisation?'

'Four years – if you can call Bavaria civilisation just at the moment. The riots are getting worse. The neo-Nazis march, the left-wing people counter-march, the two lots meet – and *Boom!*'

'The state government elections in a few days should solve all that,' Martel suggested.

'If Langer's moderates win. The trouble is Dietrich's party and the frequent discovery of Delta arms dumps may drive people into Tofler's left-wing bear-hug. Then he'll set up Bavaria as some kind of so-called Free State – detached from the Federal Republic . . .'

'You don't really believe that, Erich . . .'

'I do believe you've just been subjecting me to some kind of personal interrogation and I'm wondering why.'

Martel swore inwardly. He'd had to take the risk Stoller would catch on. Maybe he'd been stupid to try the experiment – facing a fellow-professional. He set out to repair the damage.

'Why so edgy? If we're to work together I like to know about a man. Maybe I can provide you with my career sheet . . .'

'Sorry!' Stoller raised a hand and smiled his slow, deliberate smile. The German did everything deliberately. He even sipped his coffee as though testing for a suspect ingredient.

'I am edgy,' he went on. 'You would be if you faced a crucial election – just when the Summit Express is crossing your territory with the West's top leaders aboard. My responsibility is the sector from Strasbourg through to Salzburg . . .'

'And the German Chancellor?'

'Kurt Langer boards the train at Münich Hauptbahnhof – but I still have the other three to guard through the night from Strasbourg.'

'You sound as though you expect trouble,' Martel suggested.

'I do.' Stoller stood up behind his desk. 'Shall we collect your friend, Claire Hofer, and drive to Münich?'

'Can I make one phone call to London before I leave?'

'I'll go and entertain Miss Hofer. No, no! You may prefer to talk in private.' Standing up, Martel reflected, the German was an imposing figure; not the sort of man you would expect to survive behind the Iron Curtain for two years.

'I will be in the canteen where we left her while we talked,' Stoller informed him. 'Just ask the operator for your number, press the red button and you're on scrambler ...'

While he waited for the Park Crescent number Martel studied a wall-map of Bavaria. It showed where caches of Delta arms and uniforms had been found. Flags indicated the discovery dates.

He found it strange that the rate of success was accelerating. No wonder the polls were showing increasing support for Tofler's party as Election Day approached. Each discovery increased the voters' fear of a Delta win. The phone rang and he heard McNeil at the other end of the line. He asked her to supply 'photos of the four principals ...'

'Tweed is out of London,' she told him quickly. 'He asked me to give you a message, Keith. Tomorrow, Monday, catch the first available flight to Heathrow where you will be met. You can give me the flight number? Good. And the ETA? Bring a passport picture of Miss Hofer. As soon as the meeting is over you fly back to Bavaria. Time is running out ...'

'Don't I know it,' Martel replied.

It was a hot Sunday morning in Paris.

Howard had stayed in the city at the urging of Alain Flandres for a further discussion with O'Meara about security precautions aboard the Summit Express. The train was due to leave the Gare de l'Est late Tuesday evening, June 2 – only three days' hence.

Despite Howard's protestations Flandres had insisted he would personally drive his British opposite number to Charles de Gaulle Airport to catch his London flight. Howard had a shock when he stepped out of the lift with his bag into the reception hall of the Hotel de France et Choiseul ready for his departure.

'Tim is flying to London with you,' the Frenchman announced.

'Decided I'd call at the Embassy there and check out certain unfinished business, then fly back here for *Der Tag*,' O'Meara explained. 'It will give us a chance to get better acquainted . . .'

Howard said nothing as he contemplated the two men, contrasting their styles. They were opposites – the slim, elegantly dressed Alain, every hair in place, his movements nimble and precise, and the large American in his check sports jacket who exuded aggressive self-confidence.

'I have to pay my bill,' Howard said and walked to the counter. His eyes scanned the guests seated in the lounge area. A slim, fair-haired girl, fashionably dressed and with her superb legs crossed, sat reading a copy of *Vogue*. A blue Vuiton suitcase stood by her chair and she glanced up briefly as Howard passed her.

It took only a few moments to settle the bill, he lifted his case went back to the entrance and Flandres led the way to where a blue Citroen was parked. He opened the rear door and Howard was forced to join O'Meara in the back. As the car left the kerb the fair-haired girl with the Vuiton case emerged and climbed inside a waiting cab.

During the journey the Englishman encouraged O'Meara to talk and maintained an almost uninterrupted silence. Without appearing to do so he was watching Alain behind the wheel who frequently glanced in his rear-view mirror. Howard gained the impression they were being followed.

He was on the verge of asking the Frenchman if he had spotted a tail when something made him keep quiet. At de Gaulle Alain accompanied them to the barrier and bade them an effusive farewell.

'. . . until we meet again here in Paris aboard the Summit Express,' he murmured.

He watched as the two men stood on the escalator carrying them up inside a transparent tube elevated at a steep angle. A fair-haired girl passed him carrying a Vuiton case followed by a small, stocky man wearing a trilby. The tails were in position. Renée Duval would report on all Howard's movements and contacts. Georges Lepas would perform the same operation on O'Meara. Alain Flandres was a professional, his favourite maxim *trust no one – particularly those close to you.*

Because something was wrong . . .

Münich Hauptbahnhof. The location Charles Warner had haunted on his visits to the Bavarian state capital. Martel and Claire had asked Stoller to drop them at the Four Seasons Hotel in the centre of the city. As soon as the German had departed Martel picked up both bags and shook his head at the hotel porter.

'We're not staying here . . .'

They walked a short distance before Martel hailed a cab and gave an address close to the Hauptbahnhof. After he had paid the fare they separated, each carrying their own bag. When they entered the vast station there was nothing to indicate they knew each other. Claire followed Martel at a distance, thankful for the pistol concealed in her handbag.

Both got rid of their cases in self-locking storage compartments and Martel began his search. Why had Warner found this place – and its alter ego in Zürich – important enough to record in his notebook? Knowing it would help identify him to any watcher, he strolled into the Sunday turmoil with his cigarette-holder at a jaunty angle. Behind him Claire checked for shadows. They were now in the middle of the spider's web.

Erwin Vinz felt desperate – which he knew was bad because a mood could cause him to make a mistake. After two fiascos in Lindau – Gross's unsuccessful attempt to kill Martel in the fog followed by the elimination of the wind-surfer execution squad – Reinhard Dietrich had flown into a fury in his Münich penthouse apartment.

'You had Martel! You had him in the palm of your hand in Lindau. What happens? Gross is killed by Martel while you stand by! Are you degenerating into some kind of amateur? If so, there is always a remedy . . .'

'I do have a plan . . .' Vinz began.

'Wonderful! Just as you had a plan at Lindau! I hope you also realise I hold you partly responsible for my nephew, Werner's demise?' He paused, choking on his emotion. The news had come over the phone from Erich Stoller of all people, the Intelligence creep Dietrich loathed. Vinz made a great effort.

'I am sure that Martel will surface in München. He is likely to come in by train. He uses trains a lot. He travelled to St. Gallen from Zürich by train. He left St. Gallen aboard the München express last Thursday ...'

'And you lost him,' Dietrich broke in sarcastically.

'I have crammed München Hauptbahnhof with our soldiers,' Vinz persisted. 'They have his description. The station is so overcrowded an accident can occur and no one will notice. A man falls off a platform under a train ...'

'Dangerous,' Dietrich said thoughtfully as he lit a cigar, 'to draw attention to the Hauptbahnhof ...'

'Only if the Englishman realises its significance – only if he survives to pass on the information ...'

'Kill him!' Dietrich crashed his fist on the desk, his face red with fury. '*Kill him for Werner! Now – get out ...*'

The Hauptbahnhof was an inferno: the noise, the chaos incredible. Martel was caught up in the mob of passengers hurrying for trains, getting out of the city for a Sunday break. Expresses arriving, departing ...

Saarbruecken, Bremen, Frankfurt, Zuerich, Dortmund, Wuerzburg ... The destination boards carried the names of cities all over Europe. Under the tall roof in the cavern below were platforms 11 to 26. A sign pointed to an adjoining *second* station – the Starnberger. There was even a third station for platforms 1 to 10.

Wartesaal, a huge waiting room. Rows of telephone booths. A cafeteria. *Kino* – a cinema open from 0900 to 2100 hours, entrance six deutschemarks, for which sum you could sit there all day and in the evening. A score of different exits – including one to the complex U-Bahn system.

Martel was like a sponge, soaking up data, smoking his cigarette, strolling among the hustling, shoving crowds. At the back of his mind an idea was forming. Warner had noted down this rendezvous of strangers as important. Was the reason staring him in the face?

The noise was appalling, trapped by the overhang of the roof, the noise of voices, trampling feet, tannoys booming. An assault on the nerves. The heat, again trapped inside the cavern by the roof, was exhausting – the clammy humidity, the sweat of God knew how many hurrying passengers.

Patiently, her handbag under her left arm, her right hand close to the flap and the pistol inside, Claire Hofer appeared to drift into the whirlpool as she doggedly followed the Englishman. Then she saw him. *Erwin Vinz . . .*

She was sure the killer would not recognise her. When he came into the reception hall of the Bayerischer Hof late in the evening he had not even glanced at her. But she had been trained never to make easy assumptions. From her handbag she took a pair of tinted glasses and slipped them on. She had to warn Martel.

Keith Martel's attention was absorbed by something else. He had the uncanny feeling that he was surrounded by hostile forces, that amid the surging crowd was a more compact, organised detachment of men. Then he saw a man wearing a Delta symbol in his lapel, a man waiting by the barrier where the Münich Express from Zürich was gliding to a halt.

More people poured off the platform into the station. Martel pretended to study a timetable board while he watched the man. One of the disembarking passengers showed his ticket but retained it – so it was a *return*. It happened in seconds – showing the ticket, the shaking of hands with the waiting Delta man and then they walked into the cafeteria. The new arrival also wore a silver triangle in his lapel.

'Erwin Vinz is here. Wearing the same clothes as in Lindau. He is standing by a loaded trolley behind you – he's seen you . . .'

Claire Hofer gently rubbed the side of her face to conceal the movement of her lips as she stood alongside Martel, also appearing to consult the timetable.

'Watch *yourself*,' he warned. 'I think the place is crawling with Delta types. Two have just gone into the cafeteria . . .'

He left her and she remained for a few moments studying the times and scribbling them in her pocket notebook. When she turned round Martel was disappearing inside the cafeteria. Erwin Vinz had spoken to a man she had only a brief glimpse of: she had an impression of tanned skin, large sun-goggles and the man vanished towards the exit.

Inside the cafeteria Martel ordered a cup of coffee, paid for it and selected a table close to one of the doors to the concourse. He sat in a chair with his back to the wall. The two Delta men were absorbed in conversation. The recent arrival from the express handed to his companion a thick envelope which disappeared inside the companion's breast pocket.

A glance, the briefest lifting of eyes in Martel's direction by the man who had waited at the barrier, warned the Englishman he had walked into a trap.

They crowded round the nearest exit, blocking his escape route – five well-built men wearing Tyrolean hats and carrying beer steins. One of them sat down at his table as Martel grasped the pepper pot. The man put his stein on the table, reached inside his pocket and produced a notebook which he laid on the table. He had not looked once in Martel's direction.

He put his hand in his pocket again and it reappeared holding a felt-tipped pen. He held it below the level of the table, pressed a button and the needle shot out into the action position. Martel ripped off the top of the pepper pot and tossed the contents into his eyes. He screamed – and his scream coincided with a louder sound. The explosion of shots fired from a pistol.

Martel jumped up and pushed over the table, tipping the killer opposite and his chair sprawling to the floor. The men round the door were stumbling against each other and their faces registered stark fear. They were desperate to get away from the door they had been blocking a moment earlier.

'*This way out!*'

Martel had a brief vision of Claire standing in the doorway, the pistol she had fired three times gripped in both hands and aimed at the Delta men. Her earlier shots had gone over their heads. Martel ran forward, using the stiffened side of his hand to chop down a man who made an attempt to stop him.

Then he was outside. Claire had rammed the pistol inside her handbag and he gripped her by the arm, hustling her across the concourse. Behind them they left a scene of confusion and shouted curses as frightened customers panicked and struggled to leave the place.

'*U-Bahn!*'

Martel shouted the words close to Claire's ear as he continued moving her fast among the crowds, elbowing people out of his way, forcing a swift passage towards the main exit and the escalator to the U-Bahn system.

'Tickets ...' Claire reminded him.

'I bought a couple earlier when I was prowling round – to give us a line of retreat ...'

Before entering the U-Bahn it is necessary to buy a ticket which you insert into an automatic punching machine and then descend the escalator. Still moving rapidly, still gripping her arm, he headed for the U-Bahn entrance, weaving in and out among the passengers.

He was careful now not to force his way through, to merge into the background. They had a short head-start; the U-Bahn must swallow them up before the Delta men inside the Hauptbahnhof arrived. They reached the machines, punched their tickets, went below and arrived on a platform as a train was pulling in.

As it moved out Martel was certain no one had followed them on to the train. He looked at Claire sitting beside him. She removed her dark glasses. Her forehead was glistening with beads of sweat – but other people in the coach sat in shirt-sleeves and mopped their own foreheads. She looked back at him uncertainly.

'We go straight to the Clausen,' he told her quietly. 'It's a small hotel in a side street. We can go back for our bags later – much later.'

'Was it all worth it?' she asked.

'You tell me. I know now why the Hauptbahnhofs are important.'

The Sunday Concorde flight from Washington departed 1305 hours local time and arrived at Heathrow at 2155 hours local time. The cab deposited Tweed at Park Crescent – where McNeil, forewarned by his call from Dulles – was waiting for him in his office. The clock on the wall registered thirty minutes before midnight.

'The news has just come over the telex.'

McNeil made no attempt to soften the shock she knew Tweed would receive. The one thing her chief detested was any kind of fuss.

'What news?' he enquired.

'Your old friend, Clint Loomis, has been murdered ...'

She handed the telex to Tweed and sat down, her notebook at the ready. She doodled while she waited, carefully not looking at Tweed who sank into his swivel chair and eased his buttocks into the old cushion. He read the signal three times.

Ex-CIA agent Clint Loomis killed by unknown assassins this day ... aboard power cruiser Oasis ... attorney fishing witnessed second cruiser sail alongside ... grenade attack killed Loomis and the guard dog ... FBI investigating with full cooperation CIA ...

'That damned helicopter,' Tweed muttered. 'He wouldn't take any notice ...'

'I beg your pardon?' McNeil queried.

'Sorry, just thinking aloud.' His voice became crisper, he sat up erect in his chair as he pushed the telex strip back across his desk. 'Put that in the shredder. No one else is to see it. Any word from Martel?'

'He phoned me from Bavaria. He's coming in early tomorrow and I have booked the necessary hotel accommodation at Heathrow. He has given me the flight details so you can meet him there.'

Tweed swivelled in his chair and gazed at the blinds which were closed over the windows. They were as blank as his thoughts. He was very worried.

'Things are coming to a head,' McNeil suggested.

'And only two days to solve the insoluble. The Summit Express leaves the Gare de l'Est in exactly forty-eight hours' time.' He swivelled back to face her. 'You've been going through all the dossiers. No hope, I suppose ...'

'There is something,' McNeil replied.

The call from Washington came through just before midnight and Manfred was asleep in his München apartment. He switched on the bedside light, slipped on his gloves and picked up the receiver. The identification procedure was concluded and the American-sounding voice gave its message briefly.

'Loomis' contract has been terminated. We decided not to renew it ...'

'Thank you ...'

Manfred replaced the receiver, got out of bed and began padding round the room. All was going well. Nothing could now stop Crocodile. The big killing would be carried out on schedule.

CHAPTER 21

Monday June 1

'We have the rest of today and part of Tuesday before the Summit Express leaves Paris for Vienna tomorrow night,' Tweed said.

'And in those few hours,' Martel commented, 'we have to identify the target out of the four western leaders. And we have to track down the security chief who is the rotten apple – again from four potential candidates ...'

At the London Airport Hotel McNeil had reserved three bedrooms – all in different names. The accommodation would only be used for the short time while Tweed conferred with Martel, but this would not seem strange: it was common practice among international business executives.

They were esconced in the middle room. Earlier Tweed had checked the rooms on either side to make sure they were empty. Martel was inserting a cigarette in his holder after his comment. He had arrived a short time ago on a flight from Münich. Once they had talked he would fly straight back to Germany.

'Any ideas?' Martel asked. 'Does the Loomis murder tell us anything?'

'It is pretty certain that after my signal was read out in Paris to the security conference by the British Ambassador one of the four security chiefs present reacted. He had me followed to London Airport when I boarded Concorde. There just wasn't sufficient time to kill Loomis *before* I talked to him ...'

'What about Alain Flandres? His earlier history is pretty thin in the files. Then there's O'Meara – that absence from his West Berlin base for two months Loomis told you about. It could have been spent in East Berlin.'

'That is my reading of the situation . . .'

'Except that I have another candidate – Erich Stoller of BND. He spent two *years* under cover in what he called "The Zone".'

'I didn't know that,' replied Tweed. Intrigued, he leaned forward over the coffee table. 'You dug up this fact?'

'No, he volunteered it, implied you knew about it. He also knew I was interrogating him, but on the surface it hasn't affected his cooperation . . .'

'I didn't know, but Erich is clever,' Tweed leaned against the back of his chair and stared at the ceiling. 'He may be pre-empting the possibility we'd find out in his dossier. So we have two possibles – O'Meara and Stoller. And after we've finished here I'm flying to Paris to meet Alain. I want his version of his past.'

'And Howard?'

'The least likely.' Tweed took off his glasses and rubbed his eyes. Martel noticed traces of fatigue. 'I don't like him,' he continued, 'but that's irrelevant. We're looking for a traitor who has practised his trade of treason for years . . .'

'So you're ignoring Howard?'

Without replying Tweed burrowed inside a brief-case he had propped against the side of his chair. Extracting the photocopy of a file he handed it to Martel. On the front was the security classification, file reference number and three words. *Frederick Anthony Howard.*

Martel began skip-reading as Tweed explained. 'We have McNeil to thank for that. How she got the original out of Central Registry and made that photocopy I'll never know. I think she has a duplicate key to the dossier cabinet . . .'

'Christ!' Martel looked up, stupefied at the thought of the risk McNeil was running. 'She's never told you that?'

'No,' Tweed said quietly. 'That is her way and I don't ask her questions. Have you come to it yet?'

'Come to what?'

'Page 12. Several years ago Howard spent a tour of duty with the Paris Embassy as Intelligence Officer. While he was there he took a spell of leave – six weeks. In *Vienna*.'

'Normal leave?'

'No, sick leave. He was on the edge of a nervous breakdown – "mental exhaustion" is the phrase used by the quack. The medical report is there. He was away January to February. Think of the Austrian climate. Damned funny place to go for sick leave ...'

'If he knows Vienna that will help him protect the PM.'

'That's another odd note,' Tweed commented. 'He's never made a single mention of the fact as far as I know.'

Martel handed back the photocopy and sat puffing his cigarette. Tweed produced an envelope with four glossy prints. 'You wanted photographs of Flandres, O'Meara, Howard and Stoller ...' Martel put the envelope in his pocket, stubbed out his cigarette and spoke with great vigour.

'Time is so short we have to put maximum pressure on all four security chiefs – in the hope that the unknown assassin makes a wrong move. We stir up the cauldron ...'

'How?'

'By telling each of them on the quiet the part we left out. I can deal with Stoller – you'll have to pass the word on to Howard, Alain and O'Meara ...'

'What word?'

'That the same unimpeachable source which told us one of the Western leaders is marked for assassination aboard the express also told you that the killer is among the four security chiefs.'

From an inside pocket Tweed extracted a card protected by a plastic folder and gave it to his companion. Martel studied the card, which carried his photograph, as Tweed explained while he wandered restlessly round the room. So far he had not reacted to the audacious suggestion Martel had put forward.

'Keith, we shan't meet again before the Summit Express leaves the Gare de l'Est tomorrow night. That card enables you to board the train at any point en route. No one can stop you – not even Howard ...'

186

Permission to board ... every facility to be given to the bearer, Keith Martel ... specific permission to carry any weapon ...

Across his photograph was inscribed the neat and very legible signature of the Prime Minister. She had counter-signed the reference to weapons. Martel stared at Tweed.

'In God's name, how did you get this?'

'I approached her directly through the Minister. I spent half an hour with her. I told her one of the four security chiefs may be an assassin ...'

'She must have loved that ...'

'Took it very calmly,' Tweed replied. 'She even said she would feel perfectly safe in *our* hands. She went through your dossier while I was there. Incidentally, you brought a good passport picture of Claire Hofer with you? Good. Do you trust her?'

'With my life – I *have* done already. *Twice* ...'

'Give me her photo.'

Tweed sat down at the table, produced a second card, a duplicate of Martel's but without the photo or signatures. Taking a tube of adhesive from his pocket, Tweed carefully affixed Claire's photo in position. He then extracted a pen Martel had not seen before and proceeded with great care and skill to forge the PM's signature twice. He looked at Martel over his glasses.

'I have her permission – and she loaned me her pen to do the job. Here is Miss Hofer's card. One thing I must remember to do above all else.'

'What's that?'

'Return the PM her pen. She'll give me hell if I forget. One thing more is exercising my mind – before we go. *Manfred* ...'

'What his next move will be, you mean?'

'I know,' Tweed replied. 'I have duelled with him long-distance before and I should know by now how his mind works. Sit in his chair for a moment. He has been informed that we know one of the four western leaders is marked down for assassination. When we reveal to the security chiefs that one of them is the assassin he will react – he may already have put into action the next phase of his strategy ...'

'Which is?'

'*Smokescreens.* To conceal the identity of the killer he will try to divert our suspicions to the wrong man. He will aim for the maximum confusion in our minds – simply put, so we don't know where the hell we are. And we have no time at all left to locate the guilty man.'

'You agree my idea, then,' Martel said and stood up, checking his watch.

'Yes. We tell the security chiefs one of them is a phoney. And then watch all hell break loose ...'

Reinhard Dietrich was in a state of controlled fury as he drove the Mercedes 450 SEL from his apartment to the underground garage which Manfred had designated as the meeting place. On the phone it had almost been in the nature of a summons for Dietrich to come immediately – alone and with just sufficient time to get there.

Inside the deserted underground garage Manfred sat behind the wheel of his BMW hired under a fictitious name with false papers. He had deliberately arrived early and positioned himself so his car would face Dietrich's on arrival. He heard Dietrich coming, driving on the brake.

The garage was dimly lit and Manfred timed it perfectly. As the millionaire appeared driving towards him he turned on his lights full power. The unexpected glare blinded the industrialist who threw up a hand to shield his eyes and cursed as he reduced speed and pulled up alongside the BMW. Manfred promptly turned off his lights, which further confused Dietrich's vision.

He saw a vague image of a man wearing a dark beret, the face turned towards him concealed behind large sun-goggles. Switching off his motor he lowered the window. Manfred was already talking as the window purred open.

'If you lose the election you go ahead with the *putsch* as planned. Your men in full uniform. You march on München –

188

make it as much a replica of Hitler's 1923 march on Münich as you can.'

'Hitler didn't succeed,' Dietrich pointed out. 'He ended up in Landsberg Prison ...'

'Where is the new weapons dump?' Manfred interjected. 'I see ...' He paused. 'We are so close to zero hour you should use armed guards to protect the place this time. That is all ...'

'*Wait!*'

Manfred had not even heard the plea. He was driving out of the garage, his red tail-lights disappearing round a corner. Dietrich swore again, took out a cigar and lit it. The arrangement was he should wait two minutes before he also left.

Arriving back at Münich Airport, Martel took a cab to the corner of a side street in the city. Waiting until the cab had gone, he walked the last four hundred yards to the Hotel Clausen where the Swiss girl was staying. He was relieved to find Claire safe in her room.

'I've been busy while you were away,' she announced. 'I spent a lot of time at the Hauptbahnhof ...'

'That was foolhardy – you could have been spotted ...'

'When will you learn I'm not stupid?' she flared up. 'I change my clothes before each visit. A trouser suit in the morning, a skirt and blouse with dark glasses after lunch ...'

'Sorry.' Martel dropped his brief-case on the bed and stretched his arms. 'I'm tensed up. The Summit Express leaves Paris tomorrow night and we're no nearer knowing who the target is, let alone the assassin ...'

'The dossiers that woman in London is checking? She has found nothing?'

'It could be Flandres, Howard, O'Meara – even Erich Stoller. Any one of them. But she's persisting. The Hauptbahnhof ...'

'You never told me what *you* had noticed after we ran for it,' she reminded him.

'Your impressions first.'

He slipped off his shoes, lay on the bed and propped his back

189

on the bedboard. While she talked he smoked and watched her, thinking how fresh and appetising she looked. He felt a limp, sweaty, mess: the humidity in München was growing worse.

'The Hauptbahnhof here,' she began, 'and probably in Zürich – for the same reasons – is the *mobile* headquarters of Delta. Which explains why Stoller has never managed to locate their main base. The *schloss* Dietrich has in the country is a blind ...'

'Go on.'

'It makes an ideal headquarters because of all the facilities. It is always crowded. So a meeting between two men – or several – is unlikely to be noticed. Couriers come in on trains, deliver their messages – and depart on other trains. They never actually go into München! How am I doing?'

'Promising. Do go on.'

'You observed one of those meetings – the man off the Zürich Express. Plenty of meeting-places – far less risky than any so-called safe house which might be located and watched. The cafeteria, the cinema, and so on. They even have fool-proof communications which can be used with the certainty no call will ever be intercepted. The payphones.'

'I think you've got it,' Martel agreed. 'But suppose they are spotted?'

'Look at the number of exits available. They can even rush on to a train just leaving. Remember how we escaped – by diving down into the U-Bahn ...'

'That's what I think Warner worked out – all you've been saying. And it explains his reference to the Hauptbahnhofs in his little notebook.'

'I did observe one thing which worried me,' Claire went on. 'I saw men coming in on different trains, tough-looking cus-tomers who all made for the self-locking luggage containers. They had *keys to the lockers* and collected large, floppy bags – the kind you use to conceal automatic weapons. Then they walked out into the city ...'

Martel whipped his legs off the bed and frowned in concentra-tion. 'You mean Dietrich is sending in an élite force – probably placing them in hotels close to strategic targets like the TV station, the central telephone exchange – all the key centres of control?'

'That was my guess . . .'

'We should contact Stoller,' Martel was pacing the room. 'The trouble is we don't know whether the assassin we're trying to pinpoint is Stoller. If he is, he'll thank us – and do nothing.'

'Can't we do one damned thing?' Claire protested.

'We can try . . .'

'Alain,' Tweed said quietly, 'we know one of the four passengers aboard the Summit Express leaving for Vienna tomorrow night is the target for an assassin . . .'

'We must certainly assume that, my friend,' Flandres replied.

They were eating dinner in a small restaurant at the end of a court off rue St. Honoré. *Le patron* had escorted them to a table in a secluded corner where they were able to converse without being overheard. It was an exclusive place and the food was excellent. Alain was in the most exuberant of moods.

'What I am going to tell you is completely confidential – just between the two of us – and because we have known each other all these years. How long is it?' Tweed ruminated.

'Since 1953 when I left the Army – I was Military Intelligence, you recall? I then joined the Direction de la Surveillance du Territoire. An orphan, I have spent all my adult life engaged in the traffic of secrets. A strange pastime.' Flandres sipped at his wine glass. 'I do not like your Frederick Anthony Howard,' he said suddenly. 'He is not sympathetic – like a man who fears to say much in case he reveals more than he wishes to . . .'

'I find that impression interesting, Alain.' Tweed spoke in all sincerity: he greatly respected the Frenchman's acumen. 'And you chose Military Intelligence when you joined the Army?'

Flandres laughed, a vibrant laugh. 'My God, no! My whole life has been a series of absurd accidents. Military Intelligence chose me! Can you imagine it? Two weeks after I put on uniform

I am commissioned overnight – and all because of two accidents! My predecessor got drunk, fell out of a window and broke his neck! And my second language was German – because I had been born in Alsace. So I am attached to General Dumas' staff as Intelligence Officer since at that moment he was advancing through Bavaria. Absurd!'

'And later you were demobilised . . .'

'That is so. I return to Paris. My only trump card is a commendation from Gen. Dumas. I show this to the DST and to my utter astonishment they take me on. Even the commendation is an accident. Dumas mixed up the documents! He intended it for a quite different officer! It is a mad world. Now, what were you going to tell me? Something amusing, I hope?'

'Anything but amusing, I fear . . .'

Tweed looked round the small restaurant, shook his head as *le patron* caught his eye and moved towards them. He was not happy about what he had to say – and he was enjoying a pleasant evening with his old friend.

'This is a message from a dead man – I prefer not to identify him. I believe he told the truth but I cannot prove it. He reported that the assassin who will kill one of the western leaders aboard the Summit Express is – one of the four security chiefs charged with their protection.'

'That is a really terrifying prospect,' Flandres replied slowly. He sipped more wine, his dark eyes pensive. 'Is there any clue as to which of the four is the guilty man?'

'None whatsoever . . .'

'It could even be me? That is what you are thinking?'

'I have an open mind on the subject – some people might say my mind is blank . . .'

'That is something I cannot believe. You will have ideas. You will have investigated. How long have you known this?'

Flandres was in one of his rare solemn moods. But his surface temperament had always been mercurial. Only those who knew him well realised he was possibly the most astute security chief in the West.

'For the last few days,' Tweed replied. 'I have told no one else – not even Howard. Officially I'm not concerned with this Summit Conference ...'

'And unofficially?'

'I root around,' Tweed replied vaguely.

'In Europe? In America?'

'In my mind. I do have a prime suspect. There was, shall we say, an incident? It could point in one direction only. It needs further checking. As regards the Summit Express, let no one board that train without impeccable credentials,' Tweed warned.

'I shall lose a little sleep,' Flandres assured him. 'I am not entirely happy that the train leaves the Gare de l'Est at 11.35 at night and that it will still be dark when it crosses the frontier into Germany.'

'I understand it is the normal train with a section of coaches sealed off from the rest of the express for our illustrious passengers? Plus their own restaurant ...'

'That is so. Which means there are six stops before the express reaches München. There Chancellor Langer boards the train ...'

Flandres threw up both hands in a gesture of frustration. 'All because my own President will not get into a plane – so the others agree, seeing it as a chance to confer during the journey so they present a united front to the Soviet leadership in Vienna.'

'Well, you can't alter that, so let's talk about something more congenial ...'

For the rest of the meal Flandres was his normal ebullient self, a tribute to his exceptional self-control. But Tweed thought he could see in the Frenchman's eyes an unspoken question. Who was the Englishman's prime suspect?

The caller gave the code-name Franz to the operator at Stoller's Pullach headquarters and said he would ring off in twenty seconds if he was not put through without delay. It was late on Monday evening but the BND chief was waiting hopefully in his office.

193

'Erich Stoller here . . .'

'Franz speaking again. I have more information for you – the location of the largest arms dump yet. This time it will be protected by Delta men . . .'

'Let me get a notepad, I'll only be a moment . . .'

'*Stop!* I know that trick! Make your notes afterwards. Wait until the dump has been built up – organise your raid for tomorrow, the day before the election. The location of the dump is . . .'

Having provided Stoller with the information Reinhard Dietrich had given him earlier in the underground garage, Manfred replaced the receiver.

CHAPTER 22

Tuesday June 2

FREISTAAT BAYERN! TOFLER! TOFLER!! TOFLER!!!
FREE STATE OF BAVARIA! TOFLER ...

The banners and posters had appeared overnight and were everywhere. Small planes flew over the cities cascading thousands of leaflets bearing the same message. Two days before the election Bavaria seethed in a turmoil.

There were marches by Delta men wearing peaked caps, brown shirts and trousers tucked into jackboots. They sported armbands carrying the Delta symbol.

There were counter-marches by Tofler's supporters waving banners and dressed in civilian clothes – each cavalcade preceded by small groups of teen-age girls carrying flowers – which made it tricky for the police to intervene for fear of hurting the girls.

Münich was like a cauldron with motorists shrieking their horns as planes above fluttered leaflets like confetti. Standing by a window in the office reserved for him at police headquarters Erich Stoller's expression was grim as he spoke to Martel who stood beside him.

'It's getting out of control. And the news tomorrow that we've seized the biggest Delta arms dump yet isn't going to help ...'

'Your informant again?' enquired Claire who stood behind the two men. 'There has to be an informant for you to have traced so many weapon caches recently ...'

'Yes, Franz phoned me again ...'

'*Franz?*'

'The code-name for my informant.' Stoller made a gesture of impotence. 'I really have no idea who he is – but every time we react to his brief messages we find a fresh dump ...'

'The timing is interesting,' Martel commented. 'This business of the arms dumps has been rising to a crescendo – and the climax, oddly enough – will coincide with the Summit Express crossing the Bavarian sector. There is, incidentally, an item of news I should pass on to you. Just before Werner Hagen caused his own death at the water-mill he made an alarming statement.'

'What was that?' Stoller asked quietly as he went to the table and poured more coffee.

'He alleged – and both Claire and I believed him – that ...' He swung round and stared at the German as he completed his sentence. '... the assassin who will kill one of the western leaders aboard the train is one of the four security chiefs assigned to protect those leaders ...'

A hush descended on the large room. Claire remained quite still, sensing the rise in tension. Stoller paused in the act of pouring coffee. Four sparrows settled on the window-ledge outside, which struck Claire as very strange. *Four*. There were four security men involved.

'Did – you – say – Hagen?' asked Stoller, spacing his words.

'Yes.'

'He said that just before he died?'

'Yes.'

'Which means you withheld this information for three days?'

'Yes.'

The two men faced each other like fierce dogs squaring up for battle. Stoller had gone very pale, his long arms close to his body. Martel watched the German as he lit a fresh cigarette. He asked the question casually.

'What was it like – your two years under cover in what you still call The Zone? That length of time must be something of a record – to survive undetected ...'

'And what does that mean?' Stoller asked very quietly.

'Simply that my main job is to identify the rotten apple in the barrel – O'Meara, Flandres, Howard – or yourself. And the train is leaving Paris tonight. You're going to find the atmosphere aboard rather electric. Think of it, Erich, all four of you looking over your shoulders ...'

'Why take Hagen's word?'

'Because my job is to tell when a man is lying – and I believe Hagen was telling the truth.'

'Would you think me rude if I asked you to leave? And at least you won't be on board the train ...'

'Why the hell did you do that to Stoller? God knows he's helped us,' Claire raged.

They had returned to the Hotel Clausen and Martel was sitting on her bed while she stormed round the room. The Swiss girl was in a furious temper. She sat down in front of the dressing-table and began brushing her hair vigorously.

'We're letting them all know at the last moment. It's the plan Tweed and I cooked up when I met him at London Airport. It will throw the killer off balance, may cause him to make a slip ...'

'They'll *all* know? Is that a good idea?'

'They'll be watching each other.'

'As you said, the atmosphere will be diabolical. One thing's for sure – you've made an enemy of Stoller ...'

'Only if he's guilty ...'

She swung round on her stool and glared. 'For God's sake remember what you said to him. We can't go near him again.'

'You think we're marooned?'

'Aren't we?' she challenged.

They were waiting for Tweed in his office after his return flight from Paris. Seated behind her desk, McNeil half-closed her eyes to warn her boss. Big trouble.

'This is Tim O'Meara,' Howard began very stiffly, introducing the large American who remained by the window to avoid shaking hands with Tweed. 'Someone took this photograph while you were on board Clint Loomis' power cruiser on the

Potomac . . .'

Tweed took the glossy print and examined it carefully. It was a blow-up which had been produced with great skill, doubtless in the CIA laboratories at Langley. The print provided a clear reproduction of Tweed who was squinting as though gazing into the sun.

'Well?' Howard demanded.

'How did you come by this photo? It is important that I know.'

Previously Tweed had given O'Meara one brief glance on entering his office. The question was now addressed to him. Howard went purple at Tweed's reaction.

'By God, you're going to regret this . . .'

'No,' Tweed corrected him briskly, '*you* are going to regret this if my question is not answered. I happened to notice when the photo was being taken.' He looked direct at O'Meara again. 'I need to know how you obtained this picture . . .'

'Delivered by messenger to Langley,' O'Meara said brusquely. 'I gather the messenger was held at the gate – normal procedure. He said he had been called by phone, told to go to the reception desk of a Washington hotel where an envelope would be waiting with my name on it. Another envelope contained the delivery fee and a fat tip.'

'You believe this?'

'We checked out his story, for Christ's sake,' the American snapped. 'Who took the picture we haven't a snowflake in hell's idea. It was obviously taken with . . .'

'A telephoto lens – then your technicians produced this remarkable blow-up. There was a message with the print and negative?'

'Yes,' said O'Meara, unconsciously confirming Tweed's query as to whether both print and negative had been delivered. 'It said that I might like to know an Englishman called Tweed had been aboard the *Oasis* before the unfortunate aftermath. All this stuff was flown to me top priority by Langley.'

'Manfred,' Tweed murmured.

'What was that?' Howard pounced.

'*Manfred!* He arranged it – the taking of the picture after he had had Loomis and myself followed from Dulles. He's playing his usual tactic – sowing confusion prior to launching Crocodile ...'

Tweed then proceeded to play his own diversionary tactic before Howard could interrogate him about the Washington trip. Unlocking a desk drawer he lifted out three articles and placed them neatly on his desk top. A .38 Smith & Wesson Special. A black beret. A pair of large tinted sun-goggles. He added to the collection a dark blue windcheater.

'The interesting question,' Tweed remarked, 'is who was in London last Friday morning when Manfred-Carlos was in Piccadilly?'

'We were in Paris for the security meeting. I caught the noon plane,' said O'Meara.

'I was on the 10 a.m. flight ...'

Like the American, Howard answered quickly, then stopped in mid-sentence. In a matter of seconds Tweed had reversed the roles, had become the inquisitor instead of the accused. He followed up his advantage before Howard could explode.

'That doesn't exonerate either of you. The wearer of these garments, the owner of the gun was seen by a policeman in Piccadilly at nine o'clock in the morning. As you know, shortly afterwards this little collection was found on a chair in the man's shop, Austin Reed. My question really is *who* did this mysterious man who vanished so quickly come to London to meet ...'

He broke off as the door opened and Howard's deputy, Mason, came into the room. He was closing the door when Tweed spoke abruptly.

'Not now, Mason. And next time, knock first. It is customary.'

'But I was invited to attend ...'

'You are now invited to leave immediately.'

Mason stared at Howard who looked away towards the window. He wet his lips as though about to say more when he caught

Tweed's gaze. It was bleak and intimidating and Mason suddenly realised no one was coming to his aid. With a mumbled apology he left the room.

'Did you invite him?' Tweed asked Howard sharply.

'Not really ...' Howard seemed as relieved as anyone to
see the back of Mason at this juncture. 'He is, of course, my
deputy ...'

'Who has yet to work his passage,' Tweed replied caustically.
'Returning to the subject of this strange incident in Piccadilly,
Special Branch – at my request – handed these items to their
Forensic boffins for urgent analysis. No manufacturer's labels,
of course. The beret is from Guyana, the windcheater and
goggles from Venezuela next door. Origin of the gun untrace-
able. Does their report suggest anything?'

'South America,' O'Meara said grimly. 'Carlos again?'

'Except that it is rather obvious,' Tweed pointed out. 'And we
are getting too many obvious signals. I'm looking for something
not obvious ...'

'What the devil do you mean?' demanded Howard who had
recovered his normal balance. 'And what has this to do with our
over-riding concern – the Summit Express?'

'It's a question of timing.' Tweed was still addressing
O'Meara. 'You should read a little more history. In the early part
of 1919, when Germany was falling apart, a Soviet republic was
established in Bavaria – so there is a precedent for Operation
Crocodile. Luckily the so-called people's government was
destroyed by the remnants of the German Army and the
Freikorps. Look at the map ...'

Tweed opened *The Times* atlas and showed them Lake Konstanz and how its shape was like that of a crocodile with its jaws
agape.

'That is the significance of Crocodile – it denotes the locale of
the conspiracy. Bavaria is their immediate target. The plan is to
set up a neutral government under this creature, Tofler – who
has Communist links. Bavaria has a narrow section of the Konstanz shore – and reports have reached me that a secret factory

200

in Czechoslovakia is building motor torpedo boats ...

'But Czechoslovakia has no coastline,' the American protested.

'So when Tofler takes over, the torpedo-boats are sent by road aboard giant trailers and launched into Lake Konstanz. Only a few would be needed to dominate the Rhine delta – even to help a campaign later to seize the Vorarlberg province from Austria ...'

'I find this sinister,' O'Meara muttered.

'A typically audacious Manfred plan,' Tweed assured him. 'To detach Bavaria from the rest of the Federal Republic – and then one-third of the land mass of Western Germany is severed from the main bulwark against Soviet Russia. The stakes in Crocodile are enormous ...'

'You could be dramatising the situation,' O'Meara suggested.

'No, he isn't,' Howard agreed, to Tweed's surprise. 'If by some twist of political events Bavaria were detached from the Federal Republic the Soviets have conquered western Europe. It is a scenario we have feared for years – not that I dreamt Bavaria would be the key the Kremlin would turn to unlock Western Europe ...'

'This crap about a Soviet Republic in 1919 ...' O'Meara broke in aggressively.

'Is history,' Howard confirmed. 'It existed for a short time. Now I want to know the source of your information,' he told Tweed firmly.

'Werner Hagen, the recently deceased nephew of Reinhard Dietrich. What neither of you know,' he continued poker-faced, 'is that he also revealed that the assassin is one of the four security chiefs attached to the train ...'

Howard recovered from the shock first. His expression froze and he walked round the side of the desk to stare down at Tweed. His tone was clipped.

'For this I will have you thrown out of the Service.'

'If I'm wrong, you might manage it,' Tweed agreed. 'But if

I am right you will have questions to answer at the highest level . . .'

'The guy's crazy!' O'Meara burst out. 'First he gets involved in the Clint Loomis killing. Now he comes across with this lunatic accusation . . .'

'Alain Flandres is taking it very seriously,' Tweed observed. 'I met him in Paris only yesterday . . .'

'You did what!'

Howard was almost apoplectic. He thrust both hands inside his jacket pockets to regain control. Tweed gazed back at Howard over the rims of his glasses as his chief spoke with great deliberation.

'You have no authority to involve yourself in any way in the security of the Summit Express. You have grossly exceeded your brief and will be held answerable for this dereliction of duty . . .'

'Washington will hear of this, buddy,' snapped O'Meara. 'They will be interested to hear a senior British agent has made this accusation about their security chief . . .'

'I said *one* of the four security chiefs,' Tweed reminded him. 'There are precedents. Remember Chancellor Willy Brandt's closest aide, Guenter Guillaume, turned out to be a Soviet plant – which destroyed Brandt. Now I believe they have planted someone else.' He looked at Howard. 'The assassin could have been recruited many years ago. I rather think he was. You had better be extremely careful from the moment you board that train tonight . . .'

CHAPTER 23

Tuesday June 2

Name: Alain Dominique Flandres. Nationality: French. Date of birth: January 18 1928. Place of birth: Strasbourg.

Tweed, alone again in his office with McNeil, studied the file she had handed him. Alain's personal description followed – his height, weight, colour of eyes, colour of hair. It matched the file's subject. He settled himself more comfortably in his chair to peruse the life history.

Career record: Escaped to England, April 1944. Commissioned as lieutenant in Free French Forces. Appointed to Military Intelligence due to fluency in German. At war's end transferred to staff of Gen. Dumas for French occupation of Vorarlberg and the Tyrol. Demobilised and returned to France, May 1953. Immediately joined Direction de la Surveillance du Territoire. Transferred to Secret Service in charge of special unit guarding President, July 1980.

Tweed finished reading the file and drank more tea while he ran over the details again. 'What about his marital status?' he asked.

McNeil replied from memory. 'He married Lucille Durand, daughter of a textile manufacturer from Lille in ...'

'That's enough,' Tweed interjected. 'What about the dirt?' he enquired with an expression of distaste. 'The yellow sheet – an appropriate colour for the things we record about people's lives. But sometimes that's where the clue lies ...'

'Seven different mistresses so far ...' McNeil was consulting a yellow flimsy. 'You want the erotic details?'

'No. Were all his women French?'

'The names look French to me. Who next?'

'O'Meara.' Tweed hunched forward in the chair, his eyes screwed up in concentration. 'This file will be meagre, I presume?'

'Here it is.' She handed him a slim dossier. 'And, as you say, meagre ...'

Name: Timothy Patrick O'Meara. Nationality: American. Date of birth: August 3 1930. Place of birth: New York City.

Career record: Served with Cryptoanalysis Section, CIA, Langley, 1960–1965. Assigned other duties, 1965–1972. Served with West Berlin station under Controller, Clint Loomis, 1972–1974. A two-man unit; other member (junior) Lou Carson. While in Berlin had affair with 18-year old German girl, Klara Beck. On return to US promoted to Assistant Director of Operations, Langley. Transferred to Secret Service on ...

Tweed stopped reading. 'He's married?' he enquired.

'Yes.' McNeil produced another yellow flimsy. 'He did rather well. Nancy Margaret Chase, educated Vassar and all that implies. Daughter of a powerful Philadelphia banker. What they call "the quiet money".'

'His first and only wife?'

'Yes. The yellow sheet hints his father-in-law's connections with the White House helped his rapid rise. O'Meara carries lots of clout. His next move may be to stand for the Senate ...'

'The yellow sheet says that?'

'No, McNeil says that. And you still haven't explained why you lit fires under Howard and O'Meara this morning ...'

'Just trying to arrange the key pieces on the board prior to the opening moves in the game. Again, I'm fighting Manfred long-distance – and already the bastard is breathing down my neck.'

'And your rogue piece – Martel? I wonder what he's up to?'

'I'm going to pay a call on Reinhard Dietrich at his *schloss*,' Martel informed Stoller, who greeted him with apologies on his return to police headquarters in München.

'You are completely mad,' the German protested.

'There's something very peculiar going on,' Martel continued. 'I suspect that – unknown to Dietrich – Erwin Vinz is operating a secret cell inside Delta, a cell controlled directly by the East Germans, which means ultimately by the Soviets. Dietrich is being manipulated, conned – and I think I can raise doubts in his mind. That could upset the whole Crocodile apple cart at the last moment – and with the Summit Express leaving Paris tonight *this* is the last moment . . .'

The tall German wandered over to the window with an expressionless face. 'What makes you come up with this bizarre theory – what is it based on?'

'Four attempts on my life so far, for God's sake. In Zürich, two in St. Gallen and one off Lindau. In every damned instance the killers wore Delta symbols – the worst type of publicity for Dietrich's movement. They even *left* a badge under Warner's dead body – because that didn't get there by accident.'

'How are you going to handle it?' Stoller enquired.

'I have phoned Dietrich who apparently had just returned to the *schloss*. I'm going as a foreign correspondent. Dietrich wallows in publicity . . .'

'And what paper are you pretending to represent?'

'*The Times* of London. I always carry credentials confirming my status as a reporter. I have one for *Die Welt* . . .'

'In your own name?'

'No, as Philip Johnson – who exists . . .'

He broke off as the phone rang. Stoller answered it, listened for a moment, spoke a few words and handed the receiver to the Englishman. 'It's for you – from London . . .'

At the other end of the line Tweed chose his words carefully. It was quite possible the call was being secretly recorded for Stoller to play back to himself later.

'Keith, a courier – carrying diplomatic immunity – is bringing you certain records for you to peruse in the hope that something will point the finger. The courier is my assistant. She will be arriving aboard an evening flight at München Airport. Have someone meet her. The flight details are ...'

'Thank you,' Martel said. 'And goodbye ...'

'I still think you are mad,' Stoller repeated as Martel replaced the receiver. 'You could get yourself killed visiting Dietrich at that *schloss*.'

The Englishman glanced at Claire who had remained silent during their conversation. 'At least you can't say I don't inform you of my movements on your patch, Erich. I'm driving down to Dietrich's place at once.'

'Don't delay ...' Stoller paused. 'Late tonight I have to fly to Bonn ...'

'I didn't understand what went on in Stoller's office,' Claire said later when they were leaving the outskirts of München with Martel behind the wheel of his hired Audi. 'I had a feeling that signals were being exchanged ...'

'He was just showing he was sorry for his earlier outburst. And Tweed is sending in a courier with the dossiers on the evening flight to München. We're clutching at every last straw we can lay our hands on.'

'Why tell Stoller about your suspicions about Vinz and his secret cell? If it is Stoller who is guilty ...'

'Then his reaction – or lack of it – will tell me something. Incidentally, Reinhard was most cordial when Philip Johnson of *The Times* phoned. He's looking forward to seeing me.'

'That's what worries me,' Claire replied.

'You say this British reporter who calls himself Philip Johnson has an appointment at the *schloss*? At what time? Dietrich, why did you agree to see this man?'

In the München apartment Manfred's gloved hand held the receiver tightly as he waited for the reply. It was pure chance that he had called the *schloss*, that the millionaire had then volunteered this information.

'Because I am convinced he is Martel, the man responsible for the murder of my nephew ...'

'*Why?*'

'Because I checked immediately with *The Times* in London.' A note of exasperation had crept into Dietrich's voice. Manfred questioned every decision he took. 'They confirmed they have no correspondent of that name based in Bavaria . . .'

'No correspondent of that name on their staff?'

'I didn't say that!' Dietrich rapped back. 'They do have a man with that name on their staff, he is a foreign correspondent – but at the moment he is in Paris. This man who called himself Johnson is driving here this afternoon by the direct route from Münich in a blue Audi. Any more data you require?'

'Be very careful what you say . . .'

Once beyond the outskirts of Münich Manfred drove his BMW like a maniac. The sniperscope rifle was concealed inside a zipped-up golf-bag on the seat beside him. His features were concealed behind an outsize pair of dark-tinted glasses. His hair was hidden by a soft hat pulled well down over his forehead.

He braked about half a mile from the main entrance to the Dietrich estate. His phenomenal memory had not let him down. Yes, the gate in the wall was there. And beyond it stood a ramshackle farm-cart abandoned long ago and which he remembered from his secret meeting with Erwin Vinz by the roadside.

The geography also, was right for his purpose. Beyond the gate a field rose up steeply to a ridge surmounted by an outcrop of rock. An excellent firing-point. Getting out of the BMW, he opened the gate, lifted the shafts of the cart and heaved to get it moving.

Manfred possessed extraordinary physical strength. He had once broken the neck of a man weighing twenty stone. He hauled the cart into the road where he positioned it carefully. He could have blocked the road completely – but this would have been bad psychology.

If you are quick-witted, confronted by a barrier you turn your car swiftly on the grass verge and drive like hell back the way you have come. So he used the cart to block the road partially – to force an oncoming vehicle to *slow to a crawl* and negotiate the obstacle.

It also provided against the contingency that the wrong car could arrive first and the occupants might get out and shift the cart. As the cart was positioned they would simply drive slowly round it. He next hid the BMW inside the field behind a clump of trees, not forgetting to close the gate. His target would notice little details like that.

Five minutes later, confident from what Dietrich had told him on the phone that he had arrived first, Manfred settled himself in place behind the rocky outcrop and peered through the gun's 'scope. In the crosshairs the road came up so he felt he could reach out to touch it. Then he heard the sound of an approaching car. Martel's blue Audi came into sight.

'I still don't like this idea of visiting Dietrich,' Claire said as she sat beside Martel in the Audi. 'But oh, this must be one of the most beautiful places in the world.'

According to the map Martel had studied earlier they were within two miles of the main entrance to the *schloss*. All around them the sweeping uplands of Bavaria were green in the blazing sun. At the summit of limestone ridges which reared up like precipices clumps of fir trees huddled. They had not passed another vehicle for some time.

'*You* are not going to visit Dietrich,' Martel told her. 'Before we get there I'm leaving you with the car while I walk the rest of the way. If I haven't reappeared in one hour you drive like hell to München and report to Stoller ...'

'I'm not frightened. I'm coming with you ...'

'Which means if I run into trouble there's no one available to fetch help ...'

'*Damn you, Keith Martel!* That's blackmail ...'

'That's right. Now what, I wonder, is this?'

'It's a farm-cart someone has left in the road. You can drive round it along the verge.'

Martel was driving at fifty miles an hour when he first spotted the obstacle. He began to reduce speed, agreeing with Claire that to get past the obstruction he would have to edge his way round it along the grass verge. He looked in his rear-view mirror, expecting to see one or more cars coming up behind him. The mirror showed an endless stretch of deserted road.

He looked to his right and saw a vast field running away to the foot of an upland. He looked to his left and saw ahead, close to the farm-cart, a closed gate. Beyond the gate the land rose steeply, ending in a rocky escarpment which loomed over the road. He scanned the escarpment, reducing his speed further so that he would be moving at less than ten miles an hour as he nosed his way round the ancient cart.

The escarpment was deserted. Claire followed his gaze, shading her eyes against the glare of the sun. The escarpment had a serrated edge like a huge knife with large notches. In one of the notches she saw movement. She pressed her back hard against the seat as she shouted.

'*There's someone up there ...!*'

In the crosshairs of Manfred's 'scope the windscreen of the blue Audi was huge. The sun was in an ideal position – shining from behind his shoulder. He took the first pressure on the trigger. The Englishman's features were clear – even the cigarette-holder at a jaunty angle. The girl beside him wore dark glasses, making identification impossible. It didn't matter. The car was crawling ...

'*Hold on tight!*'

Martel yelled the warning as he did the opposite to what instinct dictated – to reverse and turn on the verge. He rammed his foot through the floor. The Audi surged forward. The farm-cart rushed towards them. Claire blenched. The accident would be appalling. There was a sound of shattering glass.

Martel heard the whine of the high-powered bullet wing past the back of his neck. He kept his foot down, skidded as he swerved round the cart, regained control, drove off the verge and down the clear stretch beyond the cart.

Missed! On the ridge Manfred was stupefied. It was unprecedented. Following his normal cautious policy – which had enabled him to survive so long – he left the area immediately and drove back to München.

CHAPTER 24

Tuesday June 2

Name: Frederick Anthony Howard. Nationality: British. Date of birth: October 12 1933. Place of birth: Chelsea, London.

Career record: Joined Foreign Office, June 1958 ... Appointed to Intelligence Section, May 1962 ... Transferred to Paris Embassy, May 1974 as Intelligence Officer ... Owing to pressure of work took six weeks' special leave, January 1978 ... Appointed head of SIS, May 1980.

Studying the dossiers once again with McNeil in his Maida Vale flat, Tweed skip-read Howard's details. In any case he knew them from memory. He handed the dossier back.

'Anything?' she asked.

'I don't know. I'm intrigued by that special sick leave he took while in Paris and which he spent in Vienna. Intrigued because he has never mentioned the fact ...'

'You'd have expected him to?'

'I'm not sure.' Tweed took off his glasses and chewed on the end of one of the frame supports. 'Despite his apparent extrovert personality if you listen to him carefully he is highly vocal but says little.'

'A natural diplomat?'

'Now you're being cynical,' Tweed admonished. 'But the Vienna incident reminds me of someone ...'

'Who?'

'Kim Philby.' Tweed replaced his glasses. 'It was in Vienna that Philby was first contaminated by the plague – by a woman. So that leaves only Erich Stoller, thank God – I'm beginning to see double. Drag out his file and we'll see what we have there ...'

*

At the entrance to Reinhard Dietrich's *schloss* the noise was ear-splitting, the source of the noise terrifying. A pack of German shepherd dogs snarled and leapt towards Martel, restrained only by the leashes held by the guards. The Englishman immediately recognised Erwin Vinz. The German walked forward and stopped close to the visitor.

'Yes?' he enquired, his slate-grey eyes studying Martel.

'Philip Johnson of *The Times*. Mr Dietrich expects me ...'

'Why do you arrive on foot?' Vinz demanded.

'Because my bloody car broke down a couple of miles back. You think I'd walk all the way from München? And I'm late for my interview – so could we stop wasting time?'

'Credentials?'

Vinz extended a hand and took the press card Martel handed him. Somewhere high in the warmth of the azure sky there was the distant murmur of a helicopter. It reminded Martel of the humming of a bee. Vinz returned the card.

'We will drive to the *schloss* ...'

He led the way to the large wrought-iron gates which were opened and then closed behind them with the dogs and their handlers on the inside. The guards were dressed in civilian clothes and wore Delta symbols in their lapels.

Vinz climbed in behind the wheel of a Land-Rover-type vehicle and gestured for Martel to occupy the front passenger seat. When they were moving Martel glanced back and saw the rear seats were occupied by two burly guards.

He lit a cigarette and made a display of checking his watch. As he did so he looked surreptitiously into the blue vault of the sky over Bavaria. The tiny shape of a helicopter was receding into a speck.

It was a good five minutes' drive through parkland dotted with a variety of trees before they turned a corner in the curving drive and the *schloss* appeared. It was not reassuring – a grey-stone walled edifice like a small fortress complete with moat, drawbridge and raised portcullis gate in the arched entrance.

Vinz slowed down as they bumped over the wooden draw-bridge, crossing the wide moat of green water. They passed under the archway and the main building came into view, enclosing a cobbled courtyard. At the top of a flight of steps a man and a woman waited to greet their visitor.

Reinhard Dietrich wore his favourite country garb, riding clothes and breeches tucked into gleaming boots. In his right hand he held a cigar. His ice-cold eyes stared at Martel as he dismounted from the vehicle, but it was the woman who gave the Englishman a shock.

Dark-haired and sleek, she was dressed in a trouser suit with her jacket open exposing her full figure. There was a half-smile on the finely chiselled face, a smile with a hint of triumph. Klara Beck was obviously pleased to see their guest.

They led him inside the open doors of the *schloss* into a vast hall with a highly polished floor scattered with priceless Persian rugs. Vinz and his two henchmen had produced Luger pistols and escorted him across the hall into a large library overlooking the moat.

Martel was faintly amused at this display of weaponry – somehow it symbolised the poor imitation of Hitler's bodyguard Dietrich was aping – and the reaction helped to quell the cold fear growing at the pit of his stomach. He had not anticipated Klara Beck.

'Stay with us, Vinz – just to ensure our guest preserves his manners.' Dietrich gestured with the cigar he had lit. 'The other two can go dig the garden ...'

Wary of Vinz's Luger, Martel took out his pack slowly, inserted a cigarette in his holder and lit it. He sat down in a leather, button-backed chair in front of a huge Empire desk. An ash-tray of Steuben crystal was filled with cigar butts.

'You may sit down, Martel,' Dietrich said sarcastically. 'We can dispense with the charade of Philip Johnson, I suggest ...'

'We all seem to be making ourselves at home ...'

Martel gestured to Klara Beck who had perched herself on the arm of his chair. She crossed her legs and even the trousers could not disguise their excellent shape. Taking off her jacket, she revealed more of her superb breasts. Dietrich glared at her, went behind his desk and sank heavily into his chair, his voice harsh when he addressed his visitor.

'What suicidal motive drove you to come here? And don't tell me that if you're not away from the *schloss* in half an hour Stoller and his minions will rush to the rescue. I read the papers. The BND commissar is flying to Bonn – doubtless to escape the humiliation of witnessing my victory at the polls . . .'

'Your *defeat* . . .'

Martel was watching Beck as he spoke and caught the flicker of surprise in her dark eyes. *Surprise* – not alarm or disbelief. Dietrich exploded.

'You bloody amateur! What do you know of politics in Germany? I hope you don't imagine you will leave this place alive? Where is the witness to prove you were ever inside the grounds, let alone the *schloss*? Why the hell did you come here . . .'

'To tell you that you are being conned, Dietrich,' Martel replied harshly. He ground out his half-smoked cigarette in the ash-tray and lit another. 'You have been manipulated. Right from the start you've been a pawn in a game you were never equipped to play . . .'

The atmosphere in the library had changed. Martel could sense the change and, resting against the back of his chair, he was watching everyone in the room under the guise of an attitude of nonchalance. He could *feel* Beck's nervous reaction, the tensing of her muscles which subtly shifted the chair leather.

Vinz reacted differently. He tried to freeze his emotions but he shifted nervously from one foot to the other. Dietrich, who was no fool, noticed the movement. He frowned but concentrated his ire on Martel.

'Bloody hell! What are you talking about . . .'

'I'm talking about your betrayal,' Martel continued in the same even tone. 'Betrayal by someone you trusted. Why does Stoller keep locating the Delta arms dumps so easily and swiftly?

He has an informant – that is the only answer . . .'

Vinz took a step forward and waved the Luger. 'You are asking for a mouthful of broken teeth . . .'

He got no further. Dietrich stood up and moved round his desk with surprising agility. With the back of his hand he struck Vinz across the face. The German stood very still as Dietrich stormed.

'Shut your trap! Who do you think is in charge here? Get out of this room and go fishing!'

Martel waited until Vinz had left and then went on speaking. 'Ask yourself the question, Dietrich. Is there one other person only who knows the location of the dumps? If so, that has to be Stoller's informant. Maybe a series of anonymous phone calls? If you are wondering why, every newspaper headline reporting discovery of another dump swings the polls a few points more against you. I say you are being manipulated by a master-mind . . .'

There was a flurry of activity. The door into the library burst open and one of the guards rushed in. Dietrich glared at the intruder.

'What is it, Karl?'

'The gate. They have just phoned through. A convoy of cars is approaching the entrance – they think it is the police . . .'

Dietrich stood considering the news for a few seconds, staring at Martel. Then he barked out an order and two more men appeared from the hall through the open door.

'Put him in the cellar – he can shout his head off down there and no one will hear him. Search him first . . .'

He moved across to a bookcase and removed a volume. Behind it was a button which he pressed. A section slid back with a purr of hydraulics, an addition to the *schloss* no doubt built by his Stuttgart technicians. Martel carefully did not look at Beck as he extracted the smoked cigarette from his holder and stubbed out the butt in the messy ash-tray.

'On your feet!'

Karl had spoken and his Luger was aimed point-blank. Beyond

the dark well exposed by the secret door Martel could see a staircase curving down out of sight. He followed one of the guards
across the shag carpet as Karl gestured with his gun, walking
slowly. The muzzle was rammed into his back. As he stepped
through the opening he heard Klara Beck speak urgently.

'Empty that ash-tray – it contains his cigarette stubs . . .'

Trust lovely Klara not to overlook any little detail, the bitch.
A smell of damp, of mustiness rose to meet him as he descended
the spiral with the guard in front and Karl behind. Dietrich
called out a final threat.

'Later you will talk – or we open the moat sluices and you
drown slowly in that pit . . .'

At the bottom of the steps a doorway led into a stone-walled
cellar. Karl thrust a hand against the small of his back and shoved
him forward. He lost his balance, sprawled full-length on the
floor. When he stood up he was alone and the door was closed
and locked.

The BND motorcade, comprising three six-seater black Mercedes crammed with armed men in civilian clothes, pulled up in
a semi-circle round the entrance gates. The chief guard inside
panicked and gave an order.

'Release the dogs!'

The gates were opened and the pack of unleashed dogs rushed
out, jaws agape, snarling as they leapt at the cars. Beside the
driver in the lead car sat Erich Stoller. He gave the command at
once.

'Shoot those beasts . . .'

A window was lowered, a machine-pistol appeared and a
fusillade rattled. The vicious animals stopped, some in mid-leap
as the hail of bullets swept over them. Within seconds every dog
lay inert in the roadway. Stoller stepped out followed by two
men.

'Cut the communications in the gatehouse,' he ordered.

The two men ran forward and inside the building as one of the
guards held the phone to his ear calling the *schloss*. One man

grabbed him. The second ripped the instrument from the wall. Shaken, the guard still protested.

'That's illegal . . .'

'You're under arrest. Charge – obstructing the authorities in the performance of their duty . . .'

Outside another guard was shouting at Stoller. 'You will pay for this – killing the dogs . . .'

'I noticed one of them was foaming at the mouth,' Stoller told him. 'I suspect rabies. Tests will be carried out.' He returned to his car and spoke to the driver. 'Burn rubber to reach the *schloss* . . .'

The motorcade swept up the curving drive, spinning round corners. One minute after leaving the entrance Stoller saw ahead the walls of the *schloss*.

'Keep up the speed – they may try to lower the portcullis . . .'

He was right – as they approached the drawbridge the hydraulically operated portcullis began to move down. All three cars swept through the archway and the gate closed behind them. At the top of a flight of steps stood Reinhard Dietrich, hands on his hips. Stoller, followed by his men, jumped out and ran up the flight.

'You cannot enter,' Dietrich told him. 'And when I am elected you will be booted out of Bavaria . . .'

'This warrant . . .' Stoller waved the document under Dietrich's nose. '. . . signed by the Minister-President, allows me to do what I like – tear down the place stone by stone should it be necessary. Are you going to invite us in or attempt obstruction?'

Dietrich turned away and walked back into the hall followed by Stoller. Inside the industrialist began moving towards a room on the left. Stoller noticed a door to the right which was half-open. He made for it and entered a large library. An attractive dark-haired woman holding a glass sat on a sofa and looked at him over the rim as she drank.

'Your name?' Stoller demanded.

'This is outrageous!' Dietrich had hurried after Stoller and was standing behind a huge desk. 'I shall complain to the Minister-President . . .'

'There is the phone.' Stoller turned to the woman again and his manner became polite. 'We have full powers of search. Could you please give me your name . . .'

'Don't answer,' Dietrich told her, reaching for a cigar.

'Klara Beck,' the woman replied and smiled. 'I am Mr Dietrich's secretary and personal assistant. Is there any other way in which I can help you?'

'You can let me know the present whereabouts of an Englishman who called here within the past hour. His name is Philip Johnson . . .'

Klara Beck. One of the names Stoller had checked out when Martel had reported the conversation he had eavesdropped on in the phone booth at Lindau Hauptbahnhof. The Stuttgart number had been traced to a penthouse apartment owned by Dietrich GmbH. There was also an interesting file on Beck which went back to her early days in Berlin.

'I have been working in my office upstairs and just came down to the library before you arrived,' Beck replied. 'I have never heard of anyone by that name . . .'

'You live here at the *schloss*?'

'What bloody impertinence . . .!' Dietrich exploded from behind his desk.

Stoller ignored the industrialist, concentrating his whole attention on examining the room and questioning Beck. His men were at this moment searching the rest of the *schloss*. Dietrich knew this, yet he had left Erwin Vinz to keep an eye on them. He seemed most reluctant to leave the library, which convinced Stoller he was in the right room.

'I have an apartment in Stuttgart,' Beck replied as she took out a pack of cigarettes and inserted one between her lips. Stoller leant close to her with his lighter and ignited the cigarette. As he did so she watched him with her large eyes and there was a hint of invitation. A dangerous woman.

'It is a company apartment,' she went on. 'One of the

advantages of working for the owner.' Her eyes again met Stoller's directly. 'And I'm very good at all aspects of my job.'

'I'm sure you are.'

Stoller bowed courteously, then resumed his slow stroll round the room. The ash-tray on the desk had recently been hastily cleaned. There were smear-marks of ash round its interior. He looked up as one of his men entered the room followed by a colleague.

'Anything so far, Peter?' Stoller enquired.

The man shook his head and Stoller told both of them to wait with him in the library. He noticed Dietrich was beginning to enjoy his cigar, to relax in his chair.

'Who has told you this fantastic story about this mythical person being anywhere near my home?'

'The aerial camera – plus the co-pilot's field-glasses. The film taken will, when developed, provide the evidence. We used special film which shows the exact date and time pictures are taken – one of the products of your company, I believe?'

'Camera? Pilot? Have you gone mad?'

'A helicopter tracked Johnson up to the *schloss* – with a cine-camera recording the incident as I have just explained. What cigarettes do you smoke, Mr Dietrich? The brand, I mean.'

'I only smoke cigars – Havanas.' Dietrich was mystified by the turn events were taking and shifted restlessly in his chair.

'And Miss Beck smokes *Blend* – as I noticed when she took out her pack . . .'

Stoller was walking along the line of bookcases. He stopped and stooped to pick up a cigarette stub half-hidden in the shag carpet at the foot of a bookcase. He showed everyone the stub which he had spotted a few minutes earlier.

'Interesting. Dietrich – on his own admission – smokes cigars. Miss Beck smokes *Blend*. This stub is *Silk Cut* – a British cigarette. It was lying at the base of this bookcase. I find it hard to surmise how it comes to be there – unless it was dropped when someone walked through a solid wall. Or is the wall so solid . . .'

He began taking out volumes from the shelves and dropping

them on to the floor. To speed up the process he swept whole sections of the calf-bound volumes on to the carpet as he nodded to his two men. They produced Walther automatics and held them ready for use. Enraged, Dietrich strode round his desk.

'Those volumes are priceless . . .'

'Then show me where the catch is which releases the concealed door.'

'You are mad . . .!'

Dietrich stopped speaking as another half-dozen books went on the floor and Stoller gazed at a red button set in a plastic frame which had just been exposed. He pressed the button and a section of bookcase slid back revealing the spiral staircase beyond.

'Peter,' he ordered, 'go and see what is down there. Should you meet any resistance use your gun.' He glanced round the room. 'I doubt if I have to remind anyone terrorist kidnapping is punishable by long terms of imprisonment . . .'

'I was upstairs helping Klara,' Dietrich began.

'Was he, Miss Beck?' Stoller enquired. 'Be careful how you reply since criminal proceedings may be involved.'

'I'm confused . . .' Beck started choking on her cigarette but was saved from saying more by the appearance of Martel brushing dirt from his sleeve. There was dried blood on his knuckles where his hands had hit the cellar flagstones. Peter came into the room behind him and spoke to Stoller.

'He was imprisoned in a cellar like a pig-pen but they left the key on the outside of the door – it saved shooting off the lock.'

'Well, Dietrich?' Stoller asked.

'He is an imposter . . . I was sure he was an assassin sent to kill me . . . After he made an appointment I phoned *The Times* in London . . . They told me Johnson is in Paris . . . I have many enemies . . .'

The Delta leader was talking like a machine-gun, gesturing to indicate his alarm, the words tumbling out as he struggled forcefully to make his story sound plausible enough to make Stoller doubt the wisdom of preferring charges. It was Martel who guided Stoller to a decision.

'I suggest we get to hell out of this den of nauseating clowns. The atmosphere here smells even fouler than it did in that filthy cellar ...'

The three BND cars reached the exit, turned past the heap of dog corpses lying in the road and headed back towards München.

'In a minute,' Stoller said to Martel, 'we come to where I left Claire Hofer parked in your Audi – where you left her. She recognised me and blasted hell out of her horn to stop us. Then she blasted more hell out of me to hurry to the *schloss*. That girl likes you,' Stoller commented with a sideways glance.

'I'll bear it in mind – and thanks for keeping tabs on me with the chopper – and for battering your way into the fortress ...'

'Why did you visit Dietrich?' the German asked.

'To set the enemy at each other's throats. To convince him he is being betrayed, which I believe is the truth. It may throw a last-minute spanner in the works of Operation Crocodile. And God knows we're close to the last minute ...'

Claire made her remark as Martel drove them in the Audi back to München. Stoller's motorcade had long since vanished as he hurried to reach the airport to catch his flight to Bonn.

'I assume we cancel out Erich Stoller now as a possible assassin?'

'Why.'

'For God's sake because he rescued you from the clutches of that swine, Dietrich ...'

'And what will be the prime objective of the security chief who is the secret assassin?' Martel enquired.

'I don't follow you,' she said with a note of irritation.

'To act in a way that will convince Tweed and I that he is not the man we're looking for.'

'You can't mean Erich Stoller is still on the list.'

'Yes. He is no more cleared than the others. Let's hope those records we're collecting from München Airport do tell us who we're looking for.'

CHAPTER 25

Tuesday June 2:
1400–2200 hours

Name: Erich Heinz Stoller. Nationality: German. Date of birth: June 17 1950. Place of birth: Haar, Münich.

Career record: Served with Kriminalpolizei, Wiesbaden, 1970–1974 ... Transferred to BND, 1974 ... served as under-cover agent inside East Germany, 1975–1977 ... Appointed chief, BND, 1978 ...

Tweed again skip-read the file McNeil had handed him. Examining dossiers produced this reaction: the more you tackled the faster you absorbed them. Tweed pushed the file back across the desk to McNeil. He rubbed his eyes and yawned before asking the question.

'What do you think of Stoller? You never met him – which can be an advantage. His personality doesn't intrude, you concentrate on the facts.'

'He's by far the youngest of the four – in his early thirties. Isn't that unusual – to become chief of the BND at his age?'

'Chancellor Langer personally promoted him over the heads of God knows how many more senior candidates. He has a reputation for being brilliant ...'

'I detect a "but" in your inflection,' McNeil observed.

'Well, he did spend two years behind the Iron Curtain ...'

'But you said he was brilliant ...'

'So we start going round in circles again.' Tweed frowned and leaned forward to tap the neat pile of folders McNeil had arranged. 'I'm convinced that in one of those folders is the answer –

a fact pointing straight at the guilty man. It's at the back of my mind but I'm damned if I can bring it to the surface.'

'Maybe Martel will spot it when he reads the copies I'm taking with me to München this evening . . .'

'It worries me, McNeil,' Tweed said quietly, 'you're breaking all the regulations by taking even copies of those dossiers out of the country . . .'

'I'll be covered by my diplomatic immunity pass. Martel will meet me as soon as I get off the plane. Nothing can happen while I'm in the first-class section of the plane. I'm quite looking forward to the trip . . .'

'I'm having you escorted to München with an armed guard,' Tweed decided. He reached for the phone, dialled a number, gave brief instructions and listened. 'He'll be here in half an hour,' he told McNeil as he replaced the phone. 'It will be Mason – he says he's the only one available.'

'At least he will be company on the flight.'

Tweed looked at her and marvelled. Some of these middle-aged Englishwomen were extraordinary. They undertook the most dangerous missions as though they were taking a trip to Penzance. He watched as she packed the copy files in a special security briefcase. Her own small bag had been packed hours ago.

'You're not to chain that thing to your wrist,' he told her.

'Why not?' I'm doing this job.' She spoke sharply as she locked the case, extended the chain from the handle and clamped the cuff of steel round her wrist, snapping shut the automatic lock. Both knew why he had said that.

Tweed would sooner lose the case rather than subject McNeil to a frightful ordeal – and instances had been known where attackers used the simple method of obtaining such a case. They chopped the hand off at the wrist.

1800 hours, the American Embassy, Grosvenor Square. In a second-floor office Tim O'Meara stood holding his executive case while his deputy, James Landis, listened on the phone, said yes and no, and then replaced the receiver.

'Well?' O'Meara demanded impatiently.

'Air Force One is on schedule over the Atlantic. It will touch down at Orly in good time for the President to be driven direct to the Gare de l'Est and the Summit Express ...'

'Then let's get to hell out of here so we're at Orly ourselves in good time ...'

'A curious report came in about a half-hour back, sir – concerning the investigation into the murder of Clint Loomis on the Potomac. Apparently a nosey international operator in Washington listened in on a call which came through from ...'

'I said *come on*!' O'Meara blazed, cutting off his deputy in mid-sentence.

1800 hours, Elysée Palace, Paris. In the courtyard outside the main entrance and behind the grille gates leading to the street Alain Flandres watched the anti-bomb squad going over a gleaming black Citroen. In a few hours this car would transport the French President to the Gare de l'Est.

As always, Flandres could not keep still – nor trust anyone except himself. As two men directed a mirror at the end of a long handle underneath the car he stood to one side and watched the mirror image.

'Hold it there a moment!'

He stared at the reflection and then called out to a leather-clad man nearby. 'Get underneath this car and check every square centimetre. The mirror could miss something ...'

He ran up the steps inside the Elysée and went to the operations room where an armed guard opened the door. Two men were hunched over powerful transceivers while the third, a cryptographer, checked decoded signals. He looked up as Flandres came into the room and tried to hand his chief a sheaf of messages.

'Just tell me what they say, my friend! Why should I ruin my eyes when you are paid to ruin your own?'

There were grins at the sally and the tense atmosphere lightened with Flandres' arrival. It was part of his technique to defuse any heightening of tension. Calm men took calm decisions.

'The American President lands at Orly at 2300 hours . . .'

'Which leaves exactly one half-hour to drive him from airport to train. We had better close off the route – they will drive like hell. It is the Americans' idea of security. A demonstration by Mr Tim O'Meara of his efficiency! Long live the Yanks!'

'The British Prime Minister will land in her special flight at Charles De Gaulle at 2200 hours . . .'

'Characteristic of the lady – to allow sufficient time but not so much that she wastes any. A model passenger!'

'The German Chancellor is scheduled to board the express at Münich Hauptbahnhof at 0933 tomorrow morning . . .'

'That I know – it has long been planned . . .'

'But there is an odd signal from Bonn I do not understand,' the cryptographer told him. 'We are particularly requested to stand by in the communications room aboard the Summit Express for an urgent message from Bonn during the night.'

'That is all?'

'Yes.'

Flandres left the room, walking slowly along the corridor. The Bonn signal was a new, last-minute development which he could not understand – and because he did not comprehend its significance it worried him.

1800 hours, The Chancellery, Bonn. Erich Stoller left the study of Chancellor Langer in the modern building on the southern outskirts of the small town which overlooks the Rhine. The tall, thin German wore an expression of satisfaction: his dash by private jet from Münich had been worthwhile.

During the flight Stoller had wondered whether he could manage it: Langer was notoriously unpredictable, a highly intelligent leader with a will of his own. And it had taken only ten minutes' conversation to persuade the Chancellor.

Stoller had sent off the coded signal – prepared in advance –

while he was still in Langer's study, the signal to control H.Q. at the Elysée in Paris. Alain Flandres would by now, he hoped, have received this first signal. It was the second signal, timed to be sent later when the train was on its way, that was vital.

'I have pulled it off,' Stoller said to himself. 'The plan is working ...'

1800 hours, Heathrow Airport. Flight LH 037 took off for München on schedule, climbing steeply into the clear blue evening sky, leaving behind a vapour trail which dispersed very slowly. Two passengers had come aboard and settled themselves in the first-class section at the last moment. Special arrangements had been made in advance to receive the couple.

Neither McNeil, carrying her brief-case locked to her wrist with a metal hand-cuff and chain, nor her companion, Mason – who carried a Smith & Wesson .38 in a shoulder holster – passed through normal channels. Once identified, they were hustled to an office with a sign outside. *Positively No Admittance.*

They remained inside the locked office until a phone call to the uniformed police officer sharing the room informed them all other passengers were aboard. They ran down the covered way leading into the aircraft where stewardesses waited to escort them to reserved seats.

'Isn't it nice to be VIP's?' McNeil whispered as she sipped her champagne and the plane continued its non-stop ascent.

'All in a day's work,' Mason replied, his expression blank.

1930 hours, Heathrow Airport. Flight BE 026 departed for Paris on schedule. Tweed – who was deliberately travelling economy class – had a difficult job timing his boarding of the flight. As he knew from McNeil's private intelligence service, Howard was travelling on the same flight, but first-class.

Tweed, therefore, entered the final departure lounge just as the last-but-one passenger disappeared down the ramp. The steward on duty beckoned frantically.

'The flight is just departing!'

'So I'm just in time,' Tweed responded as he rushed down the ramp. Damnit, he had paid for his ticket.

As the stewardess ushered him aboard he glanced into the first-class section on his left. The back of Howard's head was just visible. Fortunately when disembarkation took place the custom was to let off first-class passengers ahead of the plebs. Tweed chose a seat he hated, a seat at the rear of the plane. He detested flying.

He sank into his seat and after take-off forced himself to gaze out of the porthole window. In the evening sunlight the full glory of Windsor Castle revolved below. For Queen and Country. A bit old-fashioned these days, but Tweed never bothered about what impression he might create on the rest of the world.

Flight LH 037 had crossed the German border when Mason excused himself to McNeil. 'I want to send a message to Martel confirming we are aboard this flight – the pilot can radio it for me . . .'

'But he's expecting us,' McNeil reminded him.

'Expecting is not the same thing as *knowing* we caught the plane. With what you're carrying we can't take any chances . . .'

He made his way towards the pilot's cabin and was stopped by a stewardess. He took out his identity card and gave it to her.

'Show this to the pilot. I have to send an urgent radio signal. The pilot knows we are aboard . . .'

After a short delay he was shown into the cabin and the door was locked behind him. Mason introduced himself and then turned to the wireless operator. The pilot nodded that it was all right and the agent asked for a pad to write the message. It was addressed to a Münich telephone number.

'The signature is a code-name,' he explained as the operator read the wording. Mason nodded his thanks to the pilot and left the cabin as the operator began transmitting.

Telephone number Münich . . . McNeil and I aboard Flight LH 037 from London. ETA . . . Please arrange reception committee. Gustav.

*

In the Münich apartment a gloved hand picked up the phone as soon as it began to ring. The operator checked that she had the correct number and then began to transmit the message.

' "McNeil and I aboard Flight LH 037 ..." '

'Thank you,' said Manfred, 'I have that correctly. Goodbye.'

The gloved hand broke the connection, lifted the receiver again and dialled a Münich number. It was answered by Erwin Vinz whose voice changed when he realised the identity of the caller.

'You will take a team of men to the airport ...'

Manfred's instructions were precise, although masked in everyday conversation. When the call was completed he checked his watch. It was convenient that the airport was close to the city – Vinz's execution squad would be in position by the time Flight 037 had touched down.

And Mason, who was still over twenty thousand feet up, would have been appalled had he known the instructions.

'Kill them both – the man as well as the woman ...'

Martel stood by a bookstall inside the exit area at Münich Airport, apparently studying a paperback. He also appeared to be on his own, which was not the case. At the other side of the large hall Claire, wearing dark glasses, stood with a small suitcase at her feet like a passenger.

The arrival of Flight LH 037 from London had been announced over the tannoy. Passengers who had disembarked were hurrying across the hall for cabs and the airport bus. Martel scanned the small crowd and saw McNeil, carrying a brief-case in one hand, a suitcase in the other. He also saw Mason alongside her.

'Tell you what,' Mason was saying to her, 'I'll just dash over to that kiosk and get a pack of cigarettes – you go and grab a cab and then we shan't have to wait ...'

'But we're being met ...' McNeil shrugged. Mason was gone.

Martel saw the separation and frowned. He dropped the paperback, picked it up and quickly returned it to the revolving rack. Claire was waiting for the signal and now she recognised McNeil from the description Martel had given her.

She also knew something was wrong. The dropping of the paperback had warned her. Had Martel simply returned the book to its rack it would have been no more than a recognition signal. Inside her handbag she gripped the 9-mm pistol. McNeil, an erect, slim woman headed for the exit.

A man dressed in the uniform of a Lufthansa pilot standing near the exit produced a Luger equipped with a silencer from a briefcase. Erwin Vinz, carrying a light raincoat folded loosely over his arm, walked into the hall, dropped the raincoat and aimed the machine-pistol the garment had concealed.

'*McNeil, drop flat!*' Martel yelled.

It was remarkable: Claire was amazed. The middle-aged Englishwoman fell forward, dropped her suitcase, used her hands to cushion the shock of the fall and lay quite still, hugging the floor.

Martel pointed the Colt .45 snatched from his shoulder holster and aimed at the most dangerous target – Vinz and his machine-pistol. He fired rapidly. Three heavy slugs hammered with tremendous power into Vinz's chest, hurling him backwards. His shirt crimsoned as he crashed to the floor, still clutching the weapon. He had not fired a single shot.

The Lufthansa 'pilot' aimed his Luger point-blank at his agreed target – Mason, who stood near a cigarette machine. Two bullets struck Mason who fell forward against the machine, clawing at it as he sagged to the ground. Claire aimed, steadying her pistol over her left arm. It was remarkable shooting – clear across the hall. Two bullets hit the killer and he toppled forward.

'*McNeil, stay flat!*' Martel yelled again.

Three men apparently waiting for passengers had produced hand-guns.

Martel had just shot Vinz . . . Claire was firing at the 'pilot' . . . The three new Delta professionals were aiming their weapons at the still-prostrate form of McNeil . . . There was panic spreading among the other passengers . . . A woman screamed and went on screaming and screaming . . .

A steady drum-fire of fresh shooting filled the hall and Martel watched in amazement as all three Delta assassins fell to the floor. Men in civilian clothes appeared from different parts of the hall armed with Walther automatics. One of them came up to Martel, an identity card held up in his left hand.

'BND, Mr Martel. Josef Gubitz at your service. The others you see are my men.'

'How the hell did you know ...'

'The plane's pilot transmitted the message the Englishman on the passenger list named Mason had sent, transmitted it to Stoller as instructed.'

'Who instructed him?'

'A man called Tweed in London. Any signals sent by Mason from the aircraft to be immediately transmitted to us. Stoller reacted from Bonn by sending us here. It was kind of complicated ...' The German, a small, well-dressed man, looked over his shoulder at the carnage in the hall. '... but it worked.'

'Thank God for that – and thank you.'

Claire was helping McNeil to her feet who was looking down at her grazed knees as Martel joined them. She looked at Martel. 'You know something? My nylons are ruined. Do you think I could indent for a new pair?'

Martel, Claire and McNeil were sitting in the Englishman's room at the Hotel Clausen. The two women drank tea as Martel checked the four photocopy dossiers McNeil had brought him. McNeil sat in an arm-chair next to Claire and placed her cup on the table. The Swiss girl was marvelling at her placidity.

'That tea you poured me was just right,' McNeil announced. 'It was nice and strong – just a dash of milk and no sugar. You can't beat a cup of tea after a bit of a dust-up.' She paused. 'Mason tried to get me killed, didn't he?'

'Yes,' said Martel. 'And they wiped him out because by now he had served his treacherous purpose. I'm certain he bugged Tweed's office. I'm equally sure he dressed up in the wind-cheater, beret and sun-goggles, made sure he was spotted by a policeman in Piccadilly and then took off his things – probably in a lavatory – and left them with the gun on a chair in Austin Reed's . . .'

'Why?' Claire asked.

'To confuse us. Manfred was never within hundreds of miles of London. And it must have been Mason who followed Tweed to London Airport before he boarded Concorde – then reported that back to Manfred. It's odd Howard ever took on a man like that . . .'

McNeil was watching Martel who had closed the last file. 'Do they tell you anything?' she asked. 'Tweed gave the impression he couldn't find anything but I believe it's there . . .'

Martel took a sheet of the hotel notepaper, scribbled something on it and showed it to McNeil. She read what was on it, tore the sheet into small pieces, got up and walked across to the toilet. They heard her flush the loo and she came out and sat down again.

'Well?' Martel enquired.

'I thought so, too,' McNeil replied. 'You can't trust Tweed, of course – he keeps so much to himself. The trouble will be proving it . . .'

'So we leave you here until it's all over with Stoller's armed guard on the door. Claire has some distance to travel – and I'm heading for a different destination. What scares me is we have so little time . . .'

CHAPTER 26

Tuesday June 2:
2030–2335 hours

Charles de Gaulle Airport, 2030 hours. Flight BE 026 landed on schedule. Howard was among the first passengers to disembark. His special pass took him straight through Customs and Immigration and Alain Flandres was waiting for him with a large Citroen.

'This is what I call service,' Howard remarked as they settled back in the rear and the chauffeur-driven car glided away.

'We pride ourselves on our organisation,' Flandres replied with a cynical smile. 'Since the change of government we have little else to pride ourselves on.'

'As bad as that?' Howard glanced sharply at his companion who, as always, was the soul of relaxation. 'Is everything proceeding according to plan?'

'There is something I do not understand – and in the situation we are faced with incomprehensible things disturb me. I have had a signal from Bonn warning us to expect an urgent communication from Germany during the night. Stoller is not at Pullach ...'

'Well, that's his problem ...' Howard dismissed the whole thing with a curt wave of his hand.

'It might be our problem as well,' Flandres responded.

Under Flandres' instructions French security forces at both Orly and Charles De Gaulle were checking all arrivals for known faces. But they missed one person who came in on Flight LH 323 from München via Frankfurt. The aircraft landed at Charles de

232

Gaulle at 2215 hours and the passenger, who had travelled first class, passed through the security checks unchallenged.

Elegantly clad in a black Givenchy dress and wearing a string of pearls, she also wore a hat with a veil. Porters carried her Gucci luggage to a waiting chauffeur-driven limousine. She raised her veil briefly for Passport Control.

'I wonder how many ingots of gold she is sitting on in the Bahnhofstrasse,' the Passport official murmured to a colleague after he had returned Irma Romer her Swiss passport and she moved away.

'I wouldn't mind having her sitting on me,' his colleague replied. 'She *is* a beauty . . .'

Settling herself in the spacious rear of the car the woman with the veil spoke to the chauffeur as the car was driven away from the airport.

'Emil, we have one hour before the train leaves – so you must drive slowly, kill some time. I must board the Summit Express five minutes before it departs.'

'My instructions were clear, Madame,' Emil replied. 'There will be no problem.'

'There *must* be no problem.'

Having issued this injunction, Klara Beck crossed her long legs and relaxed. It had been a rush to drive from the Bavarian *schloss* to catch the plane at Münich but she was sure she had successfully eluded the man who had tried to follow her. That would be Stoller's doing, of course.

'Stick Stoller,' she thought inelegantly and checked the time by her diamond-studded watch.

Gare de l'Est, 2300 hours. The twelve-coach express stood in the station. At the front the giant locomotive which would haul its precious cargo gleamed under the lights. It had been polished and polished again like a jewel. The chief engine-driver, Jacques Foriot, was the most experienced driver in the whole of France. He stood checking his array of dials and controls and then peered out of his cab.

The first six coaches immediately behind the engine were reserved for the train's illustrious passengers. The Prime Minister of Great Britain, typically, had arrived first. She had gone to bed without delay in Voiture One, the coach attached to the locomotive.

Voiture Two would be occupied by the French President who was at this moment climbing aboard after his swift ride from the Elysée. Alain Flandres stood on the platform, his eyes everywhere as the short, stocky President mounted the steps and disappeared inside. Flandres let out an audible sigh of relief.

'One more worry off my mind,' he remarked to his deputy, Pierre Buzier, a giant of a man with a bushy moustache who towered over his chief. 'And now one more worry on my mind,' Flandres continued with a shrug of his shoulders.

'But he is safe now,' Buzier reassured him. 'It was the drive from the Elysée that bothered us . . .'

'And you imagine that the next seven hundred-mile ride across Europe does not worry me, my friend?' He squeezed Buzier's huge arm and smiled cynically. 'It will be a long night – followed by a long day . . .'

The makeup of the express had been the subject of considerable study and much discussion by the security staff at the Elysée to ensure maximum safety. Voiture Three was reserved for the American President who was expected to arrive from Orly at the last moment. And Voiture Four would be the preserve of Chancellor Langer when he boarded the train at Münich at 9.33 a.m. on the following morning.

Behind these four coaches was attached the communications coach which carried some of the most sophisticated equipment available. One section was devoted entirely to a link between the train and the White House in Washington. The president would be accompanied, as he was everywhere, by an official carrying the black box – the sinister device for signalling a nuclear alert in varying stages of urgency.

Flandres and his technicians had devoted a great deal of energy to equipping this coach, cooperating with the Americans

234

who had installed their own devices.

As though to counter the austere purpose of this coach, the one behind was taken up by the restaurant car for the exclusive use of the western leaders. It was expected that during daylight hours they would confer at length while they hammered out a united policy before facing the Soviet leader in Vienna.

'I want more men on this barrier,' Flandres ordered as he passed through the second barrier temporarily erected on the platform, a barrier sealing off the VIP section at the front from the rest of the express.

'Surely we have enough men already,' Buzier protested.

'For practical purposes, yes,' Flandres agreed. 'For public relations' purposes, no. The Americans are great believers in numbers. Bring ten more men from outside the station. That should impress them, should it not, Pierre?' Again he smiled cynically.

'If you say so . . .'

'I know O'Meara. If I am not mistaken I can hear the approach of the great man . . .'

'The American President?'

'No – O'Meara! Accompanied by the President!'

Beyond the second barrier was the rest of the train, the public section which comprised another six coaches. Two for first-class passengers (one a sleeping-car), three for second-class and, at the rear of the express, the public restaurant.

As he passed them alone – Buzier had hurried ahead to gather up ten more men – Flandres glanced at each window. Most of the blinds in the sleeping-car were closed but the station pulsated with a sense of expectancy. As he continued towards the main ticket barrier the little Frenchman scanned the other windows and eager faces stared back. He stopped to request that a window be closed. Until the train was moving the order was all windows must remain shut.

In the corridors on the other side of the express armed men of the French security services stood at intervals. At the main barrier he saw Howard waiting and pursed his lips. Having seen his own charge safely aboard, the Englishman was going to be present when the President of the United States arrived.

The distant sirens shrieking like banshees came closer. He must feel at home, Flandres reflected. He himself had been kept awake when he visited America by the hellish wail of patrol cars dashing through the night.

'He's only just on time,' Howard commented as Flandres reached the barrier. 'Why is it that Americans have to arrive at the very last minute?'

'Because they see no point in waiting. What they accomplish with the time saved is another matter . . .'

As the Frenchman had anticipated, O'Meara made a great performance of the arrival. When the motorcade swept into the station the American security chief leapt from the leading vehicle almost before it had stopped. Several men, their coats open at the front, followed him as he glared up the platform. The President rather spoilt the effect.

'I want men facing every window before the President moves up the platform,' O'Meara demanded.

'If they're going to take a pot-shot at me, Tim, they're going to,' said the President who stepped out from his car looking as cool and unaffected as a clerk walking home from work. 'And your remark is hardly a great compliment to M. Flandres . . .' He extended a hand. 'It is Alain Flandres, isn't it?'

'A pleasure to see you again, Mr President . . .'

They shook hands while O'Meara moved restlessly and gestured for the American Secret Service men to form a circle round Flandres and the President. 'Washington, two years ago – am I right?' the President said.

'You have a remarkable memory . . .'

There was tension as the procession of men made their way along the platform, so many alert to danger which might come from any quarter – and the potential target was the most powerful leader in the western world. Flandres was disturbed and felt he must speak.

'I don't like being hemmed in like this ...'

The President, smiling and amenable, stopped. 'Tim, I think we must allow Alain to command the security operation. This, after all, is his territory.'

'More space, please!' Flandres spoke curtly to O'Meara. 'We must have a clear field of fire in an emergency ...'

At the foot of the steps leading up into his coach the President lingered to speak again to the Frenchman. 'I just want you to know that I feel perfectly safe in your capable hands. And now, if you'll excuse me, I like an early night's sleep ...'

Three minutes from departure time two unexpected events occurred. A chauffeur-driven limousine drove into the station and an elegant woman alighted and presented her ticket while the chauffeur brought her bags. The ticket collector noted that she had a sleeping compartment reserved. At the same time the Passport controller – brought to check the identity of all ordinary passengers – noted she was Swiss.

'You had better hurry, Madame,' the collector advised. 'The train departs in three minutes.'

Further down the platform at the second barrier Howard watched the elegant woman walking gracefully towards him while her chauffeur carried her luggage. She disappeared inside the sleeping-car and Howard turned to his deputy, Peter Haines, a short, wiry man.

'I wouldn't mind joining that one in her bunk,' he observed and climbed aboard the train.

The ticket collector was closing the barrier when a cab drew up.

A compact figure wearing glasses and a rumpled hat who had paid the fare earlier got out. He ran towards the barrier, carrying a small case.

He had his ticket ready and a plastic card which he presented to the Passport official. The latter glanced in surprise at the card which bore a photograph of its owner and then turned to hold up his hand to the guard indicating that the train must wait.

The late arrival moved rapidly down the platform to the

237

second barrier opposite which Howard was standing in the open doorway to get a last-minute breath of fresh air. As he saw the passenger his face went rigid and he stepped down on to the platform.

'Tweed! I don't know what the hell you are doing here but I'm forbidding you to board this train . . .'

'I don't think you have the power.' Tweed showed his card with green and red stripes running across it diagonally. 'And you are holding up the train . . .'

'Say, what the devil goes on here?'

O'Meara had appeared behind Howard. Now Flandres stepped down from the other end of the coach and ran along the platform to join them. O'Meara peered over Howard's shoulder.

'Jesus Christ! She signed the pass herself!'

'This is outrageous!' Howard exploded. 'I was not informed . . .'

'You were not informed for security reasons,' Tweed replied. 'If you are worried, why not wake up the lady and check? But I doubt whether she will appreciate the interruption . . .'

'Get aboard, my friend.' Alain Flandres had grasped Tweed's arm and was ushering him up the steps. 'You are most welcome.'

Tweed waited in the corridor as Flandres waved his hand towards the guard, climbed the steps and closed the door.

'Alain, there is one person I would like checked as a matter of top priority. At the barrier the Passport controller told me the lady who came on board at the last moment is travelling on a Swiss passport, that her name is Irma Romer. Can you use the communications set-up to radio her details to Ferdy Arnold in Berne? Ask him to confirm whether their people have issued Irma Romer with a passport – that she does in fact exist . . .'

'Why bother about her?' Howard demanded.

'Because her car was parked in a side street for sometime before it drove into the station. I arrived earlier myself, you see . . .'

The train was moving now, the huge wheels of the locomotive

238

revolving faster as the Summit Express emerged from under the canopy of the Gare de l'Est and headed east on its historic journey for its final destination, Vienna. Seven hundred miles away.

CHAPTER 27

Wednesday June 3: 0100–0810 hours

'Has anything unusual happened yet, Haines?' Tweed asked.

'Unusual?' Howard's deputy enquired cautiously. At one o'clock in the morning he had a haggard look.

'Unexpected, then.'

They were sitting at one end of the communications coach where two bunks had been installed for security chiefs off duty. Haines glanced towards the far end of the coach where the three security chiefs were gathered round the teleprinter.

The express was ninety minutes away from Paris, moving at over eighty miles an hour as it thundered through the dark. The coach swayed round a curve. No one felt like sleep.

'I'd sooner you addressed that question to Howard,' said Haines.

'I'm addressing it to you.' Tweed reached towards his pocket as he continued. 'Perhaps you are unaware of my authority?'

'There was something, sir,' Haines began hastily. 'While he was at the Elysée Flandres had a message from Bonn warning us to await an urgent signal aboard the express. Stoller has disappeared . . .'

'Disappeared?'

'Yes. We don't know where to communicate with him. The secrecy of the whole business is worrying Flandres . . .' He looked again at the far end of the coach. 'I think something is coming through on the teleprinter.'

It was Howard, beginning to look strangely dishevelled, who came with the telex strip which he waved at Tweed with an expression of satisfaction.

'Signal from Ferdy Arnold in reply to your query. The Swiss can be damned quick. Irma Romer was issued with a passport four years ago. Widow of an industrial magnate – engineering. She's travelling outside the country somewhere in Europe. So can we now forget about your paranoid aberrations?'

'Can I see the telex, please?'

'I've just read the damned thing out to you!' Howard threw the strip into Tweed's lap. 'Admit it,' he snapped, 'it's a wild goose chase.' He turned and stepped on the right foot of O'Meara who had come up behind him. 'Do you have to follow me everywhere?' Howard demanded.

'People apologise when they bump into me,' O'Meara rasped.

Tweed watched the two man over his spectacles. Already they were getting on each other's nerves – because under the surface there was a terrible suspicion that one of the security chiefs was the enemy. And with the windows closed tightly for the sake of the communication experts the atmosphere was growing torrid. Something had gone wrong with the air-conditioning.

Flandres, who had witnessed what was happening, came rapidly to their end of the coach. 'Gentlemen, we have the most nerve-wracking assignment any of us has probably faced – let us face it calmly and help each other . . .'

'What I'd like to know,' O'Meara demanded, 'is who is in charge of British security – Tweed or Howard . . .'

'I would say Alain is in supreme control for the moment,' Tweed said quickly. 'We are passing across French territory . . .'

'Still nobody answers my Goddamn question,' O'Meara persisted.

Tweed read through the Berne signal and looked at Howard. 'You left out a bit, didn't you? Arnold ends his message with the words *further details to follow as soon as available*.'

'What further details do we need?' asked Howard wearily.

'Her full description,' Tweed replied.

Nobody slept inside the communications coach as the express

sped on through the night. The atmosphere grew worse as the air became more clammy and oppressive. Conditions were not improved by the cigar O'Meara smoked as he lay half-sprawled in the lower bunk.

Tweed moved away and sat in a swivel chair screwed to the floor, his head slumped forward, apparently asleep. But he was aware of everything going on as the thump-thump of the train's wheels continued its hypnotic rhythm. The factor he found most disturbing was Stoller's disappearance.

They had arranged a duty roster for one security chief to patrol the corridors of the four coaches where the VIP's were presumably asleep. This was at Flandres' suggestion despite the armed guards from each contingent occupying the corridors of their respective coaches. At the moment Flandres himself was on duty.

The Bonn signal arrived at the ungodly hour of 0431 – after the express had left Strasbourg and ten minutes before they were due at Kehl on the German border. Tweed sat up in his chair because he saw the cypher clerk decoding the signal which had arrived. He held out his hand as the clerk walked towards O'Meara who appeared to be asleep.

'I'll take it . . .'

'What the hell is it now?' O'Meara suddenly demanded.

The American – who had obviously not been asleep – was stripped to his shirt-sleeves, exposing the holstered gun strapped under his left arm. He leaned over Tweed's shoulder and the Englishman caught a whiff of stale sweat from his armpits. Howard, who had just entered the coach, joined them as all three men perused the signal.

'Christ Almighty, what is going on?' O'Meara growled and lit a fresh cigar. Howard's reaction was a tightening of the muscles of his jaw, Tweed noted.

Urgent change of schedule. Chancellor Langer will board Summit Express at Kehl, not München. Repeat Kehl not München. Stoller.

'It's a nightmare,' Howard said. 'What does it mean?'

There were pouches under his eyes betraying his fatigue. The underlying strain of mutual suspicion and mistrust was beginning to take its toll on the three security chiefs. Flandres had now joined them and was mopping moisture off his forehead with a silk handkerchief. The atmosphere was becoming claustrophobic. Each man was conscious of being cooped up inside a confined space he could not escape. Only Tweed seemed relaxed as they re-examined the signal.

'He has given us less than ten minutes' warning. It's just not good enough. What *does* it mean?' Howard repeated.

'It appears to mean,' Tweed suggested, 'that Stoller is using his considerable ingenuity to protect his leader. That is,' he added, 'assuming Chancellor Langer is the assassin's target ...'

He was watching the three men as he spoke, searching for a clue in his blunt reference to the assassin. The American chewed at his cigar and spilt ash down his front.

'You're not making sense,' he complained irritably.

'The timetable of the western leaders for their journey to Vienna has been widely publicised,' Tweed explained patiently. 'Including the fact that Langer was scheduled to board the train at München when he had made his brief speech outside the Hauptbahnhof. By coming aboard much earlier this unexpected change may throw the unknown assassin off balance.' He stared round the trio hovering over him. 'It *has* already thrown you off balance ...'

'You're assuming Langer is the target,' Howard pointed out.

'True,' Tweed agreed. 'The target may already be on board. I am not sure ...'

'Just as you're not sure of any of us,' Flandres said amiably.

'True again. And the train is slowing down – we are at Kehl. So the fourth suspect, Stoller, should join the happy band ...'

There was a further surprise when the express drew into Kehl and Flandres opened the door of Voiture Four to find Chancellor Kurt Langer staring up at him, his lean face wearing an

243

expression of amusement. Like the French security chief, the German spoke fluent English and, wearing his well-cut business suit, could have passed for an Englishman.

'Alain Flandres, how pleasant to see you again. I trust my early arrival did not get you out of bed?'

'None of us have had much sleep . . .'

Flandres ushered the Chancellor quickly aboard into the corridor and away from the open doorway. He peered briefly out into the early morning. The gloomy platform, glowing with sepulchral lamps, was lined with BND men facing *away* from the express. Flandres frowned and turned to speak to the Chancellor.

'Where is Erich Stoller, Chancellor? Surely he is accompanying you?'

'I have no idea where he is,' Langer answered affably. 'He is as elusive as a lark. The train can leave when you are ready – I go this way? Thank you . . .'

Flandres signalled to the guard and closed the door. The train began to move again, picking up speed, the coaches swaying slightly as they started to cross Germany, heading for Bavaria. Flandres wasted no time making sure Langer was comfortable: the Chancellor was notorious for his dislike of fuss. He hurried back into the foetid atmosphere of the communications coach where the others sat waiting for him.

'Stoller did not come aboard,' he announced. 'And Langer tells me he has no idea as to his present whereabouts . . .'

'That's crazy,' O'Meara protested.

'It could also be very serious,' said Tweed.

His remark did nothing to lighten the highly nervous mood which had now spread to the communications technicians. Howard left the coach to take up his duty roster, glaring at Tweed as he passed him hunched in his swivel chair.

The early hours when morale is at its lowest crawled and no one spoke unless it was absolutely unavoidable. Friendly cooperation had long since given way to raw-edged nerves and outbursts of irritation over trivia. Only Tweed remained detached and watchful – like a man awaiting an event he has foreseen and which is inevitable.

When they had at last settled down into some kind of neutral silence the second signal came in from Berne.

Subject: Irma Romer. Height: 5 ft. 4 ins. Weight 120 lbs. Colour of eyes: brown. Age: 64. Married to industrialist, Axel Romer, 34 years. Destination: Lisbon. Arnold, Berne.

The second signal promised from Berne reached the communications car of the Summit Express as it was pulling into Ulm Hauptbahnhof at 0805 hours. Tweed automatically converted the details from the metric system as he read the message and passed it to Howard.

'The elegantly-dressed woman who came aboard at the last moment at Paris,' he commented. 'The one you said was of no significance. The description doesn't tally in one single detail . . .'

'We had better go to the sleeper coach at once,' Flandres said. 'With armed guards,' he added. He looked at Tweed. 'Coming?'

The two men passed through the restaurant coach where breakfast was being laid for the four western leaders to the end door which was kept permanently locked, sealing off the coaches occupied by the public. A guard unlocked the door and Flandres, followed by Tweed, hurried along the corridor of the sleeping car.

'Come with us,' Flandres ordered two of the guards standing in the corridor. 'Have your weapons ready. Good, there is the attendant . . .'

The uniformed attendant in charge of the sleeper was making the morning coffee and looked up in some trepidation as Flandres began questioning him. He then explained that the passenger, Irma Romer, had left the express at Stuttgart after complaining that she felt unwell.

Stuttgart . . . The timetable details flashed into Tweed's mind. *Arrive, 0651; Depart 0703.* A twelve-minute stop, the longest of the whole trip except for München. Flandres looked at Tweed and made a gesture along the corridor.

'So, once again you are right, my friend. We should examine her compartment?'

'Yes,' said Tweed.

The attendant opened the door which he had locked after the passenger had left. Tweed stepped inside followed by Flandres. The Englishman raised the wash-basin lid.

'The soap is untouched. She hardly used the place . . .'

'The bed has not been slept in,' Flandres pointed out. 'So she sat up all night . . .'

'Waiting until she reached Stuttgart,' Tweed said thoughtfully. 'I don't like this, Alain, I don't like it at all. Why should she book a sleeper, spend the night in it from Paris to Stuttgart and then get off? This business of feeling ill is nonsense.'

'Well, she is off the train – and we are moving again, thank God. I hate these stops. Let us go back and check with Howard and our American colleague . . .'

It was only a two-minute stop at Ulm. An essential element in the overall security was that at each stop one of the security chiefs climbed down on to the platform to check who was leaving or boarding the public section of the train. As they made their way back through the restaurant car Tweed asked his question.

'Who was watching the platform at Stuttgart?'

'O'Meara volunteered for the job . . .'

'And he wouldn't recognise Irma Romer,' Tweed remarked. 'He has never seen her.'

'And there was a fair amount of activity at Stuttgart. It will remain a mystery . . .'

In the first-class day coach a woman passenger sat reading a copy of American *Vogue*. Her hair had a tinted rinse and she wore horn-rimmed glasses which were also tinted. She was dressed in an American trouser suit and perched on the luggage rack above her was a case with a bright tartan cover.

She was travelling on an American passport in the name of

246

Pamela Davis and her occupation was given as journalist. Taking out a pack of *Lucky Strike* she lit a fresh cigarette. By her side the ash-tray was crammed with half-smoked butts – but on top in view were fully-smoked stubs.

After complaining to the sleeping-car attendant of feeling ill, Reinhard Dietrich's mistress, Klara Beck, had got off the express at Stuttgart carrying her large Gucci suitcase. It was, she knew, a twelve-minute stop. She made her way to the ladies' room.

She had changed into the trouser suit behind a locked toilet door. She had used a hand-mirror to adjust carefully the rinsed wig which concealed her dark hair. Inside the large Gucci suitcase were some expensive clothes but it was mainly occupied by a smaller, tartan-covered case.

She had used a steel nail-file to force the locks on the Gucci. When it was found it would be assumed it had been stolen, certain contents taken and then abandoned in the toilet. There was no way the suitcase could be linked with its owner.

She had put on the tinted glasses, filled her new handbag with the contents of the one she had carried earlier, and substituted the Pamela Davis American passport for the Irma Romer Swiss passport. In her handbag was a fresh ticket purchased in advance from Stuttgart to Vienna. The transformation was now complete.

Klara Beck had overlooked nothing. Her actions had neutralised any check which she felt pretty sure would be made on the occupants of the sleeping-car. She was now ready for the final stage of the operation.

Normally Tweed would have been standing on the platform at Ulm during the two-minute stop – and Tweed was the man capable of recognising Claire Hofer. Martel had not only given him a verbal description of the Swiss girl during their meeting at Heathrow; he had backed this up with the passport photo attached to the special card. Instead it was Howard who checked passenger movement.

Claire was waiting on the platform when the Summit Express

came in. She carried a small suitcase and her handbag. And she wore a pair of glasses with plain lenses which gave her a studious air. When the train stopped she approached the entrance to the first-class coach and showed her ticket to the waiting official.

'And your passport, Madame – or some other form of identity,' another uniformed official requested.

Claire produced her Swiss passport and this immediately satisfied the German. She climbed aboard and began moving along the corridor glancing into each compartment. The first one with only a single passenger was occupied by a tall man wearing lederhosen – the leather garb seen so often in Bavaria. His hat was tipped over his eyes and he appeared to be asleep.

She went inside, closed the door and heaved her case up on to the rack. The fact that it was a smoker had influenced her choice. And she wanted a quiet compartment so she could think. Inside the next compartment – only a few feet further along the corridor – sat another lone passenger, a woman carrying a passport in the name of Pamela Davis.

'What a pleasant surprise, Miss Hofer . . .'

She nearly jumped out of her skin. Her hand slid to the flap of her handbag which contained the 9-mm pistol. The tall man tipped back his hat as he spoke softly.

'No need for protection. I'm quite harmless,' he continued.

Stupefied, she stared as Erich Stoller stared back at her. The express began moving east again. It was exactly 8.07 a.m.

CHAPTER 28

Wednesday June 3:
0800–0845 hours

'The Blumenstrasse cemetery. I haven't much time ...' Martel told the Bregenz cab-driver.

'Where you're going they have all the time in the world ...'

The cab-driver's response was typically Austrian, taking life as it came – and went. But Martel's urgency communicated itself to him and he drove away from the solid wall of buildings along the lakeside at speed.

The Englishman made an effort to contain his impatience. Away to the north the Summit Express was speeding across Germany and, if on schedule, was approaching Ulm. At the eastern end of Lake Konstanz a grey drizzle blotted out the mountains. Through the open window moisture drifted in and settled on his face.

Arriving at the entrance to the cemetery, he paid the fare, added a generous tip and told the driver to wait. Then he plunged into the sea of headstones, his eyes scanning the maze. It was such a long shot – a remark made to him by a gravedigger when he had last been in Bregenz.

But it was the right day. He checked his watch. It was also the right time. 8 a.m.

'She comes every week without fail,' the gravedigger had told him. 'Always on the Wednesday and always at eight in the morning when no one else is about ...'

Martel buttoned up the collar of his raincoat against the rain. The only sound was the low whine of a wind. Clouds like grey smoke were so low you felt you could reach up and touch them.

As the mist parted occasionally there were brief glimpses of the forest on the precipitous Pfänder mountain. Then he saw behind a headstone the crouched form of the gravedigger. He was levering his spade, adding to a mound of freshly dug earth.

'Back again, sir.'

The old man had straightened up and turned. His moustache dripped moisture and his cap was soggy. He regarded Martel's expression of surprise with amusement.

'You didn't startle me. Saw you coming soon as you entered the Friedhof. Thank you kindly, sir ...'

He pocketed the sheaf of Austrian banknotes Martel had earlier counted from his wallet, then leaned on his shovel. Martel had one hand clenched behind his back, the nails digging into his palm to conceal his frustration. It was no good asking direct questions immediately: that was not the way of the Vorarlberg.

'You work in all weathers?' Martel enquired.

'They don't wait for you on this job ...' The gravedigger then surprised him. 'Looking for that woman who comes here each week? She's just coming through the main gate. Don't turn round – the slightest change of atmosphere disturbs her ...'

Martel waited and then glanced over his shoulder. Beyond the pallisade of large headstones a woman wearing a red head-scarf was walking briskly. She wore a fur coat and carried a spray of flowers as she headed in a diagonal direction away from them.

'She's not short of a schilling,' the gravedigger whispered to Martel. 'Saw her in town once – my wife said that fur is sable.'

'Whereabouts in Bregenz?'

'Coming out of a house in Gallus-strasse. Now's your chance.'

The woman was crouched with her back to them laying the flowers on a grave. Stooping low, Martel ran among the maze of headstones which reminded him of huge chess-pieces.

His rubber-soled shoes made no sound as he came up behind her and stopped. It was the same grave. *In Gottes Frieden. Alois Stohr. 1930–1953.* The woman stood up, turned and saw him.

'*Dear God!*'

Panic! A slim, shapely hand clutched at her mouth as she

stifled a scream. Large luminous eyes stared at Martel in sheer fright. A reaction which was hardly justified. Startled – yes, Martel would have expected that. But her reaction was too extreme – like that of someone whose dreadful secret had been discovered. He spoke in German.

'I have to ask you certain questions ...'

'Questions?'

'Police.' He produced the special pass which gave him access to the Summit Express and showed her only a glimpse. Documents were designed to delude the innocent. 'Security from Vienna ...'

'Vienna!'

'I need information on Alois Stohr – as he is called on the headstone ...'

Afterwards he could never have explained why instinctively he chose this approach – only another trained interrogator would have understood. 'Seventh sense,' Tweed would have commented tersely.

'Why do you say that?' There was a quaver in the woman's voice. She would be in her late forties, Martel estimated. Still a very handsome woman. She must have been a beauty at eighteen, say. In 1953 when Alois Stohr was buried. 'I come here to put flowers on the grave on an old friend,' she went on.

'A friend who died nearly thirty years ago? You come here each week after all this time? To recall the memory of a *friend*? The man who died in 1953 when the Vorarlberg was under occupation ...' The words poured out of Martel in a torrent as he aimed blind, hoping to strike a sensitive spot. He went on, saying the first thing which came into his head. '... occupation by French troops – that is, French officers and Moroccan other ranks ...'

He stopped.

He *had* struck home – he could tell by the brief flicker of alarm in her eyes which vanished as swiftly as it appeared. Martel felt he had a lousy job to carry out but there was no other way.

'You know then?' she asked quietly.

251

'I am here,' he replied simply. One wrong word would lose her.

'I keep a taxi waiting ...' She stooped and gathered up the loose cellophane wrappings in which she had brought the flowers. The cellophane was printed with the name of a florist and was moist with the mist. 'You want to come back with me?' she continued quietly, her voice soft and weary. 'Here ...' she gestured at their surroundings. '... is hardly the place.'

'Of course ...'

Her taxi was waiting behind his own at the gate, the drivers chatting together. Martel paid off his own driver and climbed into the back beside the woman who gave an address in Gallus-strasse.

The bookseller Martel had talked to on his previous visit had informed him it was one of the wealthier residential districts. As they drove away Martel recalled a remark the gravedigger had made about the woman. *Not short of a schilling.* It was all beginning to make hideous sense.

The four-storey villa in Gallus-strasse had cream-washed walls, brown shutters and was a square, solid edifice. Eight steps led up to the front door. Alongside the door were eight names, each with its own bell-push. There was a speakphone grille. One of the names, Martel noticed as she unlocked the door, was Christine Brack.

She had an expensively furnished apartment on the second floor. When she offered to make coffee he refused – he was desperately short of time. She removed the head-scarf, the sable coat, and underneath she was wearing a dark dress with a mandarin collar. As he had expected, she had an excellent figure.

Sitting down on a chair close to his own and facing him, she used both hands to shake loose long black hair. She was a very attractive woman.

'I suppose I have been waiting for you to arrive all my life – ever since it started ...'

'May I smoke?' Martel asked.

'Please do. You can give me one ...'

Was it a reaction to the state of extreme tension affecting him? He felt a wild desire to pick her up and carry her to the bed he could see through a half-open door. She followed his glance and crossed her shapely legs.

'Will the money stop now?' she asked. 'Not that I really care. It has felt like blood money all these years. And going to the Post Office to collect the envelope seemed undignified. Does that make sense, Mr ...?'

'Stolz, Ernst Stolz ...'

'You know, of course, I still retain my maiden name, Brack?'

'Yes, and I understand the blood money feeling,' Martel probed cautiously. 'Although I think you are wrong ...'

'We were deeply in love, Mr Stolz. When the accident happened we had just got married ...'

'It was an accident?'

He was – to use another of Tweed's phrases – creeping over thin ice. She looked startled.

'But of course. My husband was driving the American jeep alone on a dangerous road in the Bregenzerwald and it was winter. He skidded over a precipice ...'

'Who confirmed it was an accident?'

Perplexity mingled with suspicion in her expression as Martel struggled to draw her into the web of revelation. 'The two security men who brought me the news,' she replied.

'They wore civilian clothes? Had you ever seen them before? Do you speak French?'

'In the name of God what are you suggesting?' she demanded.

'It would help if you answered the questions ...'

'*Yes!* They wore civilian clothes. *No!* I had never seen them before. And *no!* I do not speak French ...'

'So, from the way they spoke, you would not be certain whether these two men were really French – because naturally you conversed in German?'

'That is correct. They explained to me how important it was

253

for my husband's death to remain a secret – he was part of a long-term anti-Soviet operation. They said I owed it to his memory that his work should continue – probably for many years. They told me that his real rank was much higher than the one he had borne – that of lieutenant – and that each month I would therefore receive via the post a generous sum of money as a pension. From the amount I get he must have been a colonel at least . . .'

'What about the burial? Who identified the body?'

'I did, of course! In a private mortuary in the mountains. He had broken his neck but there were few other injuries.'

'And who was buried in the grave? Alois Stohr?'

'My husband, of course . . .' Christine Brack was shaking. 'He was buried under a different name because the long-term anti-Soviet operation depended on pretending he was still alive. They told me he would have wanted me to agree to the deception . . .'

They had committed two murders, Martel reflected. The man whose neck had been broken – and some poor devil of an Austrian whose body had probably been weighted and dumped in the nearby lake. It had been vital to kill and remove the unknown Stohr because of the death certificate regulations and so on – when all they had needed was his name.

Christine Brack, too, would have been killed except for one snag. A third murder might have loaded the dice against the conspirators. Instead they had told her black lies and provided money. He was now at the crux of the whole business. As he reached into his coat pocket for the envelope he realised his palm was moist.

'I want you to look at these photographs and tell me if you recognise anyone. Prepare yourself for a shock. These photos were taken recently.'

Martel waited, concealing a sensation of turmoil. Everything depended on what Christine Brack said during the next minute. She spread out the glossy prints on her lap and then uttered a little exclamation. Her expression was frozen as she held out one photograph.

'That is my husband, Mr Stolz. Older yes, but that is him. I have been dwelling under some terrible illusion for thirty years. What does it mean ...'

'You are quite sure?'

'I am certain. Incidentally, I will now tell you another man came to see me recently but I told him very little.' Martel realised she was referring to Charles Warner as she returned the photographs to him.

'That is *not* your husband,' Martel said gently. 'It simply looks very like him. And you have been living under no illusion – your husband did die thirty years ago.' He stood up. 'You may well be under observation and in grave danger now I have called. Can you pack a bag in five minutes and come with me to a place of safety for a few days?'

Shock made her amenable and she agreed to his suggestion. Also she was a woman able to pack in five minutes.

Martel hurried her down Gallus-strasse to the lake front where he found a cab and told the driver to take them to a nearby airstrip. The pilot who had flown him from Münich was waiting with his plane.

'I have to be in Münich so I reach the Hauptbahnhof by 9.30 at the latest. And first I have to drop this lady at a hotel ...'

'We're going to have to move,' the pilot warned.

'Then *move!*'

As they settled into the plane Martel prayed to God that he would not be too late. It had certainly been *German* 'security' men who had fooled Christine Brack all those years ago. And he now knew for certain the identity of the assassin.

CHAPTER 29

Wednesday June 3. München

The arrival of Erich Stoller in the communications coach after the express had left Ulm caused a sensation. Howard was furious and did not resort to diplomatic language.

'Where the hell have you been? You realise the three of us – O'Meara, Flandres and myself – had to assume the responsibility for the safety of your own Chancellor . . .'

'Who is where at this moment?' Stoller broke in.

'Still locked in Compartment 12. The others are impatient for their breakfast but felt they had to wait until he emerged . . .'

'Follow me,' the German suggested. 'And surely you mean the *four* of you?' He glanced at Tweed who remained oddly silent. 'So, had someone hurled a bomb through the window of Compartment 12, you feel it would have been due to my negligence?'

'That's how I see it,' O'Meara replied.

They were following the German who led the way from the communications coach to Voiture Four. He stopped outside Compartment 16 and raised his hand to rap on the door.

'Wrong damned compartment,' Howard snapped.

Stoller rapped on the door with an irregular tattoo and it opened from the inside. Framed in the doorway stood Chancellor Kurt Langer, fully dressed and smoking one of his inevitable cigarettes. He wore a fresh business suit and an enquiring look.

'Time for breakfast, gentlemen? The others must be ready for a good German meal. May I rouse them myself so I can officially welcome them on German soil?'

O'Meara, Howard and Flandres – who had come hurrying up

behind Tweed – were stunned into respectful and bewildered silence. They stood aside as Langer, chatting amiably, returned with his fellow-leaders and escorted them to the restaurant car. When they were alone Howard exploded.

'Stoller, you owe us an explanation ...'

'He owes us nothing,' Tweed intervened. 'We are now in Germany and he can take whatever action he likes. But he may wish to tell us the latest score. Something in the public section of the train worries you, Erich?'

'It was all arranged with the Chancellor in advance when I flew to Bonn,' Stoller told them as they returned to the communications car. 'I boarded the express secretly at Kehl as a passenger while the Chancellor distracted your attention ...'

'But why?' Howard demanded.

'Because,' Tweed again intervened, 'he sensed there is danger in the public section. I suspect he checked every passenger while pretending to be one of them ...'

'Correct,' Stoller agreed.

'And,' Tweed continued, 'I imagine you checked the sleeper?'

'Again, correct.' The BND chief permitted himself a wintry smile. 'For the sleeping-car I donned a uniform and examined credentials soon after the train left Stuttgart at 7.03 when they would have had a good night's rest. I found something curious – a woman left the train at Stuttgart, said she was feeling unwell. I'm unhappy about her ...'

'All of us are,' Tweed replied and explained the mysterious disappearance of Irma Romer who had proved to be an imposter.

A subtle change had come over the relationship between the security chiefs since Stoller's arrival. Before his appearance the personality of Alain Flandres had dominated the group. Now, without seeming to, Tweed had assumed authority.

'I'm going along to the breakfast car to make sure all is well while they breakfast,' Howard suggested. 'Want to join me, Tim?'

Tweed said he would stay with Erich. Stoller waited until they were alone and guided Tweed to the end of the communications coach out of earshot of the technicians. He sat on one of the bunks and lit a cheroot. Tweed thought he looked badly in need of sleep. The German kept his voice low.

'Claire Hofer, Martel's Swiss assistant, came aboard at Ulm – she's by herself in the first-class coach. It worried me ...'

'I'll go and see her in a minute,' Tweed replied.

'You know where Martel is? He's gone missing.'

'No idea. I think you have something on your mind ...'

'I know who is the target for the assassin – it's staring us in the face,' Stoller asserted.

'I agree. But you tell me – and why you think so.'

'My own Chancellor. The state election in Bavaria is knife-edged – with Tofler, the Kremlin's creature, using the neo-Nazis to frighten the electorate into voting for him. So, what would be the effect of the assassination of Langer today?'

'Panic. A potential landslide for Tofler, leading ultimately to Bavaria becoming a Soviet republic – as it briefly was in 1919.'

'So we agree,' said Stoller. 'And you know where I'm convinced the assassination attempt will take place?'

'Go on ...' Tweed was watching Stoller through half-closed eyes.

'München. He insists on making a brief speech outside the Hauptbahnhof during the stop there and I can't dissuade him. Have you made any progress in locating the assassin?' he asked casually.

'No,' lied Tweed. 'But I'm going along to have a quiet word in her compartment with Claire Hofer. Did you bring any of those new alarm devices your boffins invented.'

'Half-a-dozen were put aboard. I'll get you one ...'

Stoller walked to the far end of the coach and returned with a square rectangular plastic box he carried by a handle. 'This is The Wailer. It's designed to look like a powerful torch – but if you press this button a siren starts up. All hell breaks loose.'

Tweed picked up the 'torch' and made his way along the speeding express through the restaurant. The four western leaders were eating breakfast and the American President, as relaxed as ever, had just cracked a joke which was making his companions laugh. As Tweed passed their table the PM looked up and smiled at him.

Tweed walked on, showing the guards his pass, and moved into the first-class coach. He heard the door being locked behind him and nodded at the two guards outside. Walking slowly along the corridor, he glanced into each compartment.

The one before Claire's was occupied by a single woman wearing what the Americans called a pant suit. He noticed she had a tartan-covered suitcase on the rack and she was smoking as she stared out of the window. He wasted no words as he sat down beside Claire Hofer and showed the pass with his photograph.

'Miss Hofer, my name is Tweed. Keith Martel will have told you about me. Where is he?'

She examined the pass carefully before returning it. 'He flew to Bregenz in Austria late yesterday evening. He ordered me to board this train at Ulm.'

'Bregenz? Then I was right. But we need *proof*. Where will he board the express?'

'At München – he was flying back this morning. I just hope that he makes it ...'

'He has to make it. The target is Langer. The attempt will be made at München. There is a thirteen-minute stop. Langer insists on making a speech outside the Hauptbahnhof – in front of a vast crowd. The assassin has to be identified and exposed before Langer mounts that podium ...'

'Which means Martel must be on the platform and ready to board the express instantly ...'

'I don't like the split-second timing,' Tweed confessed. 'And now I must go ...' He tapped the plastic box, explaining how the device worked. 'Don't forget The Wailer. You see anything wrong, you press the button ...'

Alone again in the compartment, Claire was beset with anxiety. What could she possibly hope to see that was wrong?

*

'For Christ's sake, move faster! I've paid you enough,' Martel rapped at the cab-driver. 'Use the side-streets . . .'

'The traffic – the one-way system . . .'

The driver lifted both hands briefly off the wheel to indicate his own frustration. Münich was jammed with cars. People on foot were streaming towards the Hauptbahnhof to hear Langer's speech. And Christine Brack was now safely esconced in the Hotel Clausen.

They passed the river Isar where it debouched into an intricate system of sluices. Martel remembered the rendezvous a man called Stahl never kept at the Embroidery Museum in St. Gallen. Stoller had later told him of the body found trapped in one of the sluices, a body whose only identification had been a wrist-watch engraved with the word *Stahl*. Then the memory was gone.

Martel contemplated getting out and running the rest of the way. Then he saw they were passing the Four Seasons Hotel. Too far yet. He would never make swift progress through this mob of Langer supporters.

He checked his watch again in an obvious gesture which the driver saw in his rear-view mirror. It was 9.23 a.m. The Summit Express was due to arrive at the station in exactly ten minutes' time. The turmoil following the Chancellor's assassination would be appalling. It could easily sway the election into Tofler's hands.

Like Tweed, Martel had worked out that the target was the German leader. And now he knew the identity of the assassin – but only he could confront the killer and prove his identity. He stared in the rear-view mirror and met the driver's eyes.

'Here I can try a side-street,' the man said. 'It could save a few minutes . . .'

A few minutes. They could make all the difference to the future of western Europe – of the whole of the West.

Manfred's nylon-clad hand lifted the receiver the moment the instrument began ringing. He was aware he was gripping the receiver tightly. His packed case stood by the apartment door.

'Ewald Portz speaking,' a voice said. 'I am in position ...'

'Watch your timing – it must be perfect ...'

'We have gone over it a score of times,' Portz snapped.

'Then just remember – this is not a rehearsal ...'

In a phone booth at Münich Hauptbahnhof Portz, a short, stocky man in his thirties, glared at the phone he was still holding. The line had gone dead. The bastard had rung off.

Inside the apartment Manfred picked up his case and kept on his gloves while he opened the outer door, closed and locked it. Only then did he remove the gloves and stuff them in his pocket. The main thing was that Portz – the *decoy* – was ready and in position. Armed with a pistol loaded with blanks he had to aim and fire at the Chancellor at the same moment as the real assassin. Then he would run like hell in the confusion, making himself prominent as he disappeared inside the U-Bahn.

This tactic should divert attention from the real assassin who, once he had done the job, would make his way to the adjoining Starnberger Hof, the station for trains to the mountains. Then he would travel only a few stops before he left the train, was met by a waiting car and driven to a nearby airstrip.

Getting behind the wheel of his car parked at the kerb, Manfred adjusted his spectacles and drove off to the underground garage for his final meeting with Reinhard Dietrich.

It was hopeless. The traffic was getting worse the nearer they came to the Hauptbahnhof. Martel rapped on the window, gesturing to the driver to stop. He had the money for the fare – in addition to the earlier tip – ready in his hand as he leapt out.

'You will catch your train?' the driver enquired.

'This is the one train in the world I *have* to catch ...'

Martel disappeared and the driver shook his head. What a statement. The English, they were all mad. Perhaps that was why they had won the war?

Martel barged his way through the crowd, elbowing aside men

who shouted after him as he plunged on through the milling mob. He could *see* the Hauptbahnhof now. It was 9.31 a.m. Only two more minutes before the Summit Express arrived – before the Chancellor, noted for his briskness, left the train and made his way to the specially-constructed podium Martel could see. He forced a path round the edge of the jostling mass.

Reaching the road in front of the Hauptbahnhof he encountered a fresh problem but he was ready for it. In his left hand he held the special pass which allowed him to board the express. The new problem was police guards who held back the crowd. He shouted at the top of his voice.

'*Polizei!* Make way! *Polizei* . . .!'

'Stop. . .!'

A uniformed policeman drew his Walther from his holster as Martel dashed past him and across the open space. He zigzagged, risking a bullet in the back. The voice called out with greater urgency.

'Halt or I fire . . .!'

Only at this critical juncture did he have some luck. He recognised a man in civilian clothes as one of Stoller's aides – and the aide recognised Martel. He raised a bullhorn and bellowed the order to the policeman.

'Hold your fire! Let this man through . . .!'

Martel dashed past him and the station entrance was ahead with more sightseers behind a cordon of police waiting for a glimpse of the Chancellor. Beyond he saw the locomotive of the express just stopping. He ran on . . .

As the express slowed to a halt Klara Beck was walking through the corridor towards the exit, carrying her tartan-covered suitcase. She did not even glance into Claire Hofer's compartment. Something about the way she moved made Claire study the woman.

Lindau! Claire had seen Beck arrive in the reception hall of the Bayerischer Hof. From the elevated terrace above the harbour she had observed Beck walking rapidly towards the Hauptbahn-hof. Klara Beck!

Claire stood up, grabbed The Wailer and left the compart-ment, following the woman in the trouser suit. When she reached the exit the door was open and Beck was moving along the platform towards the barrier. Claire stepped down on to the platform.

Half-way along the coach Beck paused, stood the case on the platform, twisted the handle through a one hundred and eighty degree arc and walked on, leaving the case. Alain Flandres had descended from the restaurant car and glanced quickly round as though looking for something suspicious. Then he walked swift-ly through the ticket barrier to the side of the station. Chancellor Langer had left the train and waved a hand, acknowledging the crescendo of cheering.

Claire dropped The Wailer on the platform and pressed the button. She nearly jumped out of her shoes as a hellish wailing sound like a police siren blasted out, its high pitch penetrating the cheers. Langer paused uncertainly. Stoller appeared beside him, a gun in his hand, followed by O'Meara. Beck glanced back and recognised Claire.

There was a searing flash of light as the magnesium flares packed inside the paper-thin walls of the tartan-covered case exploded. It was the five-second moment of distraction the assassin was waiting for. Ewald Portz raised his pistol and began firing the blank shots. Martel appeared behind him, the Colt .45 in his hand. He gripped the butt with both hands and elevated the muzzle.

At the side of the station Alain Flandres aimed his Luger equipped with a silencer point-blank at Langer. Martel swivelled his weapon and snapped off three rapid shots. The bullets missed the Frenchman but ricochetted all round him. He ran for the entrance to the Starnberger Hof station and disappeared.

Klara Beck was on the verge of pulling the trigger of her pistol pointed at Claire when Stoller fired once. Beck stooped forward, the pistol falling from her hand, and sagged to the ground.

O'Meara had produced his .38 Smith & Wesson and took deliberate aim at Portz. After firing his blanks the German was fleeing towards the U-Bahn. The American's bullets slammed into his back and he sprawled on the concrete, leaving behind a smear of red as he lay inert.

As Alain Flandres ran on to the platform a train was just leaving the Starnberger Hof. The timing had been vital. He grabbed a door-handle and heaved it open. A train guard shouted at him as Martel came round the corner. Flandres had heaved himself up on to the step and was about to hurl himself inside the compartment. Martel fired twice and both bullets rammed into the target's back.

The train was gathering speed as he hovered, half-inside the compartment and half on the step. He stayed poised like a figure frozen in a tableau. Then his body jack-knifed slowly, toppled backwards into space and hit the platform like a sack of cement. He was dead when Martel reached him.

CHAPTER 30

Wednesday June 3

'The Soviets – using East Germans as proxies – replaced a young French lieutenant in the Army of Occupation in Bregenz with their own man thirty years ago,' Martel said and accepted a cigarette from the German Chancellor who sat opposite him in the restaurant car of the Summit Express.

The train had left München and was heading east for Salzburg and Vienna. Martel was not in the least embarrassed by his audience which included his own Prime Minister, the American and French Presidents, together with Tweed, Stoller, O'Meara and Howard. He just felt unutterably weary.

'How did they manage that deception?' Langer asked.

'By a process of elimination, I assume. Everyone has a double. I happen to know you have your own for security reasons – and never use him. They had a man – my guess would be an Armenian – and he looked very much like the real Alain Flandres. They undoubtedly scoured the French forces in the Vorarlberg, the Tyrol and Vienna searching for their double. Poor Alain was made to order.'

'In what way?' Langer pressed. 'And drink some more cognac ...'

'The real Flandres was an orphan. No one back in France knew him well. He was being demobilised and planned to join the Direction de la Surveillance du Territoire – an outfit where everyone would be a stranger. Damn it, Chancellor – if you don't mind my recalling the episode – Chancellor Willy Brandt was compelled to resign when his chief aide, Guenter Guillaume, turned out to be a KGB agent. An even more difficult plant than Alain Flandres.'

'You're right,' Langer agreed. 'And I am most grateful that you saved my life. But how did you detect Flandres?'

'It's a tragic story. We had a previous agent, Charles Warner, who was murdered. In his notebook was an intriguing reference to Bregenz. I showed Warner's photo round the town and that led me to a cemetery – to a grave still visited by the woman who married the real Flandres just before he was murdered . . .'

'She knew about the impersonation?' Langer queried.

'The East Germans fooled her, kidded her up with a story so her dead husband was buried under another name. They had to do that if the fake Alain Flandres was going back to France to infiltrate the security services . . .'

'We were not very clever,' interjected the French President.

'Every security outfit has been penetrated at some time – even the KGB overlooked Col. Oleg Penkovsky. We worked on a process of elimination . . .'

'What exactly do you mean by that?' Howard demanded.

'Let Mr Martel continue,' the PM reprimanded Howard sharply.

'It looked like O'Meara at one time,' Martel said, staring at the American. 'When Tweed visited Clint Loomis to check up your background Loomis ended up dead . . .'

'Hell, I'm not taking that . . .'

'You are taking that – and whatever else comes,' the President of the U.S. told him mildly.

'As I was saying, Loomis ended up dead. But that was to point us in the wrong direction – Manfred's doing, we suspected. Plus a missing two months when you were in West Berlin and absent from your base.' Martel tactfully omitted to mention that O'Meara had spent time with the now-deceased Klara Beck.

'You, sir,' Martel switched his gaze to Howard, 'posed a problem. While attached to the Paris Embassy you spent six weeks' leave in Vienna. You've made no mention of this fact since this operation started – even though Vienna is our destination.'

266

'Purely personal reasons,' Howard responded stiffly and lapsed into silence.

'Then there was Erich Stoller.' Martel glanced at Tweed. 'You might like to go on ...'

'Erich was the obvious suspect,' Tweed began briskly. 'He had spent two years underground inside East Germany. Plenty of time for him to be trained by the state security people in Leipzig or East Berlin. *Too* obvious. Had he gone over to the other side, after a year or so they'd have faked an imminent exposure which made him dash back across the border. That would have built up a nice credit balance of trust. The fact he was there two years proved he was just damned good at his job.'

'So we came to Alain Flandres,' Martel explained. 'Likeable, lively Alain who seemed above suspicion. Until it occurred to us that his early background was the vaguest of all four security chiefs. And now, if you don't mind, I'd like to snatch a little sleep. I'm getting off at Salzburg ...'

'I shall also get off there,' said Tweed.

'Well,' Howard broke in boisterously. 'I think you can safely leave security for the rest of the journey in our hands ...'

'Now that *they* have located the assassin,' the PM interjected cuttingly.

Manfred received his first warning when he drove into the underground garage to keep his rendevous with Reinhard Dietrich. To his surprise he saw Dietrich's Mercedes had already arrived – although it was strictly understood that Manfred would be there first.

He checked his watch. No, he was not late – Dietrich was early. In the deserted cavern Manfred swung his car in a semi-circle and backed rapidly to position his vehicle alongside the six-seater Mercedes. He used one hand on the wheel while the other opened the automatic window and then grasped from the seat beside him a Luger with the silencer screwed on the barrel. When he switched off his motor he realised Dietrich had kept his own engine ticking over.

'You are early,' he called out. 'Another mistake – I trust you do appreciate the whole manoeuvre has failed?'

'Entirely due to you,' the millionaire replied.

Dietrich was sitting in the automatic car with the gear in drive, the hand-brake off – and only his pressure on the foot-brake preventing the car moving forward. The front passenger window was open, his right hand gripped a Walther pistol, his left hand a metallic sphere, and the passenger door was not closed.

'Your meaning?' Manfred asked quietly. 'Because Langer was not assassinated his party will win?'

'That, of course. But it is not pleasant to grasp that I have been tricked from the beginning. You supplied the arms to Delta, I told you every time the location of the dumps. You, alone – and myself – had this information. Stoller must have been delighted as you relayed the locations to him. You are a bloody Bolshevik . . .'

Both men reacted at almost the same moment. Manfred raised the Luger and fired twice. *Phut-phut*. Dietrich has used his right foot to kick the door open wide as he leant forward and aimed the Walther. He was too late.

Manfred's bullets thumped into his chest and he slumped sideways over the passenger seat. His hand holding the large sphere lost its grip and, unseen by Manfred, the 'rolling' bomb thumped on to the concrete floor and disappeared beneath Manfred's car.

The new device designed by Dietrich's boffins in the secret research section of his Stuttgart factory was like a massive grenade. The button Dietrich had been holding depressed was released, the device activated and timed to detonate in five seconds. Dietrich's foot slipped from the foot-brake and the Mercedes glided forward.

Manfred turned on the ignition at the very moment the rolling bomb exploded with tremendous power. Compressed between concrete floor and chassis, the blast soared upwards and *elevated* the car. The sound was deafening, the ruination total. After-wards they were never able to find enough of Manfred to make any kind of identification possible. He was literally blown to pieces.

The three of them – Martel, Tweed and Claire Hofer – stood on the platform at Salzburg Hauptbahnhof watching the end of the rear coach grow smaller as the Summit Express headed on the last lap for Vienna.

'I'm flying back home,' Tweed announced. 'I shan't expect you for three weeks, Keith.' He glanced at Claire. 'I expect I can keep Howard at bay until you return . . .'

They watched the compact figure of Tweed striding briskly away, his shoulders erect, looking from side to side, still observing all that was going on around him. Martel turned to Claire who spoke first.

'He'd make a marvellous chief of your SIS. He's so amazingly cool under pressure. When he came to give me The Wailer just before the train reached München the tension must have been terrific. You would have thought he was on holiday.'

'Talking about holidays, you're going back to Berne to report?'

'Yes . . .'

'On the other hand there's no rush, surely? I'm going to pick up Christine Brack from the Hotel Clausen to take her back to Bregenz. I want her to know the man who impersonated her husband is dead – psychologically it may close a long, painful chapter in her life. Bregenz is on the way back to St. Gallen. Didn't you find the Metropol a comfortable hotel?'

'I think I'm going to find it even more comfortable this time,' she replied, linking her arm inside his.